THE OUTLAW SHUFFLE

A Story of Our Heroes Brayden, Uly, Margo, and Lucas, Who Scour the Southwest During the 2020 Summer of COVID on a Quest to Find the Abducted Josephine

ALSO BY KURT JOHNSON

Las Vegas Turnaround

The Barrens (with Ellie Johnson)

THE OUTLAW SHUFFLE

A Story of Our Heroes Brayden, Uly, Margo, and Lucas, Who Scour the Southwest During the 2020 Summer of COVID on a Quest to Find the Abducted Josephine

KURT JOHNSON

A Sin City Thriller

First Published by Street Level Press

Copyright © 2024 Kurt Johnson

All rights reserved.

This novel is entirely a work of fiction. The names, characters, and incidents portrayed in it are the work of the author's imagination. Any resemblance to actual persons, living or dead, events or localities is entirely coincidental.

ISBN: 979-8-9900350-0-3

Street Level Press
www.StreetLevelPress.com

TABLE OF CONTENTS

"Most people who play gin do so to excess. This finally results in a shyness within them and they are reluctant to admit, even among themselves, that their only communicable relationship is the constant pursuit of the game."

— Ernie Kovacs, *How to Talk Gin*

1

The Abduction of Josephine

Hugh had been watching the woman for two days through the lenses of his Leica binoculars. Her eyes had caught his attention. Not the color—the irises were a common shade of hazel. What interested him was the size of her dark pupils. He'd seen a scientific study about the link between pupil size and intelligence. Larger pupils were associated with more focused concentration, better working memory, and a heightened problem-solving ability. All of which meant she was good at games of any kind, and he'd watched her for two days doing difficult crossword puzzles out of a *New York Times* booklet. He'd measured his own pupils. They were between four and five millimeters across, the average being around three. Looking through the binoculars, he could see that hers were five or more, even when exposed to bright sunlight. Then he noticed how her eyes opened wide, owl-like, taking in each detail surrounding her campsite. But it wasn't prey she was assessing—not like him. She watched for more engaging things, like the odd characters who inhabited the campground.

Would she enjoy his company? Would she find him presentable or at least inoffensive despite his appearance and their ten or so year age difference?

He'd recently come upon the idea of a new mustache. He'd worn one in college that he kept tightly trimmed to the edges of his mouth—a mustache that, along with his suit coat and tie, pegged him as a Nixon conservative. In retrospect, that look in the late sixties wasn't popular on campus and didn't help much with his social life, but neither did the blood-red birthmark below his right eye that appeared as though he'd been gored by a bull. He wore the mustache until middle age when he finally married and his wife, Florence, convinced him to shave—she did not like the feeling of the bristles against her pale skin. After her death, he continued to shave out of habit. But then, one evening while watching Fox News, John Bolton caught his attention. They both had thick gray hair parted to one side and the same wire-framed glasses. The difference was the mustache, and he thought that much of John Bolton's confidence was carried through that single feature. Hugh realized that growing a mustache for perceived confidence sounded ridiculous, but he also knew that dress and grooming reflected one's personality, where first impressions were created. So, he grew back his mustache, this time letting it extend casually past the edges of his mouth and just over his top lip. Looking in the mirror, he thought it did make him appear confident and possibly more attractive—not necessarily younger but distinguished. And he thought it gave him more *true* confidence, offsetting the lack caused by his birthmark.

He watched the woman from inside his forty-foot RV motorcoach. All the window shades were pulled down except for one cracked open a few inches to see out. He watched as she left her smaller campervan and walked the short distance to the campground toilet. Minutes later, she walked back. The toilet was nearer his motorcoach, and that's where he planned to seize her. He knew the other words to describe what he was about to do—abduct, kidnap. Words mattered, and he thought his intent was more subtle. To abduct or kidnap meant violence, ransom, killing, or perhaps rape—which he had no intention of doing. To seize or capture suggested a change in ownership. In a way, he would own her, at least for a time. And that ownership would lead to a sort of dependency—she'd learn to depend on him and eventually appreciate what he had to offer. Hugh knew that the progression from captive to companion seemed counterintuitive, but that didn't mean it couldn't be done. He knew. He'd been a trained psychologist with a successful couples therapy practice. He'd seen it displayed countless times in counseling sessions. The modern term was trauma bonding—the abuser, abused attachment. It was all about rewards and punishment, then dependency. Hugh knew the steps and progression, as Pavlovian as a dog's salivating mouth and wagging tail at the sound of a dinner bell.

Hugh put down the binoculars and closed the window shade. Back in the bedroom, he began undressing to bathe. His motorcoach had a bathroom with a large stand-in shower that stretched up well past his five-seven height. He was parked in a Nebraska state campground with no water or sewer services, but the coach contained a nearly full freshwater tank that held one hundred and fifty gallons and an on-demand hot water heater. Once out of the shower and toweled off, he dressed in fresh clothes—khaki pants and a madras short-sleeved shirt, both purchased years ago through an L.L. Bean catalog. He wanted to look and smell clean for his first encounter—non-threatening—not like some hobo living out of a van.

The ether he planned to use for the seizure had been

surprisingly easy to obtain. It was right there on Amazon. The advertisement read:

Diethyl Ether (for Photographic Applications). By ordering this chemical, you agree that you are at least 21 and that you understand this is for research and development purposes only. This product is not for drug, human, animal, or food use. If you purchase this with the intent of illegal use and we are contacted by enforcement agencies, we will divulge your identity to them. Please put your intended use for this product in the comments section.

He'd ordered it to be shipped directly to an RV park he stayed at months before back in Pennsylvania—back when he first came upon the plan. In the comments section, he wrote that he *did* need it for photographic purposes, though what ether had to do with photography, Hugh didn't know or care. He loosened the bottle cap and removed the foil, tamper-proof seal.

The RV was prepared. He'd bought the Thor Outlaw motorcoach five years earlier. At the time, Florence was incapacitated but still wanted to travel. The storage room in the back of the motorcoach—a feature called a "toy hauler"—had a lift gate that swung down to load anything from motorcycles and ATVs to kayaks and bicycles. Hugh used it to allow his wife to drive directly onto the RV with her three-wheeled Medicare-covered scooter. The toy hauler room was now padded and soundproofed with a comfortable bench seat that folded out into a full-size bed. Beneath the seat were unbreakable plastic bins with bedding, clothing, sundries, and two jugs of store-bought water. A porta potty no bigger than a lounge chair ottoman sat on the floor in a discreet corner partially obscured by the bench seat. There was even a flat-screen TV mounted to the wall. A camera with a microphone and speaker was attached just above the door leading to the rest of the RV so he could communicate instructions and monitor any shenanigans. The Thor Outlaw was just one of many forty-foot Class A motorcoaches that all looked similar and were as common in RV parks as outhouse toilets and running-wild children.

The rest of his plan developed from a simple memory. Florence had volunteered at a local animal shelter for years. She loved animals, especially dogs, though they never owned one—a pet would have been a distraction in their relationship. He remembered one afternoon at a campground, Florence—and he didn't like it when others called her Flo—heard someone cry for help, "My dog needs help. Can anyone help, please!?" Florence nearly ran to the man's aid. She followed him into his RV where the dog was pathetically struggling to get to its feet. Its left paw and left leg were all palsied, and the dog was half out of its mind, panicked, and squirming. Florence comforted the dog and helped it settle down. For the next few hours, she stayed by its side until the dog could finally get to its feet, recovering from what had been a stroke. What stayed with Hugh was the thought that Florence had rushed into a strange man's RV without considering her safety. So that was his plan, a nonexistent dog in distress.

In a storage compartment next to the door of the motorcoach, he hid an ether-doused rag sealed in a Tupperware bowl.

Funny how a masked man in pandemic times was considered not only normal but someone concerned for the welfare of others. He recently bought the red, white, and blue neck gaiter at a Pilot J truck stop along I-80 in Iowa. It was a not-really-a-mask, which suggested that he was no weak-kneed liberal. As far as he was concerned, the whole masking business was like wearing a necklace of garlic to repel vampires. And if he was forced to wear one, he wanted people to know he was against it.

He stretched the top of the gaiter up over his nose. The sky was clear, the wind calm, and the temperature in the comfortable seventies. He left the coach and sat waiting on a cinderblock wall with a clear view of the women's outhouse toilet. He'd watched her use it before, and sooner or later, she'd need to pee again. He'd deploy his plan then.

———

Jo stood over the small two-burner stove inside the campervan, stirring a simmering pot of spaghetti sauce made with hot Italian sausage, onions, garlic, peppers, crushed tomatoes, and spices from an herb pack labeled Italian Blend. The sauce was boiling too rapidly, and the rising and popping bubbles spit flecks of red sauce up and over the lid and onto the stovetop and backsplash. She was distracted by the look of the splatters, like the makings of some Jackson Pollock creation, and complacent about the mess. Jo turned it down, then went back to thinking about her crossword puzzle and the last five-letter word needed to complete volume thirty of the *New York Times* Sunday crossword puzzles. The clue was "Feeling of boredom." She'd gone through all the possibilities—tired, spent, empty, faint, irked, fed up (really two words), bored (too simple), weary, and even blasé. None fit with the other words that intersected, and she'd gone over those in her head like a hundred times. Though she was getting desperate, the thesaurus on her phone was off-limits.

One fleck of hot spaghetti sauce arced up like a Fourth of July fireworks display and exploded against her forearm.

"Fuck."

She quickly turned the flame further down to a low simmer and placed the lid over the pot. The flecks of sauce now seemingly completed the Pollock, and she left the painting to bake and cure onto the enamel of the hot stovetop. She hated to clean, and the reason was simple. Her father had run a restaurant, and she'd grudgingly washed dishes for years until finally leaving for college. Cleaning for her was next to torture, and she avoided it like flesh-eating fire ants. "Fuck it," she said and then reached into the mini-fridge for a can of beer—she'd clean up later.

Jo left the van and sat down outside in one of the folding camp chairs.

The beer label read "Hopgoblin" with an illustration of some mythical elf figure slicing a yellow and red mango with a samurai sword. She got it, a pun on hobgoblin. The kind of beer she drank these days was something she could never have anticipated twenty years earlier, back when she drank Budweiser or Miller High Life. Now, it seemed every town had a local brewery, and her husband, Bray, would visit as many as possible to sample their hoppy ales. He considered himself a connoisseur and, before COVID, would happily talk about the subtleties of flavor with anyone foolish enough to listen. He'd describe the beer like fine French wine: *toasty, buttery, with a slight oak nose* and *a cardamom aftertaste*. What Jo noticed more than the taste was the proliferation of puns on the word hops: *Hop Dish, Hopping Mad, Hoptastic, Hopalicious, Hop Hash, Modus Hoperandi, 2Hop2Handle*. Bray had a favorite T-shirt with "Hoptimist" stamped across the front. Names, words, and puns could occupy Jo's mind in a long string of thoughts. They came to her in a trance-like fixation, and before she knew it, she'd be fifty miles down the road or have finished making dinner or, in her present situation, sitting twenty minutes later with a second fresh beer in her hand. She had no memory of walking into the campervan, checking on the spaghetti sauce, opening the fridge, finding a new can—this one called *Hopmama*—and sitting back down. And then, it occurred to her. That five-letter word for boredom—ennui. Jo didn't need to get up and write it down; she could imagine just where it fit in the puzzle.

The RVs in the campground were neatly arranged in a herringbone pattern with maybe fifty feet of separation between each. As Jo sipped her beer, she observed people going about the activity of camping, a loosely defined term these days. A couple in a custom Mercedes Sprinter campervan were taking photos near the reservoir's edge, rows of corn far in the distance. Jo guessed they were in their mid-twenties. Both were drop-dead gorgeous and, despite their different sexes, looked almost identical, like pups from the same breeder. The boy stood stripped down to a pair of board shorts with a retro-seventies sunset design. His straight blond hair hung to his shoulders. The girl had the same straight blonde hair but longer with ends that slightly curled in and pointed toward her perfect breasts, ones that could fit into champagne coupes. Jo thought *her* breasts were once that good, maybe better, larger, the size of red-wine goblets. That was before cancer, before her double mastectomy.

The girl posed on the bed of the campervan with the back doors opened as the boy snapped photos. His equipment was bulky and professional. Jo knew because she was a professional wedding photographer on hiatus—all her gigs had been canceled due to the pandemic. Right off, Jo knew the two were Instagram influencers trying to make a living representing #vanlife. Jo and Bray were doing the same. Their Instagram page, @vanlifevagabonds, had just under two thousand followers, definitely not enough to make money from sponsorships or by selling ads.

The boy had the girl step down from the bed and stand in the open back door of the van. Jo could just hear his instructions on how to pose, and he sounded like a cliched fashion photographer, "Now hold on to the side and thrust your head and chest out. Now, shake your head so that your hair spills into your face. Now smile, now laugh."

The sun was out, and the wind had been calm all day, but now a gust came from seemingly nowhere. It spun the girl's hair in a vortex of blonde streaks. Then, the wind caught one of the opened campervan doors, and it slowly moved. The heavy steel door quickly picked up speed, and before the girl could react, before she could retreat back into the van, it hit her smack in the head, like a slapstick bit—*CABAMM.* The girl sat back on the bed and put her hands to her head. She screamed out, loud enough for the whole campground to hear, "Fuck you, Lucas!" Jo wanted to laugh, but she thought it was in bad taste—and bad karma (*there by the grace of God . . .*). Still, the theater of the Instagram couple *was* funny, and then she did laugh.

Closer, camped next to Jo and Bray, was a single woman in her fifties. She drove a Subaru Forester towing a small teardrop-shaped camper. The camper itself was half the size of the Forester and had a tiny submarine hatch that opened to a sleeping area and not much else. The camper's rear popped up like an old roadster rumble seat to reveal a slide-out kitchen with a stove, two storage compartments, a refrigerator no larger than a dresser drawer, and just enough counter space to slice up an onion. The strange part was that the owner of the Subaru traveled with an enormous old basset hound, the biggest one Jo had ever seen. She figured the dog had to weigh more than one hundred pounds. When standing, the belly of the hound touched the ground, but it rarely stood and mostly lay on a piece of brown remnant carpet while the woman sat in her folding camp chair reading a paperback. The evening before, Jo had watched as the woman set up a ramp, just a twelve-inch-wide board, so the dog could get from the carpet and through the submarine hatch, just over a foot off the ground. Jo figured that the camper was designed so two adults could sleep comfortably—she knew the woman and the hound could physically fit—but how close do you really want to snuggle beside your pet, an aging one-hundred-pound basset hound with foul dog breath? Jo tried not to stare in the woman's direction.

The campground was set up in clusters like suburban cul-de-sacs, each accessed by a gravel road with the herringbone parking areas all within a short walking distance from a unisex pit toilet, or what she grew up calling a biffy or outhouse. Jo could see a huge forty-foot-long Class A motorcoach on the next cluster over. The base color was a dark silver, but the sides were custom painted with brown and gold swirly things that Jo guessed were to elicit the feeling of movement, like flames on a hot rod. A satellite TV dome and two air conditioning units were perched on the roof. Beneath the coach, tucked into the undercarriage, was a generator Jo couldn't see but had listened to the day before from sunup until nine o'clock, the campground's generator curfew. The sound pissed her off. Continually running generators were why Jo preferred to camp off the grid, free, on the federal lands throughout the West. Jo had never seen the person or persons who lived in the big Class A motorcoach, and she'd been watching for whoever it was. But someone did live there because the God-damned generator ran nonstop. Just then, she noticed the door to the motorcoach was slightly ajar.

Jo thought about the crossword answer, ennui. It was fitting—that's how she felt—weary, tired, bored. The last time she'd heard the word must have been in college, all that time locked away in her mind like the memory of her own birth.

Jo took another sip of beer. Bray was off getting firewood and knowing him, he'd stretch that simple task into a holy quest that could last an hour or more. She thought she loved him, but he was sometimes such an annoying pedant, getting worse as he aged. She stood up and walked toward the biffy to take a pee.

———

A bundle of firewood from the campground host cost seven dollars and fifty cents. Bray had a ten and five in his wallet. If he bought two for fifteen dollars, he'd avoid the transaction of germ-ridden change. What made him nervous, though, was that the firewood was hard oak, and each bundle weighed around twenty-five pounds; he couldn't carry both bundles at the same time. He thought about leaving one behind and making two trips—that would be the obvious decision—but he'd left a bundle behind once before, and the host had put it back under lock and key. Bray had been forced to explain the situation to the host, who only grudgingly opened the cage again. He didn't want the hassle. The other issue was that he couldn't leave the second bundle unattended in the open. Campground inhabitants were notorious wood thieves. You could leave your camper unlocked, your cookstove out on the picnic table, or even an open cooler of cold micro-brewed beer in plain sight, and no one would touch a thing. But cut firewood? It was like a quarter on the sidewalk—*it's yours*. He guessed people conveniently assumed the chunks of split wood were like random branches that had fallen from the nonexistent trees in the campground. Bray wasn't going to leave behind a bundle unattended, and he didn't want to bother the campground host for a second transaction that involved ringing her doorbell and exchanging filthy, COVID-ridden coins. He'd find a better way. Bray paid for the two bundles with the ten and five.

Normally, Bray and Jo didn't stay in campgrounds. They lived full-time in their twenty-foot Winnebago Travato campervan, so at twenty-five bucks a night for most campgrounds—and some charged as much as forty—they'd go broke fast. Instead, they could usually find free places to park and sleep. The best free camping was west of the Rockies, where the federal government's Bureau of Land Management oversaw millions of acres open to anyone. RVers needed a potable water supply, a toilet with a holding tank, and a stove for cooking. All that was built into the Travato. Then, there were interstate rest stops. They could easily park beside the big rigs, close the curtains and sleep. Worst case, Walmarts and Cracker Barrel restaurants allowed RVs to stay free overnight in their parking lots. Due to the pandemic lockdowns that led to shuttered businesses, more and more people were living out of their cars, and at the last Walmart just outside Omaha, the lot was crammed with homeless people living in everything from large conversion vans to small two-seaters. The place was well lit, probably safe. Still, the light illuminated every condensation-covered window, every guy smoking a cigarette, every woman taking her kid outside to pee in the shrubs, or God forbid, poop. He and Jo had moved on from the Omaha Walmart, finding a rest stop further down I-80. The Nebraska state campground they were at now, just near the Colorado border, cost only fifteen dollars and included shared bathrooms, a fire pit at each site, and firewood for sale.

Bray figured the best way to get the firewood the few hundred yards back to the campervan was to leapfrog with each bundle. Kids were running around everywhere, so he strapped on his Chinese N95 mask to reduce the chances of infection—those kids passed around COVID germs like headlice and without ever showing symptoms. He lifted the first bundle, walked about twenty feet, and then set it down. He returned for the second bundle and walked *it* another twenty feet past the first. By the time he'd done this relay race five or six times, he could see RVers reposition their folding camp chairs in his direction to watch the show he was putting on. Bray now felt self-conscious and moved more quickly. Ahead was a couple he'd passed before. They owned a monster pickup with twin "dually" back tires that towed a thirty-foot camper trailer that, in turn, towed a trailer hauling two off-road vehicles, like dune buggies with knobby tires. At least one American flag sticker was slapped on anything with wheels, and little American flags waved from long antennas attached to each off-road vehicle. All of which implied they were patriots, Republicans—Trumpers. Bray knew his N95 facemask labeled him a liberal communist Trump-hating tree hugger, a Democrat, and he could see them snicker.

Then the unthinkable happened—he dropped a bundle, and it split open. Chunks of heavy wood bounced off each other and made a sound like toppled bowling pins. Bray loaded his outstretched arm with the loose chunks and kept going. He started to sweat, and the couple with the off-road buggies laughed outright. Bray turned their direction as he walked and delivered a stern look that said, "How dare you!"

The man stood up and walked toward Bray.

Bray stopped.

The man had beefy tattooed arms and a prominent gut beneath a T-shirt with an imprint of an off-road vehicle and the lettering, "I Like it Dirty." He stepped inside Bray's socially-distant, six-foot, CDC-recommended perimeter. The man towered almost a foot taller with a huge cartoonish nose disproportionate to his face.

He said, "Hey bud, can I give you a hand?"

It was a nice gesture, one RVer to another. A gesture that said, *Let's put aside our petty politics.* But the man wasn't wearing a mask, and Bray imagined a dragon's breath of germs spewing from that nose. He stood there with the loose chunks, his arms getting tired. Sweat was raining down his brow, and he could barely breathe through the thick virus-filtering membrane of his mask. All he could think about was COVID-19, getting infected by this man, sick in the middle of nowhere, and then trying to find one of the few scarce ventilators at some backwoods clinic that specialized in tractor-related dismemberments. *All we can do is ease the pain.*

Bray said, "Thanks, I'm good."

The man said, "Suit yourself," and walked back to his front-row seat.

Bray continued shuttling wood and just stared ahead, ignoring the peanut gallery, focused on his mission.

He was close to his Travato campervan and passed the lady with the enormous basset hound. Bray had grown up in Minneapolis but spent summers as a boy on his grandparent's farm in Iowa. They planted corn and alfalfa but also raised a few hogs. One of Bray's chores was to slop the hogs each evening after supper. He'd take any leftovers that'd been scraped into a galvanized pail—chewed corn cobs, chicken bones, bits of mashed potatoes covered in white lumpy gravy, carrot peels, and unfinished milk—and toss the disgusting mélange over the pen fence into the horde of waiting, squealing, and jostling hogs. And that's what Bray thought of when he passed the basset hound—it looked like a greedy hog. The woman sitting in her chair and reading a paperback barely looked up as Bray leapfrogged by with his firewood, one bundle busted.

Bray stacked the wood next to the fire pit and went inside the campervan. The stove was on, the pot of spaghetti sauce simmering under low heat. Jo was nowhere. He didn't think it was a good idea to leave the sauce cooking unattended over an open flame, and it bothered him that the sauce had splattered all over the stove. Why couldn't she just clean up after herself? Bray turned off the burner, scrubbed the counter and stove, and then looked outside for Jo, calling her name. Jo did not answer. She'd most likely gone off somewhere, on a hike or to the outhouse.

He decided to shower and wash off the sweat that had soaked through his shirt. He undressed and could smell the stench of his body. He deposited his clothes in the drawstring duffle they used for a hamper, then stepped into the combination bathroom and shower, called a wet bath, to take what was referred to as a "navy shower," performed to conserve the fresh water in their twenty-five-gallon tank—get wet, turn off the water, soap up, and rinse quickly. Bray could take a shower and get clean with less than two quarts. He knew because he never switched on the floor drain pump that moved the water from the shower basin to the gray water tank until he was finished, and more than once, he'd scooped out the contents to take a measurement. Jo always used more, which was a continual source of irritation between them that turned into heated discussions—that and her slovenliness. The thought made him think of her—whether or not she was back from wherever she'd gone. He looked out the windows on all four sides and saw only the lady with the portly hound.

After he pumped out the water and dressed, Bray wiped dry the floor of the wet bath with a micro-fiber towel he kept for just that purpose. Then, he unscrewed the drain cover to clean the thimble-like screen filter inside. It was completely covered with a collection of fine lint, dead flakes of skin, and tangles of hair. All this invariably shed from his aging body during every shower. The detritus repulsed him but would otherwise clog and destroy the drain pump should he not keep the screen filter in place. He flung the bits of lint, skin, and hair into the trash receptacle beneath the sink. Then, out of some weird compulsion, Bray put the screen to his nose before inserting it back. There was no smell he could discern.

Bray took a beer from the refrigerator, a hazy IPA called *Juicy Lucy*, and sat outside in one of the two folding camp chairs. A can of *Hopmama* was in the beverage holder of the other chair, and he lifted it up to feel the weight. The beer was still cold and half full, and he thought it odd that Jo had taken off and not finished a beer that cost them over a dollar and a half. He decided to drink what was left of the *Hopmama* before opening the *Juicy Lucy*. *Waste not, want not,* he thought and took a sip. He tasted the tropical fruitiness from what he surmised were Simcoe hops.

He sat, drank, and waited.

He liked to just look at his Travato, its lines, and accessories—admiring it like a sculpture in a museum. It was a National Parks edition with upgraded suspension, alloy wheels, long-life lithium batteries, a weBoost hotspot signal booster, and an enhanced graphics package. Instead of a bike rack on the back, he'd installed a motorcycle carrier that held his prized 1969 BMW R69S. On their periodic vacations, he'd enjoyed visiting vintage motorcycle shows around the country and talking shop while Jo took photographs they'd post on their Instagram page, @vanlifevagabonds.

Now they really were full-time van life vagabonds—Bray had been laid off from his physical therapist job at the assisted living center (the tenants were now all locked in their rooms like convicts), and Jo had lost all her wedding photography gigs. Both had state unemployment insurance plus the fat six-hundred-dollar per week per person national CARES Act cash. They were doing fine as long as they didn't waste money on things like campground fees. And if they could increase the number of Instagram followers to at least 10,000, they might conceivably make $100 per post. It was his one goal for their vagabond life.

Jo still hadn't come back, and Bray was now worried. He called her cell phone and heard the simultaneous ring emanating from the Travato. He let the phone ring and followed the sound to where she'd left it docked on the van's dashboard. She hadn't taken her phone, which concerned him even more.

The woman next door with the basset hound was still reading in her chair. Bray strapped on his facemask, walked into her campsite, and stood a respectable, socially-distant ten feet away. The woman looked up from her paperback. Her gray hair was jelled into a crazy hairdo—coiffed and clean but unruly and haphazard like she planned it that way. It looked like sculpted steel wool.

Bray spoke loudly through his mask, "Say, have you seen my wife? About five-seven, graying hair, hazel eyes." As he said that, he realized he'd just described a big chunk of the female population. He knew eyeglasses set someone apart, and Jo had once worn large, red-framed ones like the show host Sally Jesse Raphael, but that was before the Lasik surgery. Then there were hats. He added, "She usually wears a tan sun hat," which didn't help.

The woman answered with lips pursed together, her words like baby talk. "I know who she is."

"That's great. Have you seen her? Because I just came back from getting firewood and she hadn't told me she was leaving. I guess I'm worried."

The woman took her time and looked down at the basset hound that hadn't moved a muscle as he approached. It appeared almost dead except for the droopy eyes that followed Bray's every movement. Finally, she said, "Went with an elderly gentleman into that big fancy motorcoach parked over there." She nodded in the direction of the pit toilets.

Bray looked at the toilets and beyond. He couldn't see any big motorcoach, though he remembered seeing one earlier. He said, "Where?"

"Well, it's not there now."

"What do you mean it's not there now? And why would my wife step into another man's RV?" Bray heard the tone of his voice and knew before she responded that his words had come out wrong, like maybe he was implying that she'd fabricated the whole story.

The woman's lips squished even tighter and wrinkles formed all pruney around her mouth. She raised her voice. "It ain't my business to know why your damn wife runs off with another man. She's your wife—why don't *you* know? Or maybe you're the kind of folks that fool around, have a party, put your keys into a punch bowl, and sleep with whatever Tom, Dick, or Harry pulls out the lucky set."

The response shocked him—those words out of that lady's mouth.

She added, "I mind my own business and expect others to do likewise."

"Sorry, sorry, I didn't mean to imply . . . I didn't mean to suggest . . ." and he stopped himself there without knowing how to finish the sentence.

He started over, "So, you saw my wife, Jo, follow a man into the motorcoach parked over there." He paused and pointed past the toilets. "Then the motorcoach drove off?"

"It's what I saw."

Bray looked toward the empty campsite. He tried to imagine what had happened and to think of any plausible rationale for why Jo would walk into another man's RV and drive away. Bray scratched his head—he couldn't.

———

Jo woke up groggy, a bitter and metallic taste in her mouth. She was lying sideways on a padded bench seat with her hands bound behind her back. She could feel the road moving beneath the room she was in. The details of what had happened came to her in blurs of images at first, a mixed collage of details. Then, it all made sense.

She remembered not wearing a mask when the older man stepped up and said, "I need your help. My dog is having a stroke or something." The man was wearing a mask, an American flag gaiter pulled up over his nose. His head of ash-gray hair was neatly parted to one side, and Jo noticed he wore the old-fashioned wire-rimmed bifocals with a line separating the readers. He stayed a respectable six feet away.

Jo said, "What?"

"My dog, inside the RV," and the man pointed toward the big motorcoach parked not a hundred feet away, "is having a stroke. He's a big lab, and I need help holding him down so I can give him his medicine. You need to hurry." His voice was whiny, nasally, and slightly muffled by the mask. Then he turned and walked in quick strides toward the coach. He looked back and did the come-on motion with his hand. He said again, "Please, hurry."

Jo didn't think. Her response was all instinct, muscle memory, a pre-programmed reaction—someone needed help, a struggling dog, no less. She followed the man.

He opened the coach door and two steps mechanically slid out from beneath the threshold. The two steps led to another flight of two steps up into the huge RV. The man walked up the stairs and stood in the narrow corridor between driver and passenger seats. Jo followed and passed him into the coach. She'd never entered such a big fancy rig and was awed by the space and luxury. The man motioned her toward the living room area. "My dog is in the back. He won't bite. Just let me get the medicine from the glove compartment."

Jo moved through the living room, looking for the pet. She saw a white leather couch across from a dinette with two matching white leather bench seats. Above one seat was a built-in TV as big as the dinette table. Beyond that was the kitchen and a hallway that led to what Jo guessed was the master bedroom. Jo kept going. She opened the door to the bedroom but didn't see the pet. She yelled back, "Where?"

What she noticed before the man smothered her mouth was the size of the bedroom, nearly as big as the one back at her old condo in Minneapolis. On the nightstand was a single pack of playing cards, and the room's wood laminate floor was covered by a rug with a pattern of card hands—not poker hands—three-of-a-kind hands and runs in the same suit. Gin rummy hands. But there was no dog.

Jo remembered all those details. She knew she was still in the motorcoach, probably in the way back, and it was moving down some highway, moving fast and far from the campground and Bray. Her head was pounding from the aftereffects of whatever drug the man had used to subdue her. She closed her eyes and relaxed, trying to focus on something other than the pain in her head, in her shackled wrists, and in her stomach. She tried to answer the simple question: what happened? The answer came to her quickly—right before she threw up.

I've been abducted.

2

Outlaw Shuffle

Hugh avoided the interstates and drove the Thor Outlaw on less-traveled roads south toward Kansas. He wanted to put at least three hundred miles between the motorcoach and the campground in Nebraska, far enough so that a one or two-day search by her husband would yield nothing. Driving three hundred miles in the Outlaw was easy, six hours at fifty miles per hour, like watching an old western in a La-Z-Boy recliner. He'd previously topped off his eighty-gallon diesel fuel tank, and even at a conservative ten miles per gallon, his range was eight hundred miles. He could avoid gas station cameras for days, finding independent stations in Podunk towns that he knew didn't have any fancy surveillance apparatus. He'd use his ample supply of cash instead of credit cards. He'd be long gone without leaving a trail before any posse mounted a serious search.

In the rear storage room, he had some surveillance

apparatus of his own. A monitor on the dashboard was hooked into a camera that allowed him to watch the woman even as he drove. He'd seen her finally wake from the ether and spew vomit over the side of the fold-out bed. He didn't slow down and wouldn't pull over until he was safely in Kansas. He already planned a place to rest, a huge Love's truck stop where he could park among the big rigs with their diesels that ran continuously, drowning out any sound that might escape the back room. He just kept driving and, from time to time, glimpsed over at the camera and watched as the woman squirmed. He knew he was supposed to feel sympathy, but what he felt was the thrill of accomplishment.

He'd thought through the details of the woman's probable responses. She wouldn't cooperate at first, fearing violence or rape. She would eventually realize that wasn't going to happen. She'd need to eat and drink if she wanted to stay alive. She'd become reliant upon him for that sustenance. That was the trick to trauma bonding, the unconscious emotional response to the terror of being held captive and the protection that's entirely in the hands of the captor. She'd eventually come around. Humans are social beings, way more than other animals. They crave interaction like they need food, water, and shelter (he, too, was prone to loneliness). She'd give in and eventually want that interaction—TV, talk, and possibly card games.

He didn't think the transformation from captive to something like friendship would take long. The older reference to trauma bonding was the Stockholm Syndrome. In that situation, two machine-gun-carrying criminals entered a bank and took four hostages for five days. During that time, the hostages grew to be reliant and eventually supportive of their captors. One woman later became engaged to one of the hostage-takers.

In Hugh's practice, he'd witnessed many newlyweds with the dysfunction of trauma bonding already firmly established. He remembered one young woman who came to her husband's defense after Hugh uncovered the fact that the man had cut her with a knife. He remembered her exact words, "There was a time I trusted that he knew what was right for me." She was a bright young lawyer. Hugh thought he could make the transformation happen in the span of two weeks, at which time he planned to compete in a gin rummy tournament in Las Vegas. Two weeks was all he needed, but for the moment, he didn't even know her name.

Hugh reached the Love's truck stop just after one a.m. and parked between two semis with tall trailers that concealed his motorcoach. He put up all the shades and then pressed the button to start the generator.

His camera system had microphones and speakers so they could talk back and forth. She was still lying on the bed, but Hugh could see some movement.

He said, "Hello."

He expected rage, a caged animal throwing itself at the bars. What he heard instead was soft crying. In therapy sessions over the years, he'd heard hundreds of people cry. Crying to him always seemed unproductive—he would rather people simply *communicate*—but Hugh knew he had issues with empathy. And empathy still eluded him—he could never feel what others felt. Over time, though, he'd learned to translate those emotions into concrete expressions of thought. To Hugh, it was obvious her crying was the emotional expression of the inevitable realization that she'd been abducted.

He said, "I won't hurt you."

The woman looked up toward the source of the sound but

said nothing.

"My name is Hubert, but except for my deceased mother, everyone calls me Hugh." He thought that the "mother" comment was funny and might trigger, if not laughter, a little anxiety relief. He added, "Please tell me your name."

She sat up on the bed and stared down at her shoes centered in the pool of vomit. Her arms were pinned awkwardly behind her back, and he could see her fingernails scratch at the nickel-plated handcuffs. For minutes, there was silence, and Hugh knew better than to force the dialogue.

She finally looked up again at the camera. "You abducted me, and you don't even know who I am?"

Hugh chose to ignore the question. The answer seemed too long and too subtle, and he wasn't sure she had the capacity to comprehend and really understand his explanation at just that moment. He said again, "I won't hurt you."

She screamed. Hugh stared at the woman's face, the contortion of features. Then, with each deep breath, she screamed again and again. So unproductive.

He tried to pulse his words between screams, "No one . . . can hear you . . . the motorcoach . . . is soundproofed."

He waited until the screams subsided—until she resumed crying. "You'll find water and other supplies under the bench seat and a porta potty in the corner. I promise I won't watch when you need to go."

She looked up silently at the camera. The look on her face showed, he thought, bewilderment. She finally spoke. Compared to her screaming, the woman's response was like a squeak. "My hands are bound. How do you expect me to—"

He cut her off. "I'll uncuff your hands if you just tell me your name." He didn't like that he hadn't let the woman finish her sentence. It was a cardinal rule in therapy that you let the person finish their thoughts and then allow a moment for them to amend the thoughts. Hugh was out of practice and needed to remember his training.

Now she shouted, "Fuck you. Tell me why I'm being abducted? Do you want sex? Do you want money? Are you some serial killer who'll get off on my death?"

The words coming from her mouth were just so harsh. The "why" was very simple. He was lonely, his practice was in shambles, he didn't do the whole online dating thing—didn't have any online presence that he knew of—and he knew he was not attractive to women. The other piece to the "why" was that he *could*. In his youth, he'd been more impulsive, one time coming close to beating a boy to death who'd called him a circus clown because of his facial birthmark. He spent six months in a juvenile detention center. He still had impulsive thoughts, but long ago, he'd learned to be methodical in their execution. He'd gotten away with plenty in the past, and he'd get away with this.

He replied, "I don't want any of those things, and I mean you no harm."

"No harm? Look at me; I'm handcuffed and standing in my own vomit. I was lured into your RV and then drugged. No harm? Fuck you." Again with the *fuck you*.

Hugh had to remind himself that he had a process. The first step was ensuring she relied on him for everything needed to stay alive. He started there. "You have water under your seat along with snacks, clothes, bedding, and toiletries. There are paper towels to clean up your mess. I'll provide a meal later today. Again, I won't watch when you go to the bathroom. I give you my word. But I also won't stand for any escape attempts. If you try to escape, there will be consequences." He said it but fully expected her to try. She needed to make that attempt within his controlled environment to put the thought of escape behind her.

"What consequences? What can you do to me that you haven't already done?" Here, she paused.

He knew the woman could think of worse—she already had: rape and death. He wasn't prepared to do the first, but he had pepper spray, drugs, and a gun. Death was an inevitability in life, a point that could be reached earlier rather than later.

She asked, "What is it you want?"

"For right now, I just want to know your name."

"Take these handcuffs off first."

The conversation wasn't going his way. He thought he should hold his ground and show who was in control, but he didn't want that kind of relationship. With Florence, their relationship hadn't always been rosy, and they'd fought often. Eventually, he agreed to see a marriage counselor, a woman. In their first sessions, he'd tried to out-clinician the clinician, like a pissing match between two professionals. Then, one day, the woman said he didn't need to win every argument and that it was important to show vulnerability. She added that empathy could allow him to see both sides and, often, it was best for the relationship if he just accepted the other's perspective. It was important to sometimes say, "I'm wrong," or "I'm sorry." Of course, he'd said some of those same things to *his* clients, but hearing it directed toward him made him understand the *usefulness* of empathy and vulnerability. He'd understood their literal meaning but hadn't understood their magnitude. He wasn't ready to tell the woman he was sorry, but he would. And sooner or later, the handcuffs would come off.

"Okay, this is how it will work. When I come into the room, you need to be lying face-down on the seat with your hands behind your back. I'll come in and take off the cuffs, but you'll need to remain face-down until I leave the room. If you move or attempt to escape, I'll use my pepper spray. I don't want to use it, so I'm hoping that we can have that understanding. Okay?"

She made no sound, which he took to mean she'd acquiesced. He tested this. "Please lie down with your face against the bed and your hands up behind you." He added, "Please." He'd found that "please" was such a powerful word, almost as powerful as the words, "I'm sorry."

She did as he asked.

Hugh walked to the back of the RV. The door to the storage area was heavy double-walled aluminum sandwiching an inch of Styrofoam insulation through which he'd installed a one-way peephole and a steel slide bolt. He could see her still lying face-down on the bench seat. He'd brought the can of pepper spray and kept it ready in his left hand as he unbolted the door and entered.

She remained still and silent. The small cylinder of pepper spray, the size of an empty toilet paper roll, came with a belt clip, and he attached it to the edge of his pocket. He reached into his other pocket and took out the handcuff key.

He looked at her hands as he unlocked the cuffs—nails clipped without polish, skin freckled with liver spots. He said, "Please stay down until I step away." He stepped back toward the door and again held the can of pepper spray. "Okay."

She sat up. Her face was red from crying, and she looked at him with obvious anger. "So, what is it you want?"

He asked, "Are you hungry?

"No. What do you want?"

"I want to know your name."

"Fuck you. What is it you want? Sex? You want sex?" Then she did something very unexpected. With two hands, she quickly pulled up her shirt. Hugh lifted the pepper spray eye level and nearly pressed the button. The woman wore no bra, and her breasts were exposed like grinning headlights. And that thought was strange because her breasts did have grins—wide smiley-faced scars that ran horizontally from edge to edge—mastectomy scars. She held her shirt up long enough for him to get a good look and until his stare moved from her amputated breasts to her eyes.

He said, "Definitely not." Hugh left the room quickly and bolted the door. He felt unnerved and also misunderstood. He'd said twice that he wouldn't hurt her. Yes, he'd tricked the woman into entering his RV, and yes, he'd drugged her and kept her confined. But now and in the future, he didn't want to hurt her. Just the opposite.

Back behind the steering wheel, Hugh watched the woman on the TV screen. She massaged her wrists and slowly paced around the room, no doubt assessing her situation. He switched on the microphone. "I can provide everything you need. It's all here in the motorcoach, and it's just you and me. I want to be friends or at least civil and provide you with food and entertainment, but for now, please tell me your name."

"Josephine."

For Hugh, the name conjured up an image of the eighteenth-century empress married to Napoleon. A great beauty and lover of the arts. "Oh, I like that name." He did like it.

"But everyone calls me Jo."

And that somehow spoiled it for him.

———

Jo woke up to the smell of diesel exhaust and the sound of big rigs on each side of the RV. She was still there; it wasn't a dream she could awake from. The time on her digital wristwatch was 9:15 a.m. She'd finally gone to sleep late into the night after she'd shown the man, Hubert or Hugh, her scarred breasts.

She'd found the lump almost ten years earlier while in the shower. The size of a lima bean, the lump swelled just underneath her right breast. She felt it, felt it again, and later had Bray feel it. Nothing was said out loud other than, "You should have that checked." A month later, after a stage-three diagnosis, a surgeon offered up a lumpectomy or double mastectomy. She wanted them gone so that they never, ever, caused her more harm. Now, the fat, wormy scars that stretched across each breast implant were far from eliciting desire. She'd shown them to the man, who'd claimed he didn't want sex, and now it was really off the table.

She started to cry, but then something stopped her. It was the thought that crying was admitting helplessness. Her situation seemed helpless, but she knew that was never the case. There could be a solution, and Jo was the kind of person who would find it. The solution, she thought, had to be tied to the man's motivation. If it wasn't sex, then it could be money, and there was the possibility he was holding her for ransom. If Bray paid the money, she'd be set free. But she and Bray hadn't accumulated any real money. Their savings were still in the low six digits. They were living off unemployment checks, and in the future, they planned to live mainly off social security. Then Jo remembered the man didn't know her name, so obviously he didn't know or care if she had money.

He'd said he wanted to be friends, but there had to be easier ways for the man to make friends, ways that wouldn't risk a lengthy prison sentence. So what was his motivation? Jo was a wedding photographer and had gotten to know countless couples. She'd seen plenty of best buddies who married after a long courtship. The attractive, infatuated ones who liked the *appearance* of the perfect couple and saw their relationship as perceived through the eyes of others. The shotgun marriages of necessity (a baby on the way or already born) and marriages blatant for money or power. She'd also seen marriages of pure desperation. These were unions between individuals who'd rarely had previous relationships; maybe one or both physically unappealing, extreme introverts, or plagued by other emotional maladies. She remembered one couple, the man thin with arms that hung at his side like dead weights, the woman much larger with mannish features. The preacher said, "You may kiss the bride," and the two barely touched lips, like nervous on a first date. This was the motivation Jo sensed—the man was desperate, plagued by emotional maladies, and possibly just plain crazy.

Sunlight beamed in through a skylight in the ceiling so now she could see her prison cell in full. She stood and took the few steps that navigated the entire room, each step sticky with congealed vomit. She wouldn't clean it up, even with his paper towels. For all she cared, let the vomit stink up the place. The walls and ceiling were covered, insulated, and soundproofed with thick sheets of hard, pink foam. Jo lifted the bench seat. Beneath were jugs of water and three storage tubs of supplies. She opened each. One had bedding: a cover sheet, a flat sheet, a pillow, and an older wool blanket. She could see how the bench seat folded down into a bed. Clothes were stacked in the second tub, but she did not rummage through to inventory what the creep had bought her. The third tub held an assortment of stuff: toothbrush and toothpaste, deodorant, a travel cosmetics kit in a clear vinyl case, toilet paper, the roll of paper towels, an assortment of cereal bars, and a TV remote. She lifted out the remote, pointed the device at the mounted flat-screen TV, and clicked it on. The television came to life, already programmed to re-runs of *Judge Judy*. She clicked the program off just as a stout white man with a locked expression mouthed the words, ". . . four months' back rent." She put the remote back in the bin. In the corner next to a plastic trash can was the porta potty. She knew the kind—a bowl above a holding tank that could be pulled out and dumped when full. There was no wall or screen for privacy. What had the man said? He wouldn't watch? Sure thing. The camera perched above the one door on the opposite wall pointed in that direction. She guessed he might be looking at her even now, waiting for her to pull down her pants. She had a fleeting instinct to give him the finger. But what would that accomplish? Jo had to think.

The engine of the motorcoach came to life, just a small vibration in her feet. Then the coach started moving, turning, then accelerating. She sat down on the bench seat. From time to time, the coach slowed and stopped, and sometimes, through the skylight, Jo could see a streetlamp. She figured they were on rural highways going from town to town, putting more distance between her and Bray.

She had to pee and just decided, *fuck it, let him watch*. He'd already seen her half naked. She squatted and did her business. Later, she drank from one of the jugs of water. She didn't eat until that night and not until after they were parked again, this time at a remote place where she could hear nothing, not even the sound of the generator. She ate a sugary cereal bar coated with chocolate. The man, Hugh, didn't speak to her, and she could just barely hear him move throughout the vehicle. She pulled out the bench seat so it lay flat into a full-sized bed. She made the bed and lay down. She remained wide-awake for hours, finally drifting into a restless sleep.

Then the nightmares came. She remembered just the last one where she was wrapped like a mummy but still alive. She tried to scream but couldn't get her mouth to move air, as though all the oxygen had been sucked from her lungs. When she finally startled herself awake, the bedsheets were soaked through with sweat. She opened her eyes to almost total darkness. She screamed, but no one came.

The rising sun slowly illuminated the room. Lying in bed, Jo focused on one thing: a simple hand crank that held down the domed acrylic skylight seven feet from the floor. She realized it could be opened to vent air but also used as an escape hatch if the motorcoach were in an accident and tipped on its side. It was wide enough for her to slip through, with no lock she could see.

She was startled when the speaker emitted a noise, the man clearing his throat and then swallowing. He said, "Good morning, Josephine."

She didn't respond.

"I'd like you to come into my living quarters. We can eat breakfast and maybe play a game of cards. Is that okay with you?"

The room still smelled of the vomit that had now dried and covered much of the floor in a milky, yellowy film.

She replied, "Yes."

3

Brayden's Heroic Journey Begins

The night of the abduction, after speaking to the basset hound lady, Bray calmed himself. Maybe the lady had seen Jo enter the motorcoach but hadn't seen her leave, and maybe Jo was just off taking a nature hike somewhere. That wouldn't be unlike her. Jo had often wandered off by herself without telling him. It was like shopping at the Mall of America. He'd be walking beside Jo, having a conversation and thinking they planned to visit the Gap or Macy's. Then, all of a sudden, she wouldn't be there anymore, and he'd be forced to search each store they'd passed. It was no use telling her to communicate, that if she wanted to go off by herself, to let him know. He tried that, and it hadn't stopped her wandering. It was as though she unknowingly followed her own muse to wherever it took her. Bray thought it possible that Jo did leave the man's coach after entering it and then just took off on a hike somewhere. Bray firmly believed in Occam's Razor, that the simplest answer to any dilemma was usually the correct one. And that's what he decided or latched onto—she'd taken off on an impromptu hike.

Bray finished making dinner. Jo had started the spaghetti sauce, but instead of pasta, they'd planned to try a new gadget called a spiralizer that turned zucchini into long spaghetti-like threads called "zoodles" that could be used as an alternative— he'd been trying to cut down on carbs. Bray assembled the gadget, a lathe contraption like the old apple peeler machine his grandmother had used each fall when making pies. But instead of apples, trimmed lengths of zucchini fit between the crank and a cutting wheel. He cranked, and the spirals delightfully appeared. Bray set the table and opened the *Juicy Lucy* IPA he'd taken out earlier. He waited. He checked his watch—just after six.

He felt the beer start to cloud his mind. By seven p.m., he'd lost his appetite and the zucchini spaghetti sat cold. It occurred to him then that the simplest answer might not be the correct one.

The basset hound lady was eating her dinner outside on the site's picnic table. The hound lay beneath, and Bray watched her slip the beast a piece of meat. He approached with his N95 mask covering his nose and mouth, then stood ten feet away.

She said, "Mister, I'm having my supper."

Bray apologized but proceeded to ask questions to confirm what she'd said earlier. He got a rough description of the motorcoach: possibly forty feet, brown with swirly designs, an expensive Class A rig. Bray vaguely remembered the vehicle.

He checked with others nearby. Two remembered seeing the motorcoach. One said it had a "toy hauler" feature. None remembered seeing Jo.

Bray walked toward the Mercedes Sprinter van parked near the reservoir. The sun was setting, and the couple were around a campfire with flames that looked dangerously high. The young woman sat on a heavy wood stump with her back to the burgeoning sunset, her blonde hair spread over bare shoulders. She looked near naked. The guy crouched from the other side of the campfire and took photos from different angles. Bray heard the guy say, "Nice nipples," and to that, the woman replied, "Hurry up, Lucas, it's getting fucking cold out here."

Bray cleared his throat, his way of announcing himself before more awkward dialogue poured out. He walked up and stood a safe ten-foot distance away. "Excuse me, I'm wondering if either of you saw that motorcoach parked earlier just over there?" Bray pointed.

Behind the couple, the van's back doors were open, and Bray could see the custom interior: a platform bed above a storage area with two mountain bikes, bedding with a faux fur comforter, walls of reclaimed wood, a row of handcrafted storage compartments along the roof line, and antique sconces converted to LEDs. Bray admired the craftsmanship. He'd always wanted to do something really custom like that, but the Winnebago Travato he and Jo purchased came fully outfitted. He had, though, done a variety of "hacks" to make the campervan more livable. One involved a collapsible table between their twin beds that could flip up and swivel. Before either could answer his question, Bray said, "Nice van."

The guy had lowered the camera to his lap. Bray noticed his straight blond hair that hung to his shoulders. He looked like everyone's idea of a cool surfer dude, and in fact, the van did have California plates. He responded to the compliment, "Thanks."

Bray waited seconds to see if the guy would answer his initial question. When he didn't, Bray asked again, "Any chance you saw that motorcoach?"

"Maybe. I don't know. Why?"

Until then, Bray had planned to say he was just trying to find the owner of the motorcoach. He'd kept it vague, not wanting to startle anyone with the threat of danger; he still envisioned the possibility that it was all a mistake, that Jo would just show up. But now, for whatever reason, the very real thought of malfeasance struck him. "I think my wife might have been abducted." With that, his mouth twisted into a pained expression, and he let out one quick cough-like sob.

The girl said, "Oh no!"

Bray shook his head, "Oh, yes!" Bray looked down, put a hand to his masked mouth, and tried to regain some composure. He focused on her bare legs tucked into sheepskin Ugg boots.

He said, "The lady next to me with the basset hound saw her walk into the motorcoach and never come out. The coach later drove off. My wife left her phone behind, and she *never* leaves her phone behind."

The girl said, "I won't let anyone even touch my phone." She reached down and picked up a flannel shirt that she draped over her shoulders and wrapped around her chest.

The guy said, "We've been taking photos all day. We could look. Maybe it's in the background in one of the shots."

Bray's outburst of emotion was spent, and he wiped at his tears. "I'd appreciate it." Then added, "My name is Bray."

The guy said, "I'm Lucas and this is Margo."

Bray stayed where he was, masked and at a safe distance. Lucas walked over to the van and came back with an iPad. He sat near the fire, and as Margo looked over his shoulder, he swiped through seemingly hundreds of photos, looking for the motorcoach. Margo shouted, "Stop."

Lucas moved two fingers on the screen to zoom in. He turned the iPad so Bray could see. "Is that it?"

Bray stepped nearer, stopping at the imaginary six-foot COVID boundary. He leaned in and over the boundary like a kid getting closer to a caged zoo animal. He could barely see the motorcoach above a closeup of Margo's knee. He said, "I'm sure that's it. Can you send me the photo?"

Margo said, "We'll post it on our Instagram page. You can see it there, at fabvanlife."

Bray repeated, "Fab-Van-Life."

She added, "We can post something if you want. Like, 'Have you seen this RV?' We have over ten thousand followers, many living on the road in campervans."

Bray thought of his own Instagram page, @vanlifevagabonds—only two thousand followers, but he could link to their page, get the word out, and find Jo. He said, "Wow, that would be great. I can message the details and keep you updated. That would be a great help."

Then, somewhere in the back of Bray's mind was the germination of a thought. At ten thousand followers he'd have access to Instagram tools and links otherwise denied him. He might be able to ramp up his follower count and find a sponsor to offset the cost of gas and food.

He thought, *Wouldn't that be something?*

————

Back in the Travato, Bray connected his laptop to the campervan's Internet hotspot, began following @fabvanlife, and waited. Fifteen minutes later, the photos were posted. One showed Margo posed with the motorcoach in the background. The next showed the motorcoach up close, though blurred. The color wasn't so much brown, more a swirly mess of black, gray, and white over a base of silver that, combined on a palette, looked brown overall. The photo only showed the side and not the back or front with a license plate. He zoomed in closer to where he could just make out some lettering. He counted six letters beginning he thought with an O or Q. The next letter he thought could be a U, which didn't rule out the Q. But then he could see that the third letter was definitely a T, which now made the first letter definitely an O. OUT_ _ _. The last letter he thought was a W. Bray's quick *Wheel of Fortune* mind filled in the blanks. He shouted, "Outlaw!"

From there, a quick Google search found that the motorcoach was a Thor Outlaw with the Thunder Canyon paint scheme. He posted the information on @fabvanlife and then linked @vanlifevagabonds to it. He created his own post with a description of what he thought had happened to Jo and asked for anyone with information to contact him. He posted a headshot photo of Jo and reposted the photo of the motorcoach. All this information was then posted to his Facebook page. From there, he reposted the photo and information to the Travato Owners Facebook group with over fifteen thousand followers. Some Bray knew; many were on the road now and could help in the search.

Bray finally felt he had enough information to bring Jo's abduction to the attention of the authorities. The closest police station was in a small town eight miles away called, simply, Settlement. He pressed 'GO' on his navigation system and drove off into the night.

He found the police station on the main street of the small farming town. The entrance was lit by an antique globe that read "Police" and the plate-glass door was flanked by frosted windows that curved away like angel wings. Bray masked up and opened the door. What struck him was the resemblance of the whole office to the one he remembered from *The Andy Griffith Show*—Sheriff Taylor's office in the small town of Mayberry.

A uniformed officer sat at a heavy wood desk. Behind the desk was a knee-high railed-in area with another, larger desk that Bray assumed was reserved for the sheriff. Instinctively, he said, "Deputy?"

A young man stood up. His body was almost as wide as he was tall, but Bray could tell the man's weight was the kind with muscle behind it. This was no Deputy Fife. The young deputy said, "How can I help you?"

He'd planned in advance what to say—no beating around the bush. "I need to report that my wife's been abducted."

"Okay, have a seat and tell me what happened." He motioned toward a high-backed wood chair next to the desk.

Bray walked nearer and saw a table-tent nameplate, Officer Otto, not Deputy. "Thank you, Officer Otto. My name is Brayden Osterhockenberger." He knew it was an unusually long and difficult last name, one his wife had initially been reluctant to take. "Her name is Josephine Osterhockenberger." Bray sat within the six-foot distance suggested by the CDC, and the officer did not strap on a mask. This was rural Nebraska, and Bray knew not to push it. He continued, "We've been camping near the Dirt Slip Reservoir for the last two days. I went out to purchase firewood, and when I came back, Josephine, or Jo, was gone. I asked a neighbor, and she said Jo walk into this Thor Outlaw motorcoach with a man, who then drove off. I'm sure she's been abducted." His voice began to quiver as he finished. Just describing what he thought had happened made the abduction more real, and he felt the loss. He held back tears and forced himself to be more stoic.

Bray noticed that the officer wasn't writing any of this down.

Officer Otto asked, "Was she forced into the motorcoach, or did she go willingly?"

"The woman who saw it said Jo *followed* the man into the motorcoach."

"So, there was no indication of a struggle of any kind?"

"Not that I know of."

"And how long has she been missing?"

Bray counted the hours approximately. "Since just after three o'clock, seven hours."

The officer still hadn't lifted a pen or powered up his computer. "Had the two of you been getting along?"

Bray knew where this was headed and wouldn't have any of it. "Listen, can't you just put out an APB or something? An Amber Alert?"

"Amber Alerts are for children seventeen years of age or younger. Is your wife a child?" The officer looked at Bray without smiling or even a trace of a smirk.

Bray was not an angry man; he had never been an angry man. In fact, he avoided confrontations like the plague, like COVID. The emotion made him doubt everything he thought he was—a good man, a smart man, a calm, thoughtful man— and shook his self-confidence. But now Bray could feel the anger rising in him like bile. He wanted to shout something but held back and dodged the confrontation by simply saying, "My wife is fifty-eight years old." He avoided meeting the officer's eyes and looked past him toward a photo of the forty-fifth President of the United States, Donald Trump. And, somehow, Bray felt that the situation he was in was all this president's fault.

"I'm sorry, mister," pausing there, unable to say Bray's last name, "I can't issue an Amber Alert for your wife, and I can't even take a missing person's report unless she's been gone for forty-eight hours. It sounds like your wife willingly entered the other man's RV—no indication of a struggle. We find that in most of these cases, like pretty much all cases, the wife will come back, call, or file for divorce. I suggest you wait."

Bray knew that the forty-eight-hour waiting period was a fabrication made up by the writers of cop shows. He pressed the issue. "You're required by law to take a missing person report if I ask for one." He wanted to cry again but wasn't sure the emotion now had anything to do with Jo.

The officer slowly opened drawers. His thick fingers flicked through stacks of paper. He found what he was looking for in the bottom drawer. He handed the poorly copied form to Bray. "You can fill out this here form at the counter over there by the door. When you're done, I'll enter the information into the computer. I'll give you a case number once the form is entered. At that point, you should leave the station. You may call back, preferably during regular office hours when I'm not around, to see if the case has been updated in any way." The man stood, "Now I have other things to attend to."

Bray looked at the officer standing above him, large and imposing—a real fireplug of a man. Bray avoided confrontation like he avoided dog turds on the sidewalk, like teenagers with saggy pants, like small barking dogs. He asked politely, "May I borrow a pen?"

With that, Bray wrote the report, received a case number, and left the hick town police station with its small-minded officer.

Bray couldn't just go back to the campground; he couldn't

just do nothing, and he knew sleep would never come. On his navigation system, he voiced the command, "Find campgrounds near me," and started his journey.

43

4

Avoid Speculating

He made Jo lie on the bench seat, face-down, with her hands behind her. He was clear in his instructions. If she moved, he'd fire a stream of pepper spray in her face. He snapped the handcuffs shut, then helped her to stand. She walked in front of him while the man kept his one hand in control of her wrists. He opened the door and guided her past the master bedroom and into the main living quarters of the motorcoach. She remembered seeing it two days before—sleek, modern, lots of white leather, and nothing out on the counters. The only personal item on the walls was a large color photo of the Grand Canyon that Jo suspected came with the coach, one more optional accessory. He'd set the table with a napkin and spoon—no knife or fork for her.

The man had Jo sit at the dinette while he uncuffed one wrist and then re-attached the one open handcuff to an eyebolt he'd drilled into the tabletop. He asked, "Would you like some coffee?"

Jo was now beyond crying and past hysterics. To get out of this situation, she knew she needed to be careful about what she did and said. She could be analytical and pragmatic at times, and she'd developed a test of sorts. She thought most problems or issues could be solved by simply answering the question, *How does this change things for me?* She didn't think finding answers that way was selfish; it was more that if she did anything to upset the applecart, then she'd better get an apple. So, Jo had asked herself, *If I'm angry and vindictive, how will that change things for me?* It wouldn't and might result in the opposite—he'd allow her less freedom and fewer opportunities for eventual escape. She answered the man, Hugh, by saying nicely, "Yes, please."

He poured her coffee from a thermal pot into a non-breakable plastic cup. The coffee was lukewarm and passed her lips without burning. She figured the guy was not going to allow her to toss scalding liquid in his face or slash him with a shard of coffee cup. He'd seemingly thought of everything. Then he said, "I hope you like bran flakes. It's all I eat for breakfast. I find a large morning meal sits in my stomach all day and makes me feel slow and bloated. I've also taken to drinking this." He held up a quart bottle of almond milk. He added, "Lactose intolerant."

The cereal box was on the counter along with the faux milk, but the cereal wasn't bran flakes. It was Fiber One, probably eaten to produce a daily stool. She said, "That would be fine."

He served her the cereal in a soft-sided bowl, like Tupperware. He sat across from her with his coffee and cereal, and they ate for minutes in silence. Jo hadn't realized how hungry she was and ate quickly, greedily. He poured more cereal and more almond milk into her bowl. Finally, he said, "It's my first time doing this."

Responses swirled through her mind: *There's a first time for everything; First time for me, too; Well, you sure made it look easy; Third time's a charm.* With a straight face, she chose an answer, "First time for me, too."

He laughed at that, and Jo looked up to see yellowed teeth beneath a bushy ash-gray mustache. Then, the words just flowed from his mouth. "I know this all seems crazy to you, that I must be crazy. I can assure you that I'm not. I'm a trained psychologist, and I've treated crazy people, so I know. What I've done isn't crazy; it's just against the law, and honestly, I believe I'm above all that. I believe in freedom, including the freedom to follow my desires. My wife—her name was Florence—died some years back. Since then, I've had one other relationship that I pursued within the law, and it only led to pain and disgrace."

He stopped there, maybe catching himself before he detailed a sordid story from his past. After listening to Hugh's caveman ideology rant, the word "relationship" stuck with her. He'd said before that what he wanted was friendship. Now, "relationship," a word with new and different connotations. It all frightened her, and she focused on staying composed and in control. She had to get out of this somehow.

The man then stood and opened a storage locker above her head. As he reached in, his stomach pressed against the tabletop, and Jo had the urge to punch it or rake his flesh with the fingernails of her free hand. But in that moment, she realized there would be no benefit to her in striking out at him. She would still be shackled to the table, and escape would remain impossible. The result would only be a snootful of pepper spray or worse. Hugh pulled out an ashtray and a pack of playing cards. He placed both in front of her. He lifted a cigarette from a pack in his shirt pocket and lit up.

He asked, "Do you smoke?"

Jo had quit smoking many years before, and now the smell

was revolting to her. "No."

"Do you like to play cards?"

"Sometimes . . . with friends." She glared at him and let that comment settle.

"Do you know how to play gin?"

"Yes."

"Gin rummy?"

The windows in the RV were closed with the shutters pulled down. The air in the confined space was now fouled by his lit cigarette. Slivers of light from the LED bulbs beamed through the swirls of smoke. Jo could feel the skin on her neck redden in hives. She responded, "Aren't they the same?"

The man laughed in three quick bursts of air that sent billows of smoke wafting into her face. "Definitely not. But let's try straight gin. Okay?"

"How about if you quit smoking."

"Very well." He snubbed the cigarette out into the ashtray, opened the pack of cards, shuffled, and dealt. Afterward, he said, "You have eleven cards. It's your discard."

They played in silence. The winner was the one who melded all their cards with three or four of the same rank or a straight of three or more of the same suit. Jo thought it was mostly a game of chance, getting the right cards at the right time, but Hugh beat her five games to two. She found she did not like losing to this man.

Afterward, he said, "With exceptions, of course, you should avoid picking up a discard that does not complete a meld or add to an existing one. That's called speculating. It's always better to draw from the deck."

And in a warped way, she guessed their relationship had just begun.

For the rest of the day, her third as a captive, Hugh drove while Jo sat on the bench seat in the pink soundproofed room. She studied the closed air vent with its unlocked cover. She could also see the small red handle labeled 'EMERGENCY,' which she figured was the latch that bypassed the vent crank. The porta potty in the corner was high enough for her to stand on and get well within reach of the vent. First, she used it for its intended purpose, pulling down her pants and crouching. When she finished and closed the lid, she moved it just slightly. The porta potty was heavy, probably filled with a few gallons of water for flushing, but at least it wasn't bolted to the floor. She hoped that once they stopped for the night, she could drag the potty to the center of the room, stand on it, reach up, and open the vent. She was sure the opening would be wide enough for her to squirm through. An unknown was if she had the strength to pull herself up and out, but she was determined to try.

The motorcoach was again parked somewhere remote. She put her ear to the pink foam insulation and tried to listen for the sound of nearby trucks or people moving about. Nothing. But right before Hugh switched on the generator, Jo thought she could hear the distant sound of a semi truck's loud horn, most likely on a busy highway nearby.

Over the speaker, he asked if she'd join him for dinner, and he performed the same routine to get her handcuffed to the dinette table with one hand shackled while the other was left free to eat with a spoon. They ate canned Dinty Moore Beef Stew heated in the microwave and served in plastic bowls. He made a salad from a bag of mixed greens that he smothered with ranch dressing. From his choice of foods, it was apparent he was not an accomplished home cook and probably didn't have a selection of chef's knives in one of the drawers, but for sure at least one, and for sure, a couple steak knives. There was an old movie she'd seen, *Wait Until Dark*, with Audrey Hepburn playing a blind woman stalked by a killer. In the final scary scene, set mostly in the dark, Hepburn slashes at the man with a knife and then finally stabs him. Hepburn was such a small and vulnerable woman, but her character had shown the fortitude to kill the killer. Did Jo think she could kill this man, stab him with a kitchen knife? She knew people were, on some primal level, capable of the worst heinous acts—just reading the news, it seemed women stabbed their abusive partners all the time. But could *she* kill a man, her abductor, with a knife? She thought she could but did not know for certain.

After dinner, they played gin again. This time, Hugh showed her how to score points at the end of each hand, twenty-five to the person who ginned plus the un-melded points in the other's hand, with aces scoring one and face cards ten. The first player to reach two hundred points won. Hugh kept score while Jo held her cards in the one wrist shackled to the table, sorting and discarding with the other. Right off, she was dealt a hand with three kings and three sevens, along with another two matching cards. Hugh's first discard gave her the third match. She ginned after four more draws. He laid his hand out and wrote down the score. She was up by thirty-three points. Hugh said, "Very nice."

During the second hand, Hugh asked a personal question, "What is your husband like?"

Jo was focused on her cards. She'd been dealt garbage, but in the first few discards, she had picked up matches and a complete run. The question took her off guard, and the first consideration was whether she should even answer. Finally, she decided she would but give him an answer with connotations. "He's a gentle man who would never harm a fly. He's a good husband who obeys the law and would feel guilty even picking up a stray quarter off the sidewalk without trying to find its owner."

Hugh smirked, a little smile with a twitch of his brushy mustache. She'd seen the same facial expression twice now, and it bothered her. This man thought he was so above it all and the whole rest of the world just a bunch of suckers.

"If I saw a loose quarter on the sidewalk, I wouldn't even exert the energy to bend over and pick it up."

"Well, that's the difference between you and Bray."

"Bray's his name? Like the sound a donkey makes?"

"Oh, that's original. It's Brayden." Jo didn't look up and kept her focus on the cards. She was close to ginning and picked a card from the deck, then quickly discarded it. Hugh picked up her card from the discard pile and said, "Gin." She showed her hand. The one card she'd been waiting for was a king, which left the two kings in her hand worth twenty points. He wrote down the score, his forty-five points to her thirty-three.

When he finished dealing the next hand, he asked, "Is Bray exciting?"

A strange question that she wasn't going to answer. The truth was, he was not exciting. She'd thought about that in the past. What kind of couple were they? Why did they get married? They'd waited well into their thirties before tying the knot. They had the "friends" type of marriage, which lasted because of that, maybe the convenience of it all. But he was never exciting, and there'd never been any passion. Sex, when they still had it, was perfunctory at best, boring in reality, and a topic they never discussed. The sexiest thing about Bray was his cherished BMW motorcycle. Before they'd met, Jo had also ridden motorcycles and loved riding with Bray. But then, after their one daughter, Rose, was born, they both decided to stop—Bray thought riding motorcycles was too dangerous and risky while raising a dependent child. She sold hers, but he kept his vintage BMW, an *objet d'art* to be admired but never taken for a ride.

Then came the campervan. Friends thought traveling throughout the US was exotic and exciting. The reality was anything but. For Bray, it was all fussy choices of where to camp, how much money they could save, gadgets to make living on the road easier, and finding the best accessories for every activity. The only thing she genuinely loved and found exciting was hiking in the mountains, desert, and forest. But even then, Bray had his obsessive considerations, such as the best trekking poles, protein bars, water bottles, and boots. Bray was a fussy man, which sometimes drove Jo to want one more of his fussy IPAs. But she'd never tell Hugh any of this.

She answered, "None of your business."

He won the next hand and the hand after that. Hugh said, "Try to discard your face cards and other high-rank cards early in the game if they're un-melded. Tomorrow, I'll teach you gin rummy. Less luck, more skill."

"Why? What's in it for me? Will you eventually let me go?"

He looked up at her and paused before answering. He appeared to be in his early seventies with ash-gray hair brushed to the side, bifocals in wire-rimmed frames, a mustache that probably hadn't changed in style since he first grew it as a young man, and wrinkles like skin on a wilted peach. His high-pitched voice, almost helium-like, came from deep within his nasal passages. "I'll let you go when you can consistently beat me. But I can guarantee that won't be easy."

Jo wasn't sure she could believe him.

5
Clipped Wings

She made the bed, turned off the one light, and lay under the covers, fully clothed, the same clothes she'd worn since the day of the abduction. Jo guessed she stunk, and the room still smelled slightly of vomit. She lay silent and listened for any movement. Two hours later, she heard his footsteps getting louder as he moved toward the master bedroom. She waited another two hours before lifting her legs over the edge of the bed and standing in her socked feet. Enough moonlight came through the vent so she could just make out the porta potty steps away. She moved slowly and quietly. She slid the porta potty inches at a time until it was positioned beneath the vent. Standing on top of it, Jo's head bumped against the vent's bug screen, with the red handle of the escape hatch nearly touching her nose. She pulled it slowly, increasing the downward pressure until suddenly it popped. The bug screen released and dropped, hitting her head and crashing to the floor. The screen was plastic mesh and the frame light aluminum, but the sound it made amplified in her imagination like a breaking bottle. She quickly stepped down and slid back under her bed covers.

The porta potty was conspicuously left out in the middle of the room.

Jo waited and listened. If caught, she didn't know what the man would do. He didn't seem the violent type—he'd provided meals, played cards with her, and always spoke in soft tones using "please" and "thank you." But he'd drugged, abducted, and shackled her. She had to assume he'd use the pepper spray if needed. She thought he could physically overpower her even though she was more than ten years younger. Could he kill her? She had to assume that he would. She lay in bed for another half hour without hearing any footsteps or movement.

Again, Jo stood on the porta potty. The vent cover was hinged, and she was able to push it up and over without making a sound. She could peek above the edge and see the roof of the coach. The size of the opening was nearly two feet, greater than the width of her shoulders.

She moved each elbow up and over the vent casing, enough to hook the edge. She took two deep breaths and tensed her arms. She leapt from her toes. Her shoulders breached the opening, and for a split second, she could see trees nearby and headlights in the distance, maybe a quarter mile away. She tried to pull herself up but didn't have the leverage or strength. She lowered herself back onto the porta potty. Her breathing was deep and loud, and she tried to muffle the noise with the crook of her elbow. She waited until she could catch her breath and breathe easily.

She thought she could do it if she jumped up just a few more inches. Jo tensed her arms and bent her knees. Summoning all her strength, she leapt from the balls of her feet. Her shoulders breached the opening and then her elbows.

Her forearms and chest now rested over the edge. Seconds later, she pushed with her arms against the lip of the vent. With her waist now over, she was finally able to inch the rest of her body up and out. She lay prone on the RV's roof.

Now, she could hear cars in the distance. The motorcoach was parked on a scarcely used side road that paralleled the highway. She wormed across the roof on elbows and knees to the edge of the coach. Below was a drop of twelve feet to a gravel road. She had not thought past getting through the vent.

She looked around. Many RVs came with attached ladders that looped over the roof, but she couldn't see a reflection or shadow of any curved aluminum in the moonlight. She'd have to jump to the ground.

The top of the coach was cluttered with an air conditioning unit, a satellite dome, antennas, and vents. She held on to a vent close by and slid over the edge with one foot, searching for the lip of a window or anything else to anchor a toe. She kept sliding, now with both feet dangling, searching. Nothing. She did not have the strength to pull herself back up.

She let go and let herself drop.

She landed on the hard-packed gravel, her right ankle taking most of the weight of the fall. She collapsed onto her side, and the pain in her ankle shot up through her leg. She lay there holding the ankle, then touched it to test for a sprain or fracture. She hoped it was just a sprain and started crawling to the edge of the motorcoach, heading toward the highway on the opposite side. Even if she had to crawl the entire quarter mile, she thought she could reach the road by dawn. There, she could flag down someone for help. Jo crawled and turned the corner at the front of the coach.

His smell reached her first: smoke from a lit cigarette. Then, she could see his feet beneath the bumper. He'd been waiting.

She collapsed to the ground, curled into a fetal position, and sobbed. She'd been so strong up until then, calculating and even accommodating. She hadn't cried or screamed since that first day. She'd put all her physical and emotional strength into this one escape. Jo closed her eyes and let the emotion of the futility drain through her tears and sobs.

He stood over her as she lay crying. He must have known that her ankle was twisted and sprained because he didn't move to quickly cuff her hands. He just stood above and smoked his cigarette and let her cry. Slowly, her sobs diminished until all that was left was her self-pity. She looked up and saw the hem of his khaki pants, threadbare above his heavy brown walking shoes. She saw the cigarette butt drop to the ground, then the heel of one shoe shifting to grind it out. His knees dropped forward into a crouch, and she felt her wrists being pulled behind her, then handcuffed. Jo let her body go limp, let him do what he wanted. A hand reached under her arm and helped her to stand on the one good ankle. She limped and hopped to the door of the motorcoach. He helped her up the stairs.

He said, "Now your wings are clipped."

Lying on the bed, she realized it had all been too easy. An unlocked vent with an escape hatch in the ceiling of her prison cell? Really? She knew he probably didn't put it there, more likely some motor vehicle safety regulation, but he'd attached soundproof insulation over every surface of the room. He'd thought of everything else, from the handcuffs to plastic tableware. Hugh might be a crazed psychopath, but he wasn't stupid—he could have locked the vent and bolted the porta potty to the floor.

Then she understood. He'd wanted her to attempt an escape.

6

Hal Attocious

After leaving the police station and driving through three other campgrounds, searching for the Thor Outlaw and finding nothing, Bray drove back to where it all started, where Jo might show up if she could. He parked in the same reserved spot next to the Subaru. The spot where the motorcoach had parked was still empty and vacant. He knew he needed sleep, and at four in the morning finally closed his eyes.

He was startled awake three hours later by the bark of the basset hound. The sound was unmistakable, a lazy expulsion of air through tired vocal cords, the range between bass and hoarse. He pulled up the shade and looked out. The woman had the makeshift ramp set up outside the rear hatch of the Subaru and was pulling at the dog's collar. It wouldn't budge. Bray thought she must have done this hundreds of times, the basset hound accustomed to it by now. But it wasn't moving and maybe the hound was getting too old—its lack of effort the beginning of the end. The poor woman would mourn that hound like a lost spouse.

The thought made him instantly think of Jo and what she might be going through. He'd Googled it—half of abductees, mostly children, never came home alive.

The woman kept pulling at the collar. Then, with her other hand, she grabbed the dog's tail and began pulling both the collar and the tail simultaneously. The sound of the dog's bark moved into the baritone range, and it finally began to shuffle up the plank. Minutes later, the dog was finally settled in the back of the vehicle on its remnant square of brown carpet. The woman shut the hatchback door and then hitched up the teardrop camper. She drove away as the sun crested the trees.

Bray put on the kettle to make coffee and opened his laptop.

Between his Instagram account and the Travato Owners Facebook group, Bray had over a hundred messages through comments and DMs. He started going through each. One said they'd seen a Thor Outlaw with Florida plates at a rest area near Denver, another at a truck stop near Phoenix. Then another who said they'd seen a platinum-colored Thor Outlaw with Colorado plates near Orlando. Someone asked if his wife had blonde hair because they'd seen a young blonde woman with this old guy at a campground in Yellowstone, but the motorcoach was a Fleetwood and not a Thor. On and on. Bray felt overwhelmed by the superabundance of information. How could he know which messages were reliable? Where do you start? The obvious place, he thought, was right there in the campground. The hosts would have a record of the Outlaw, but he wasn't sure they were allowed to give out that information. Unlikely, but he'd try.

He and Jo had met hundreds of campground hosts. Without exception, they were retired couples provided a modest income to monitor reservations, keep the bathrooms clean, make sure the rules for music and generators were obeyed, and sell firewood. The hosts were given a campsite with water, electric, and septic hookups. In the world of retirees living full-time in their RVs, the host gig was coveted, and the same people came back year after year until either sickness or death intervened. Then, other queued-up retired couple would take their place. The day before, he'd met one of the hosts while buying firewood. She seemed pleasant enough.

Bray walked the campground loop past the site where the man had offered to help him carry wood—the guy with all the American flags. Thankfully, the dune buggies were gone, and no one was sitting out front to remind him of his firewood debacle. He put on his N95 mask at the host's site and knocked on the door. It cracked just an inch and the same woman peeked through. He could see she wasn't dressed for the day yet, still in gray sweatpants and a faded black sweatshirt that read, "Harley Davidson," and beneath that, "I Ride My Own." Her gray hair was bound in some netting, and without the slightest bit of makeup, she looked a hundred years old. Somehow, he couldn't picture it—the woman riding her own thousand-pound Harley Davidson motorcycle.

She wasn't wearing a mask, and Bray stood ten feet back. She said, "What?"

"I'm sorry to bother you. Is it possible to find out who was parked near me yesterday in spot 206? Their name and phone number?"

"Why?"

Bray knew he couldn't bring up the abduction. The possibility would cause alarm; the woman would call the police to intervene, and he knew they'd do nothing. He'd thought it through. "Seems he left behind a two-burner stove, a nice GSI 460. I'd like to let him know, maybe he'd come back for it, or maybe we're heading in the same direction." The GSI propane stove was one of the best you could buy, and he owned one himself.

"I can't give out that information, but you can bring it here. We have a lost and found. I'll try to call 'em in the meantime."

"Thank you."

Bray hadn't expected a lost and found, but he should have. Now, he was obliged to follow through with the whole ruse. A half hour later, Bray was back with his own GSI 460. The woman had changed into jeans and a faded blue work shirt with a nameplate on the breast pocket that read, "Gladys Holmgren." She sat outside at a plastic patio dining table with the umbrella cranked up to protect her from what looked to be a hot sunny day. She was drinking coffee from a black mug with a Harley Davidson logo.

He pointed at the mug and said, "I own a motorcycle, too, a vintage BMW."

The woman sipped her coffee, still maskless. She said nothing. There were Harley people, and then there was everyone else—another cultural demarcation in a rapidly polarizing America. He shouldn't have brought it up.

He quickly changed the subject. "Were you able to call him?"

"I was. It was the wrong number."

"What happened?"

"I called the number. The gentleman who answered said that I'd reached the White House. You know, like in Washington, DC? I asked for Henry Attocius. The gentleman just laughed and said that 'Hal' no longer worked there. I have no idea what was so funny. Well, I tried. You can leave that stove right there. I'll let you have it if you're still around in a week."

Bray stood back more than six feet. He tried to think of how he could hold onto his stove that cost him one hundred and twenty dollars. If he refused to give it over, she'd think he was stealing it, and he couldn't come up with a good lie. He left the stove on the ground and then walked away.

Minutes later, he got it, Hal Attocius, *halitosis*, bad breath. The man had given a fake phone number and a stupid alias. Bray made a mental note to call the police later with the fresh lead.

On his way back to his campsite, he stopped where the motorcoach had been parked, site 206. He searched the area for any clues. The fire pit and picnic table looked like they'd never been used. He could see the tire tracks of the big vehicle and the footprints that came and went from where the door was positioned. One set looked smaller and possibly had the same sole pattern as Jo's trail hiking shoes. He used his cellphone to take photos, then took photos of the tire tracks. He'd seen some whodunit movie where the investigators tracked down the murderers from tire tread patterns. On his way back to his campervan, Bray remembered the movie *My Cousin Vinny*. Marisa Tomei was the sassy car expert who figured out something about positraction. He'd send all this information to the police station. *The squeaky wheel gets the grease.*

When he reached the Travato, the site next to him had already been occupied. The new RV was an old campervan from maybe the eighties, and Bray wasn't sure whether it was cool and vintage or just a piece of junk. An obese man in denim overalls with a graying beard sat just outside on an extra-wide camp chair. Bray thought, *just a piece of junk.*

Bray called the police station. A man answered, "Officer Zweiback, how can I help you?"

Little toasts—that's what he remembered. Zweiback were little toasts his mother had bought for special occasions to eat with pickled herring or braunschweiger. By the time he and Jo had Rose, Zweiback was marketed as choke-proof baby food made by Nabisco. Rose had teethed on those little toasts. She was now a mother herself. It took him a second to regain his train of thought and answer the man. "Yes, I put in a Missing Person report last night, and I'm just checking to see if you have any updates." He gave the officer the case number.

"Just a moment," and Bray thought he could hear the tapping of keystrokes through the receiver, "sir, there's been no updates since you filed the report eight hours ago. The report says the woman has been missing for less than twenty-four hours. Often, they just show back up."

He was adamant, "My wife's been abducted."

"That's what it says here, but it also says there was no evidence of a struggle, that she entered another man's RV of her own free will. Seems there was no foul play involved."

Bray felt the same anger and frustration welling up. Why didn't they believe him? He knew Jo better than anyone else on the planet, and she wouldn't just abandon him and drive away with a strange man. But how do you convey that to a jaded and apathetic officer of the law? He knew if he went into a long explanation, it would do no good—those officers had heard it all before.

He decided to keep going, be the squeaky wheel. "I have a photo of the motorcoach. I have over one hundred leads from the Internet. I have the joke alias the man used, Henry Attocius. Please give me your email address, and I'll send the photo, the leads, and the alias." Bray wanted to explain the joke behind the perpetrator's fake name but didn't think he had the time, and he didn't think the joke was *pertinent* to the investigation.

His professionalism slipping, the officer said, "Okay, bub, suit yourself," and gave Bray the address, "info at . . ."

Officer Zweiback then abruptly hung up.

7

Then Came Uly

What they didn't tell you about retirement is the fucking boredom. Who were 'they?' Uly guessed *they* were the ad agencies that published magazine photos and television ads featuring happy-go-lucky couples in their dotage playing tennis, traveling, or eating out. Okay, then what? He could only watch so much TV. He enjoyed books but not ten hours a day, every day. Now, he was traveling the country in his thirty-five-year-old Dodge Xplorer campervan. Actually, he was living in his van, and it wasn't as exciting as it sounded. You could only drive so much, and frankly, he wasn't the back-to-nature, hike-the-mountains kind of guy—his knees hurt just standing still. He also wasn't the kind of person who could find purpose in the little things like discovering the perfect brand of men's briefs or the best way to light a campfire—fussy things just didn't do it for him.

He knew he needed a real purpose, a mission of some kind. So, when he saw the Instagram post about the woman's abduction and realized the incident had occurred in the very same campground where he was currently parked, he was all in.

His full name was Ulysses Walker, and maybe purpose lay in the meaning of his name. His father was a Civil War buff and had named him after the eighteenth president, Ulysses S. Grant. Still, he liked that his name originally derived from the epic poem, *Odyssey*, and he liked to think of himself as an adventurer and possible hero. Though "hero" was maybe the wrong word—more like "protagonist" or "mentor," or maybe "life-guide," though that sounded, well, too fussy. As for his last name, Walker, it did suggest movement, but he could barely walk from his van to the bathroom without bone-grinding knee pain.

Until a year prior, his life had been anything but boring. He'd lived in Las Vegas for more than thirty years, moving there from Baltimore after his father had died following a long and futile battle with lung cancer (he'd been a pack-a-day smoker of unfiltered Lucky Strikes). Uly was twenty-three then and had helped his mother care for him. Dying slowly from lung cancer was in Uly's mind like being eaten away from the inside by earthworms. They first consumed his innards so that the man could barely eat, then the fat and muscles so he looked like some Nazi concentration camp victim, and then his brain so he often hallucinated.

A week before his dad died, maybe in one of his morphine-induced fantasies, he grabbed Uly by the collar, looked into his eyes, and said, "I know what you're going to do—start a business, become an entrepreneur!" At the time, Uly barely knew what the term meant. But he looked it up and, for years, carried that thought with him like some prophecy from a cave-dwelling oracle.

Once his father passed, his mother sold the family home and bought a condo in Florida to be near her own parents. He had two older siblings, and they'd moved from Baltimore years before. Uly was left family-less and, for the next year or so, felt lost. He worked as a bartender at a tourist restaurant in the Inner Harbor and spent most of his tip money on booze in the myriad bars of Fells Point. He met a woman there one night, a cocktail waitress at a place called Surfside Sally's. Her name was Merlene, but everyone called her Merl. He moved in with Merl and thought he was in love. Then, he made the mistake of asking for her hand in marriage. The proposal was a spur-of-the-moment thing, and he didn't think about the diamond ring business until after he'd blurted out his whole speech. Turned out he didn't need the ring. Merl just laughed and said, "What, are you crazy?" Then added, "Uly, I just need your rent money." Waking to a minor hangover the next day, he realized he'd been desperate to replace his family, desperate like a jilted lover on the rebound. Then he got fired from his bartending job for giving away too many free drinks to friends, and then he couldn't pay rent. Merl kicked him out, and he became homeless.

Then, he had too much time to think, and while sleeping on a friend's couch one night, Uly thought about his father and his parting prophecy—*an entrepreneur!* It was as though any plans for his future in Baltimore were wrapped up in that patriarchal foretelling and that fatherly blessing. The prophecy was now like an anchor wrapped around his neck. He felt like a failure. What that meant was the belief he had no future in Baltimore—he had to escape his hometown.

He bought a VW bus he converted into a camper, then hit the road. He considered a few cities. St. Louis, just west of the Mississippi, didn't seem west enough. Snow fell the first day he arrived in Denver, so cold, and he didn't know how to ski, nor did he have the inclination to learn. The small towns in between seemed just inbred, close-knit, and scary. Uly was on his way to Los Angeles when he stopped in Las Vegas. He had five hundred dollars left in his wallet, a seemingly pathetic amount to show up in LA with, and saw a sign on the side of an apartment building just off the Strip that offered a studio apartment for $225 per month. He took it.

The following years seemed to go by in the blink of an eye. He found another job as a bartender. He married a cocktail waitress named Bunny with a kid from another marriage whom he adopted. He and Bunny saved up enough to buy their own bar that became a hangout for other East Coast expats.

Over time, he also fell in love with Las Vegas. It was exciting. He loved betting on sports and horses and loved that the city never shut down. He liked talking to strangers and even liked that most of the locals were originally from somewhere else, determined to start fresh. He really loved the all-you-can-eat buffets and late-night forty-nine-cent breakfasts. He had fun, loved his wife, and sort of liked his adopted son.

Unfortunately, their marriage fell apart. Business at the bar slowed when other, larger bars with big-screen TVs and happy hour buffets crowded him out. He worked shorter and shorter hours, stayed out late, ate in the casino buffets at odd hours, and just wasn't present like he should've been. He became morbidly obese, up to three hundred and fifty pounds, and a doctor helped him apply for Social Security disability. Then he sold his half of the bar to his stepson, who'd grown to think of Uly as a pathetically poor entrepreneur. He continued to live with Bunny, but the relationship turned sour. She complained that he snored too much and had him sleep in his stepson's old room. Bunny had always owned the house, and now she asked him to pay rent. Uly could sometimes be slow on the uptake, and it took him a few weeks to realize that it was Merl all over again. It was time to escape once more.

There was little discussion and no argument when he told Bunny he was leaving. Actually, he'd taken the coward's approach and just texted her. She texted back, "Don't let the door hit your fat ass on the way out."

He'd saved a little money and had his monthly disability check. He decided to go back on the road and travel America, reinventing himself for the third time. The Xplorer was a piece of junk he bought off Craigslist for fifteen hundred bucks. He rented a room at a dump called the Jackpot Motel with weekly rates. Uly stayed there for three months while fixing up the campervan. He overhauled the engine in the parking lot while the feral kids staying in the motel with their drug-addled parents watched and taunted. He opened space in the van's dinette by taking out a bench seat and moving the table so his belly could slide beneath. The bed was a nice full-sized mattress, though only six feet long, which was okay with Uly because he was well under that mark. The hard part was getting in the small bathroom that doubled as a shower. The width of the door was only twenty-four inches. Even if he *could* get inside, the space for the toilet was equally as tight. With a demolition Sawzall, Uly cut out the entire door and interior wall, replacing both with a shower curtain. Finally, he was ready to escape Las Vegas. He had misgivings and regrets, but his mind was made up, and he committed himself to the journey. He left in the Xplorer just as the temperatures in Vegas soared to over one hundred degrees and headed east toward higher, cooler campgrounds.

Uly had followed @fabvanlife for months. The site was eye-candy, with Margo posing here and there, water or mountains in the background, and with the cool stuff in their custom van. Part of him was intrigued and maybe a little lustful, then part was cynical as hell. What they didn't show were the rainy days stuck inside their tin can bored to death or the times when the van or its complicated systems broke down—and they always broke down. Regardless, he watched for their posts and consumed them like Chili Cheese Fritos. So, when she'd posted the story of the abduction and the photo of the motorcoach, Uly knew right off that he was staying in the same campground and knew right where the Thor Outlaw had been parked. Then he clicked on the link to @vanlifevagabonds and followed that page also. Uly thought he could help find the woman, and he decided to drive over and meet the guy, Bray. And, frankly, Uly was bored to death and just needed something to *do*.

Then something else. Uly had been watching old episodes of *Then Came Bronson* saved on his computer. He remembered watching them as a kid back in Baltimore. It was about a guy, Jim Bronson, who traveled around the country on his motorcycle, going from town to town and often inadvertently helping others. Bronson had only the belongings on his bike and a little money. In the show's pilot, what pushed him onto the road was the suicide of a close friend. For Bronson, life suddenly seemed short, and the rat race of daily work pointless. Uly'd had the same epiphany and thought he should be more Bronson-like. Somehow it all fit—Uly's life on the road, the pointlessness of what he'd done with his life, few belongings, little money, and the need to just see, *really* see the country, and help others when he could. So, this abduction story seemed to Uly like a new episode of *Then Came Bronson*, and he felt helping with the search was almost a spiritual inevitability.

His name was Ulysses, and he was embarking on an epic,

Bronson-like journey.

He found the man, Bray, sitting outside an expensive Winnebago Travato.

The Internet leads kept coming in, some very random and weird. One said, "Your wife is at coordinates 37.234264 / -115.815434, left there by illegal aliens after an encounter of the fourth kind." Bray knew that an encounter of the fourth kind involved alien experiments. He typed in the coordinates and found the Nevada location—Homey Airport, also known as Area 51. Some joke. He kept reading the messages and hoping for something more specific, more real. Five thousand people were now following @vanlifevagabonds. It had taken him and Jo years to get two thousand followers, and in one day, he'd more than doubled that.

In the corner of his vision he saw movement, and he turned. An obese man was stumbling straight toward him. The man was massive, with folds of fat constrained by faded overalls held up with shoulder straps let out to their lengthiest setting. The man was really, really fat. And then that thought bothered Bray. He was being a *fatist*—acting prejudiced based on a person's appearance, and he abhorred that base instinct. The fact was, thoughts like that plagued him. He didn't like when he stared at kids with weird haircuts, didn't like that he grew up scared of homeless people—that he was still scared of homeless people (though technically Bray *was* homeless and living out of a van). Bray always tried hard to subvert those unsympathetic instincts. He tried to be a compassionate person and avoid looking at kids with face tattoos and piercings; he forced himself to say, "Hello" to homeless people and hand over a dollar if he had one—and he avoided staring at fat people. Bray tried but often failed, and now he kept looking. The man was morbidly obese, like he'd undoubtedly die if afflicted by the COVID virus—obesity was an underlying risk like heart disease, diabetes, and old age. For that matter, the man probably did have diabetes. Now Bray thought the man's weight problem was also a safety issue and that he wasn't just being a *fatist*, but sensitive to the man's plight.

Also, the man wasn't wearing a mask.

"Hi, you must be Bray?" He stood there smiling, a big grin that popped dimples in his gray-bearded cheeks. His hair was thinning on top, red flakey skin poking through a wispy comb-over. He looked like Burl Ives, the guy who sang, "Have a Holly Jolly Christmas."

"How do you know who I am?" And in just that split second it took to respond, Bray thought, *Oh no!* Was this guy going to hand him a ransom demand? The thought of an abduction and ransom was something he hadn't considered because he and Jo had no money to speak of. But he knew ransom was a common enough motive in kidnappings, and his Travato was a pricey model.

"I've been following the Instagram posts. I was near and thought I could help. My name is Uly."

Sudden relief. Bray exhaled. "You know that my wife was abducted? You're over here to help me find her?"

Uly sat down fifteen feet away at the picnic bench made of turned steel piping and rot-proof wood-like plastic composite. The table barely shook. He said, "Sure, why not. I could be useful. I can help with posts on the Internet and help track down leads. I've got a CB radio to speak with truckers."

"They still have those?"

"Sure." Uly's voice was rough, like gravel in a cement

mixer.

"I've already contacted the police and sent them all the leads I've gotten so far. Over a hundred."

Uly pushed the back of his hand beneath his nose—a scratch or a leak. "The police won't cross county lines, and unless you have a ransom note or copious amounts of blood, the FBI will just file your report under, 'Another Jilted Husband.'" His rubbery lips turned into a big smile showing large teeth gapped like a picket fence.

Bray wasn't offended. He knew what Uly said was true. They didn't care—not one bit. But why did this guy care? Then the thought crossed Bray's mind that maybe he *was* just another jilted husband. No, the woman with the basset hound had seen Jo enter the motorcoach, *lured*, and then the coach drove off. Jo had been abducted—he was sure of it. "Why do you believe me?"

"You've never seen this Thor Outlaw before? You have no idea who owns it?"

"Never, no."

"So, I believe you."

"But why do you want to help?"

"I was in the campground already. I'm retired and not doing anything." Uly looked up at the blue sky overhead, squinting. He added, "Growing up, did you ever watch *Then Came Bronson?*"

The name sounded familiar, but he hadn't watched that show. What he did remember was watching re-run episodes of *Star Trek*. He answered, "No. Why?"

The man looked at Bray and, for a moment, seemed unable to answer. He finally said, "Um," and then he paused, thinking over whether or not to go into the explanation. He decided not to and said, "Never mind."

Bray looked at the man, tried hard to get beyond the imposing and uncomfortable issue of his weight, and beyond the fact that the man wore no mask. Was he some kind of conspiracy buff, some virus denier? And what was all that about *Then Came Bronson?* He decided to ask the man, get him to commit one way or the other—believer or denier, realist or fantasist. "Why aren't you wearing a mask?"

Uly touched his face for the second time. "Oh, sorry, I forgot."

———

Uly sat at the picnic table and looked at all the leads on Bray's laptop computer, nearly two hundred, and they kept coming in. He'd gone back to get one of the blue surgical masks he wore, and now with his readers on, the hot moist breath leaking from the top of the mask fogged the lenses. He pushed the glasses up to his forehead and leaned closer to see.

The problem was, what to do with the overwhelming information? Uly started by putting the leads—ones that looked like they hadn't come from complete wackos—into a Google spreadsheet they could share. Next, he figured that in the time elapsed since the abduction, the motorcoach couldn't have crossed the border into Mexico or traveled east past Chicago, so he deleted those. Now, the number of leads was down to a manageable forty-two. He had an idea and walked back to his Xplorer campervan and brought out an old road atlas that had belonged to the previous owner. Each page had a separate state with its spiderweb of streets and highways. He'd plot each lead.

Bray was a funny guy. He wasn't really tall, but he wasn't short. His face and lips were thin, and his mouth continually open to the possible wanderings of a stray fly. He appeared to project himself as an outdoorsy type with things carried on his belt like a Ray-Ban sunglass case and a sheath holding a Leatherman multi-tool. His movements were all jerky, and the kinetic energy of his body made Uly anxious.

Bray had told him all about his wife, how their lives had changed since the pandemic, and how both had lost their jobs. Since then, they'd been on the road continuously and had covered over ten thousand miles. They'd rarely stayed in the same place for more than a few days, and they'd certainly never met anyone with one of those big, fancy Class A motorcoaches. Bray said he vaguely remembered the Thor Outlaw but had never seen anyone come or go from it. Uly knew the type who lived in those rigs. They had everything a cement condo would have, and they rarely left the coach to sit at a picnic table or use the public bathrooms. And they rarely mingled with the neighboring riff-raff in the campgrounds. Those guys thought they were special. Bray's wife would never have had a chance to meet this guy, and Uly thought it entirely plausible that she *was* lured into the coach and abducted. What could he have said? "My wife fell, and I can't get her up." "My cat is stuck behind the refrigerator, and I can't get it out." Uly could think of lots of ways.

He had Bray mark each supposed sighting of the motorcoach in the atlas along with a date and time if they'd been provided. After an hour at the picnic table, they took a pee break. Bray went inside his campervan while Uly used the public pit toilet. When he came back, Bray had two cans of beer waiting. Uly liked beer, wasn't too particular about what kind, but enjoyed a good IPA. The can label said hop-something-or-other and had an illustration of a hippie girl with a peace-sign necklace. He took a long drink, one that consumed half the can. It was good. He looked at the illustration again and sounded out the name *Hopadellic*. Now he got it.

Eventually, a few patterns appeared. Two large groupings were in Arizona and California. The problem was that those sightings seemed random, unlikely they were the *same* RV, and both places were prime tourist and retirement destinations with larger concentrations of the big motorcoaches. Just three sightings were in southwestern Kansas. Interestingly, all three fit along a secondary highway that ran in a neat line south toward New Mexico. Before Uly went back to cook dinner, both agreed to wake up early the next day and drive.

8

Knock, Knock?

Jo sat handcuffed to the dinette table while Hugh went on about the concept of knock in gin rummy.

"To knock is to end the hand early when you believe your opponent is ready to gin. To knock, you must have fewer unmelded points—deadwood—in your hand than the knock card, which is a card that's turned up after the twenty-one cards are dealt. So, if the knock card is a king, you can go out if you have less than ten points in your hand that are not paired in melds. To go out, you say, 'Knock.' If the knock card is an ace, then, of course, you have to play until someone gins. Are you following?"

"Yes," she said.

"Timing is everything. What's fascinating about the knock is that it takes much of the sheer luck of cards off the table. If you're dealt a winning hand, then you need to concern yourself with your opponent shedding all their high-point cards and knocking. Conversely, if you see your opponent searching for that one card to gin, then you can knock and rob him of his bonus."

Jo listened. She'd spent two days mostly alone in her prison room with the pain of her ankle. She'd been fed, and for the ankle, Hugh had given her narcotics, Percocet, but she refused to take them. So she lay on the bed, felt the throbbing pain, and watched as her ankle swelled to the size of a grapefruit, turning splotchy purple. With her limited knowledge of medicine, the contusion probably meant something must have torn—a muscle or ligament. Escape seemed out of the question . . . for now. She resolved to play his game. He said he'd let her go if she won consistently—that seemed a pipe dream—but what else could she do? It was either sit in her prison room with no hope or play with *some* shred of hope. So, Jo sat quietly at the dinette table and let Hugh expound.

"Scoring is a little more complicated. If you knock, you don't get the twenty-five-point gin bonus, but you do get the total points of the un-melded cards or deadwood in my hand. Two caveats: First, I can lay off my deadwood on your melds to reduce my exposed point total. For example, if you lay down three kings, and I have a deadwood king in my hand, then I can lay off that king against yours so you don't get those ten points. Are you still following?"

Jo was hoping Hugh was close to the end of the lesson because she was beginning to get confused. But she did follow and said, "Sure."

"Second caveat: If you knock with, let's say, eight points, but after I've laid off that king, I have only five points in my hand, then I undercut your knock. Now I get the difference in points, three, plus a twenty-five point bonus."

She looked up at him with a forced smile. "Knock, knock?"

He ignored her sarcastic joke and did not respond.

Hugh continued, "Some people liken the knock to the nuclear solution. Conventional war breaks out. One side is losing and sees no hope, so its leader presses the nuclear button and wins the war. Though, personally, I think that analogy is off base. I liken the nuclear solution to the concept of trump in bridge, hearts, or whist. It's a hidden power play; it takes away the current rules and applies the new, more powerful rule of trump. Knocking is different. It simply allows a player with an inferior position to win, not from power, a trump card or a nuclear bomb, but from weakness. You see?"

Hugh began dealing cards. Jo was scarcely paying attention. Who put this much thought into a game? Nuclear solution? She didn't get it and said, "Not really."

Hugh paused in his dealing. His mouth stretched into a tight-lipped smile, enjoying his little discussion. "Humans like to understand things through metaphors. Electricity *flows* like water; I *spent* time at work today. Did you know that the term 'come to a head' refers to pus in a pimple? Funny, I know. Anyway, I've had difficulty finding a metaphor that helps one understand the concept of knock. Again, something weaker that overcomes something stronger by the inherent power of its weakness. I think it's fascinating."

Jo thought for a second, his dilemma now a puzzle of sorts. "A man's power is overcome by the women's lack of power through the withholding of sex. Keeping his power in *check*."

"That's very old-fashioned of you." Hugh finished dealing and then turned up the last knock card—a queen. He looked up. "But that's why man invented rape."

Jo met his smile. She did not know how to respond to this man without screaming in anger, so she said nothing.

He said, "Your discard."

Jo picked up her cards and sorted the hand over and over as though she might conjure up more than the one measly meld of sevens she held. She did have three face cards with a potential inside straight, but they were poisonous at ten points apiece if he knocked or ginned. She discarded a jack of hearts. Hugh picked up the jack. Jo still held the king of hearts, so it was likely that Hugh had three jacks. Jo made a mental note that her other two face cards were likely safe to discard.

Hugh discarded a king of diamonds which again would be poisonous if she tried but failed to get the third king. Jo drew a two of hearts from the deck and discarded her king now that it seemed safe to do so. From the deck, he picked a card that he kept, then discarded a five that matched the two fives in her hand. Jo had gotten rid of her last face card three exchanges later but had just the two melds plus the two of hearts, a three of hearts, and two nines. She had a weak hand but still had multiple ways to gin.

They exchanged cards from the deck, neither finding the match they needed. Jo instinctively knew that Hugh was about to gin. She guessed it by the way he picked up a card from the deck, glanced quickly, and then discarded it.

She drew a nine, discarded her three upside down, and called, "Knock."

Both laid their hands across the table. She had only the un-melded two. He'd been waiting for just one card to go out, seeking a last card to go with the jack he'd picked up earlier, a card which he chose not to discard.

She'd won her first game of gin rummy by using a rule that had been explained to her only minutes earlier. She felt a tinge of exhilaration and, for a brief moment, wasn't consciously aware of her cuffed wrist or swollen ankle. She looked up at

Hugh with a smile.

But an insight came to her while he shuffled the cards for another hand. He'd picked up the jack when he obviously didn't need it. Even Jo, as a rookie player, would never have held ten points without the immediate possibility of a meld. She'd been fooled at cards just like she'd been fooled into trying to escape. He knew she would take the escape bait dangled before her. Then he waited until after she jumped from the heights of the huge motorcoach, waited until she crawled around the coach with her injured ankle, before recapturing her. Why, why, *why?*

The cards she understood. He'd wanted to involve her in the excitement of the game by providing a win. It had worked up until she understood that he'd thrown the game. The escape? He'd stood there casually smoking that cigarette, waiting. It was the opposite of throwing the game; he'd wanted her to understand the futility of escape. And he'd wanted Jo to possibly injure her ankle. Hugh had allowed her to escape to break her spirit, to force the idea of freedom out of her system. What he didn't know was that the escape attempt had been exciting. Clipped wing or not, she'd try to escape again.

And while Hugh dealt the next hand, she thought once more about the concept of knock. She said, "You know, knocking may be about winning with a losing position, but it's also about the hubris of holding on too long to a superior hand. I think another metaphor for knocking might be, 'Leave on a high note,' or more to the point, 'Quit while you're ahead.'"

Hugh ignored her at first and finished dealing. He looked at his cards, then muttered, "Marvelous." He sorted his hand, then added, "Your discard."

9

I HATE KANSAS

Uly read the latest lead appearing on Bray's computer. *Saw a Thor Outlaw with a toy hauler pull into the Love's on I-70 just east of WaKeeny, KS. Sorry, I can't tell you more.* Truck stops were filled with transient RVers spending the night between destinations, and Uly knew they'd most likely find nothing. But it was a place to start. The Love's truck stop was three hundred miles away, and both he and Bray left the next morning before sunrise with the understanding they'd meet there later in the day.

Uly crammed himself into the driver's bucket seat of his 1985 Dodge Xplorer campervan, turned over the engine, and let it warm up.

As he waited, he fed the mouse that had been with him now for a week. One morning, he'd heard scratching sounds from the dashboard glovebox while lounging in bed. When he finally got up and pulled open the door, a mouse lay in a nest made from a travel-size packet of tissue paper. The mouse didn't seem frightened and just stared up with imploring eyes. To Uly, it looked forlorn, like a lost pup, and he just closed the glovebox door. He named the mouse Calypso after the woman in the *Odyssey* who entertains Ulysses. Uly assumed the mouse was a she, figuring it was the female who built nests. Since then, he'd fed Calypso small pieces of cheese and bread crusts. He hoped the mouse wasn't pregnant, though it did look plump.

Uly followed Bray's newer Winnebago Travato out of the campground and onto the highway where the newer rig sped away at what seemed like seventy miles per hour. Uly's thirty-five-year-old Xplorer had a carbureted engine that could only push the heavy van along at sixty, tops. Fifty-five with the air conditioning on high, and Uly needed it. Within minutes, the Travato was out of sight.

Uly crossed into Kansas and felt an ominous foreboding. He'd had trouble there years before when first moving out west, a whole week when everything seemed to go wrong. It all started just past Kansas City on I-70. His VW engine began making funny noises, and then the red warning light on his dash flashed on. The engine lost most of its power near a town called Hogleg and began spewing a dark, oily exhaust. He just barely made it to the next off-ramp and into the parking lot of a closed and dilapidated Stuckey's restaurant.

His engine was beyond repair. Then, the closest replacement was at a junkyard in Wichita 150 miles away. He had no choice but to hitchhike. His first and only ride was from a guy in a souped-up Plymouth, tweaked out on crystal meth but going all the way to Wichita. Right off, the guy told Uly that the license plates on his car were expired and that the cops had a warrant out for his arrest. As though being chased by phantom police, he drove at over a hundred miles per hour on back roads that zigzagged south and east. Thankfully, the tweaker didn't plow his Plymouth into the ditch or head-on into a truck.

Then, in Wichita, Uly had no means to ship the junkyard engine back to Hogleg, so, again, he had no choice but to hitchhike, though now standing on the side of the road with the one-hundred-sixty-pound hunk of steel and hoping for a truck with a compassionate driver. Two days and just a hundred miles later, he was confronted by a state trooper wearing his Smokey the Bear campaign hat. The trooper told him that hitchhiking was illegal on the interstate and to start walking. Uly said he couldn't lift the engine by himself and that he needed the engine to get the fuck out of Kansas. The trooper wrote him a ticket and said that he'd be arrested if Uly were still there in two hours. Uly had no choice but to continue hitchhiking, and thank Christ, he found another ride quickly. Then, once back at the dilapidated Stuckey's, he had to pull out the old engine and bolt up the replacement—a task he could actually do himself. Since that time, he'd vowed never to travel through Kansas again.

Yet, here he was, back in Kansas. The bad feeling was compounded by an asshole in a pickup truck who drove so close to his bumper that Uly could see in his rearview mirror the lump of chew in the man's cheek.

The man wouldn't pass. Uly rolled down his window and waved at him to go ahead and do it, pass him—no one was coming the other direction. Instead, the man leaned on his horn. Uly knew assholes. He'd run a bar populated by loud drunk assholes. He'd lived in Las Vegas, where assholes flaunted their asshole-ness. Uly kept a handgun under the driver's seat for just that one time when an asshole might go too far. He slowed the Xplorer down to forty-five. Minutes later, other drivers were piled up behind the pickup, waiting for the guy to make the first move. After it was apparent he wouldn't, each passed them both, one by one. Did the guy think he was hassling some modern-day hippie? He remembered the one sticker he'd left on the campervan from the previous owner, a small black and white peace symbol. That had to be it.

Uly kept driving, now slowed to forty, and thought if the guy just touched his bumper, they could both shoot it out at the next exit. The man leaned on his horn for the second time. Uly considered pumping his breaks, forcing the asshole to hit him, but decided he had more to lose. He could picture the Xplorer pushed into the ditch and then rolling like one of the tumbleweeds that cluttered the Kansas highway. Finally, he just slowed more, creeping along at thirty-five. Uly was glued to his rearview mirror, barely watching the road ahead (it was straight—he was going the speed of a tortoise). Then he saw a plume of diesel exhaust blow out the rear of the pickup and saw the guy swerve into the oncoming lane just as a semi was coming the other direction. The pickup passed Uly, the guy giving him the finger, and then barely swerved back into his lane before being hit. And flying high above the bed of the pickup, now in front of him and speeding away, were two huge Trump 2020 flags.

He hated Kansas.

————

Uly reached the Love's truck stop by noon. Bray was already there in the parking lot waiting. As expected, he'd found nothing.

They looked again at the few leads in the area, and Bray added two more—one near Wichita and the other in a small town called Hooker just over the border in Oklahoma. They decided to split up, one going east through Kansas toward

Wichita, the other south into Oklahoma. They would search the truck stops, campgrounds, and known off-the-grid boondocking campsites on federal lands.

Uly said he'd take Oklahoma, get the fuck out of Kansas altogether.

By the next morning, Uly was in the small town of Hooker. He knew the area from books about the Oklahoma Dust Bowl in the thirties. Hooker was close to ground zero for the dust storms that rose out of the plains and deposited waves of dirt and dust over crops and homes. The tragedy had been man-made. Flat in every direction, the land was originally covered with buffalo grass that the sodbusters turned over to plant wheat. When the wheat prices dropped after World War I, following a year-long drought, the farmers gave up on their crops. But the topsoil, no longer rooted to the earth with buffalo grass or wheat, was exposed, and the winds picked up the loose dirt and spread it as far east as New York City. Most people in places like Hooker left, mostly west to California or north to Idaho, Oregon, and Washington State. The people who stayed behind were the obstinate, stoic ones with little imagination and a hatred of meddling outsiders. Their offspring, the ones with any sense and a high school diploma in hand, also left. Brain drain had been going on for eighty years.

In Hooker, he started with Nora's RV Park. Nora's had just ten sites, five for permanent residents with rigs that had seen better days—patched roofs, useless TV antennas, cracked windows. All five had American flags out front, some on makeshift poles, others on mounts drilled into the hoods of their rigs that never moved. Next to the park, across a gravel alley, stood a prefab home with a carved wooden sign, "Office." Uly parked his Xplorer down the block so the owner, he assumed Nora, wouldn't see it or the peace-sign sticker. He opened the office door and walked in without a mask, which would've just spooked her. He stepped through the threshold, and a buzzer sounded. Uly stood and waited.

A wood desk faced the center of the room with an old desktop computer on top that might have still run DOS. Opposite stood a three-tiered bookcase with a sign above that read, "Take one, leave one." The books were all paperbacks: thrillers, mysteries, romances, and family sagas. Uly saw a Grisham novel he might like to read but had no book to exchange. Above that was the fabled and phony jackalope, a stuffed rabbit with little deer antlers. He remembered reading a Dust Bowl story about rabbits. Before the dust storms hit in earnest, there'd been a pestilence of locusts that ate every cash crop and kitchen garden that had survived the drought. And before the locusts came, there'd been a rabbit pestilence. Legions of them roamed towns looking for anything to forage. The locals killed and ate what they could, but there were just too many. The town folk then organized clubbing parties that commenced after church on Sundays. They worked the edges of the towns, banging sticks against cooking pans to funnel the rabbits toward chicken-wire pens. Once there, the town folk clubbed the rabbits with axe handles and baseball bats. Thousands of them at a time. Uly wasn't much for religion and the Bible, but it made him think—first pestilence and now a pandemic.

After a few minutes, he heard rustling inside the house. Then, an old woman wearing a straw cowboy hat and smoking a cigarette opened the door. Perched on her nose were a pair of wire-rimmed spectacles that, at one time, Uly remembered, were called granny glasses.

"How can I help you?"

Using his most officious voice, he asked, "I'm wondering if you *could* help me. Are you Nora by chance?"

She didn't wear a mask; almost no one in Oklahoma did, and she stepped closer to Uly. He stepped back. She said, "I am." Then, "What is it now?" She said it as though this were the fourth or fifth problem she'd dealt with that day.

He started with the truth, "I'm looking for a man who is thought to have abducted a woman. We have a message that said they'd possibly seen his Thor Outlaw motorcoach—big forty-footer, a Class A rig that looks like a tour bus—near here."

"I know what they are. You call the police?" She stubbed out her cigarette in a half-full ashtray the size of a dog bowl. She pulled another from a pack on the desk, Chesterfields, a brand Uly didn't know was made anymore.

He moved into a lie, "No, this isn't a police matter. We did file a report with the FBI, but they seem to be dragging their feet. I'm helping out a friend. Doing the legwork, so to speak."

The woman nodded at that—the FBI was to-the-bone unpopular in these parts. She did have information, and it leaked out in answers to his questions. A big Class A motorcoach had stayed at the park the other night. Didn't know if it had a toy hauler feature. The older guy paid cash, and no paperwork was exchanged—the federal government needn't know these things—and the guy did not want a receipt. Medium height, gray hair, mustache. She didn't see a woman. The color of the rig, she wasn't quite sure of. "Swishy things all over, you know, like tiger stripes or something."

Uly asked if she remembered the plates or the state.

Nora stuck the Chesterfield in her mouth and inhaled what looked to be enough smoke to fill a birthday balloon.

Then, while exhaling, a puff of smoke punctuated each word. "I always look at the plates. I like to know where people come from. I've had people here from every state in the union except Hawaii. Little keystone between the numbers and letters." She stopped there, a quiz.

That was easy. "Pennsylvania."

Nora took a drag from her cigarette and then gave him a wink. "Bingo!"

After Hooker, Uly followed Highway 54 southwest toward Albuquerque. If the lead was plausible, the motorcoach would likely be headed that way.

He talked to Bray in Wichita, who'd found nothing credible there. The motorcoach that had been seen may or may not have been a Thor, and none of the other leads coming in were pointing in that direction. Bray decided to head back west and check places across the state line in Colorado. Uly told him about the sighting in Oklahoma and the Pennsylvania plates.

The search during the next two days seemed desperate and ultimately futile—there were hundreds of places to look. Uly searched over twenty campgrounds, every truck stop he passed, and every rest stop. He found nothing.

Then Bray called with another lead. A woman camping in federal land near Taos, New Mexico, was parked near a Thor Outlaw with a toy hauler feature that had pulled in just that day. She'd seen one older man come and go but no woman. Bray had messaged her back and asked for the color scheme and what state the plates were from. The woman answered that it was a swirly combination of brown, dark gray, and silver, which met the color scheme of the Thunder Canyon model. The plates were from Pennsylvania. The woman said she'd stay there until Bray showed up.

Uly and Bray both turned toward Taos.

10

Lunchables

Jo had no idea where the coach was parked. She knew it was hot outside, the air conditioner blasting throughout the day, so she figured they weren't in the mountains. She guessed somewhere in the southwest, but of course, it could have been Texas or even Florida for all she knew. Alone in her room, Jo thought continually about escape. The skylight vent with the emergency release and hand crank were still intact, but Jo knew Hugh wouldn't let her climb out that way again. She was sure the vent was somehow sealed from the outside. And even if she could get through, her ankle was still swollen and unbearably painful to walk on. She would need to bide her time until the ankle healed enough to hobble. Or maybe she could signal to the outside world. Or wait until the police or Bray found her. She knew Bray had to be worried sick, and he'd be doing everything he could to track her down.

At lunchtime, Hugh's nasally voice came over the speaker, "Okay, I'm coming in." Jo knew what she had to do: lie face-first on the seat with her hands behind her back. He opened the door, walked in, and handcuffed her wrists. He helped her to hop on the one good ankle into the main room of the RV where he shackled her to the dinette table. The periods when Hugh was near and she was briefly un-handcuffed were possibly openings when Jo could do something—hit him or run—but he was never without the can of pepper spray. Jo didn't think she could withstand the spray and overpower him, at least not with her injured ankle.

Hugh seemed to have a limitless supply of pre-packaged food that needed only microwaving or nothing at all to serve. That day, they ate Oscar Mayer Lunchables, compact slices of turkey, cheddar cheese, and crackers. Jo remembered that her daughter, Rose, had pestered her for the expensive snacks packaged in little divided plastic receptacles—very environmentally unfriendly—all for maybe one hundred calories. Jo had bought them once for Rose but never again. Lunchables were for children, and that's what he served her, a mature woman in her late fifties.

"Why don't you buy some basic ingredients so that we can eat a real home-cooked meal?

"I don't cook. Florence always did the cooking."

"You weren't really the modern husband, were you?"

The comment was sarcastic and maybe funny, but Hugh took it seriously. "I provided by working *outside* of the household. Florence provided by working *inside* the household. Do you really think it would matter if our roles had been reversed? Who's the intolerant and prejudiced one now?"

"I just think a man should learn to cook."

"And a woman should learn to shoot a gun and mow the lawn?"

"I don't think anyone should learn to shoot a gun. But mow the lawn, yes."

"That's all fine, but Florence and I liked our—what would you say? Yes, our gender roles."

"To each their own, but now I'm stuck eating a child's Lunchables snack. Why don't you buy some real food and let me cook? Handcuff me to the stove if you want."

"Maybe, but right now, the nearest grocery store is forty miles away, so just eat your lunch and play cards."

Hugh dealt as he ate. This was the second time they'd played since the escape and since he'd let her win that first hand with a knock. Now, she noticed he sat up stiffly in his seat and focused intently on the cards before him. He shifted his hand around one card at a time, careful not to reveal any groupings. Jo discarded a king, and Hugh drew from the deck. He now played to win.

They played to one hundred and fifty points. Jo ginned once and added eight points from Hugh's hand to her twenty-five-point bonus. Two hands later, she was about to gin again when Hugh knocked. She'd held onto two eights and a seven while waiting to either get a third eight or build the seven and eight of hearts into a straight. In the next four hands, Hugh ginned or knocked to put him over in points and win. Each time Hugh went out, he seemed to know or sense the cards she held. Jo was exasperated and said, "How lucky can you be?"

Hugh smiled. "Luck is in the cards dealt, but then it's all skill in how the cards are played. And the longer a hand lasts, the less luck is involved."

Jo said nothing in response.

He went on, "In the mid-sixties, a Las Vegas casino did a mailing to promote a gin rummy tournament. The post office wouldn't take the mailing because it was illegal for them to promote a game of chance. The casino then took the postal service to court with the testimony of both expert players and professional statisticians. They convinced the judge that gin rummy was, in fact, a game of skill. They won their case. True story. That's why I can say that I'll let you go when you can beat me consistently. Because I'm an exceptionally good player, maybe one of the best. I've won the gin rummy tournament in Las Vegas four times. No one has ever won a fifth."

"I may surprise you."

"And I hope you do. I hope you can make me a better player."

"So you can win in Las Vegas for your fifth time?"

"Yes."

"So, that's where we're going?"

Without hesitating, Hugh said, "Yes."

11

Starsky and Hutch

Bray's Travato was built on a modern Dodge ProMaster chassis that could keep up with the flow of traffic on any highway, and frankly, he wasn't going to convoy with Uly's tired piece of history. He reached the spot in the high desert outside of Taos hours before the Xplorer. The woman he met there was parked among a cluster of juniper trees. Bray thought the camping spot looked perfect, with the mountains in the background and shade from the hot afternoon sun. Jo would love it here with the artist community in Taos less than an hour away and the fact that the spot was so remote and private. Not to mention that camping on the federal land was free.

The woman came up to the Travato as he pulled into the campsite. She looked his age, early sixties, and attractive, with thick gray hair braided down her back. She wore a floppy felt hat with an eagle feather dangling from a thin leather headband. Her face was covered with a homemade mask stitched together from some flower-patterned fabric. Bray didn't trust homemade masks and instinctively strapped on his

Chinese N95. In the distance, he could see her white VW Eurovan camper with the pop-top raised. A man, presumably her husband, sat on the ledge of the side door. She said, "You must be Bray from vanlifevagabonds. I'm Julie."

"I am." Bray stepped out of the Travato and put on his Ray-Ban "The General" aviator sunglasses that he carried in a case looped to his belt. She led him back to their campsite and introduced him to the man sitting in the VW. She said the man's first and last name, George Deschennie, pronouncing the last name in three distinct syllables, De-shen-nie, making it clear to Bray that the man was Indigenous. And he did look Indigenous with his long black hair, dark almond eyes, light-brown skin, and wispy mustache.

"Hi, I'm Brayden." And because of COVID, because they weren't supposed to shake hands, Bray raised his hand in greeting. George looked at the gesture, and just then, Bray realized that his hand raised stiffly like that usually went with the stereotypical Old West movie greeting, "How." Bray quickly wagged the hand back and forth so there'd be no misconstruing his deep liberal values.

The man said, "Hello," but from then on, he never uttered another word, and as time went by, Bray had the sneaking suspicion that George thought all the abduction business was just hooey.

Julie said, "Let's walk," and led him along a hiking trail through stubby juniper trees and pinyon pines. He first saw the top of the motorcoach, the collection of air conditioning units, vents, and satellite TV dome. They stopped about a hundred yards out and watched.

She said, "I had my binoculars yesterday and confirmed the Pennsylvania plates. I've seen the older man again, but no sign of a woman passenger. He keeps the blinds drawn at all hours. You think it's him?"

Bray looked. He had his phone and checked the photo at @fabvanlife against the motorcoach in the distance. Nearly identical. Both had the Thunder Canyon color scheme and the toy hauler feature. On the back of the lift gate was an American flag sticker the size of a pillowcase, something Bray hadn't noticed in past photos, but with the Pennsylvania plates, it had to be the one. He said, "I think it is."

"What are you going to do?"

The question took him by surprise. He had not thought about what he'd do if the coach and Jo were actually found. He couldn't call the police back in Nebraska; the crime was now out of their jurisdiction. He hadn't filed a report with the FBI, and by the time he drove the hour into Taos and convinced anyone to help—assuming they even would—the motorcoach could be long gone. He had to do something, but what? For now, he'd watch and wait for Uly.

Bray answered, "I don't know."

She looked at him and said, "Well, don't go shooting anyone."

He'd never owned a gun, never wanted to shoot one, and he was a little offended by her remark. "I don't believe in guns." His response was honest, something he'd said a thousand times, but then he knew guns weren't really something you believed in or not. Guns weren't like Kris Kringle or the Easter Bunny. They were real and deadly, and everyone in the West seemed to be packing one. The reality for Bray was that guns scared him. He added for no other reason than the thought had just crossed his mind, "I'm afraid of guns."

Julie said a word that sounded American Indian, "*Aho.*"

Bray took it to mean *amen.*

That evening, Bray and Uly watched the coach from behind a stand of pinyon pines. Lights shined through the shades, and they could see the silhouette of a person moving inside. Bray was sure this Thor Outlaw was the same one Jo had been lured into back in Nebraska. It had to be.

Bray was scared, really scared. Nothing from his past compared to the situation he was in. Maybe his daughter's birth or when Jo first found the cancerous lump, but that kind of scared was more like a fear of the unknown, like an impending doom. Now, his feeling of being scared was more visceral, like what he imagined a soldier felt on the front line of a war (Bray had been too young for Vietnam, too old for Desert Storm). And perhaps, like that soldier on the line preparing for battle, Bray couldn't decide what to do— go over the wall or hold up and wait. He wanted to wait. It was dark, and the darkness itself was just plain scary.

Furthermore, he had to poop. He knew it was nerves, like the time he ran a half-marathon in Minneapolis. He hadn't been the only one and remembered the lines to the portable toilets were ungodly long. He'd held it then, and the feeling passed. He wasn't sure he could hold it now.

He said to Uly, "Let's wait until it's light out, then we can . . ." He stopped there not knowing how to finish the sentence.

Uly asked, "Can what?"

"I don't know." He thought hastily. "Maybe just knock on the door and confront the man."

"He could be gone by tomorrow."

There were so many decisions to make and contingencies to consider, but he knew Uly was right. They needed to act while the motorcoach was parked and the engine off. He said, "Okay, one of us should do it now: knock on the door and confront the man." He didn't specify who and secretly hoped Uly would step up to do the confronting.

"What if he says he doesn't know what you're talking about and asks you to leave?"

Now, Uly was assuming Bray would do the knocking. Okay, fine, he'd do it. "I just won't leave. I'll demand to see inside the coach. We know it's just one elderly man."

"What if he says no? What if he has a gun?"

Bray thought, *guns again*. Why do people need to carry guns? Why aren't there more gun laws? He realized his political leanings had nothing to do with the bare facts—Americans were armed to the teeth—and anyone who had the moral deficiency to abduct a woman would have no reluctance regarding the use of firearms. He said, "I don't know."

Uly looked at him. "I've got a gun."

"What?" Bray was stunned.

"A gun. I have a handgun in the van."

"Why?"

"I lived in Las Vegas, and I've had troubles. And everyone carries in Vegas. Then, on the road, you never know what can happen."

"What can happen?" Bray genuinely wanted to know. He'd run into uncomfortable situations with other campers but never anything that threatened to escalate to violence. If you don't have a gun, you're unlikely to escalate, period. Why do people need guns?

Both were standing behind a tree and looking through branches at the motorcoach. The sun had set, but there remained enough light from a three-quarter moon to see without headlamps.

Uly responded, "Are you kidding? Someone just abducted your wife."

"Right, of course." What was he thinking? Who was he kidding? "So, what should we do?"

"We should both go over there. You knock on the door, and I'll be behind you. Tell the guy something to convince him to step out. We need to assume he has a gun, but it'll be hidden. Once he comes out, I'll pull my gun and get him to raise his hands. I'll cover him while you check for your wife."

The plan seemed well thought out. "I can tell him that my tire is flat, and my jack is broken. He'll have a jack in one of his external storage compartments."

"Good."

The time was just past ten o'clock when both were ready to move. Bray was still scared and tense, and what was about to happen felt out-of-body, like he was an actor in a TV drama.

Uly held the gun in one hand concealed behind his back.

Before they left, Bray said, "I gave my word to the woman that we wouldn't shoot anyone." Bray knew that sounded stupid, but he didn't want anyone hurt.

"I won't, but if the motherfucker pulls on me, then I'll have no choice."

Then what flashed through Bray's mind as they walked toward the motorcoach was that he still needed to poop. Their plan was in motion and he just couldn't. He clenched his cheeks tight and kept moving.

At the motorcoach, Bray knocked on the door. No one answered. He knocked again. Then he heard footsteps. The coach door opened by a mechanical arm operated from inside. Steps automatically pushed out, like a robotic tongue. The man stood atop the stairs, high above Bray, and looked down. He said, "Hello. What can I do for you?"

Bray said what he'd planned—the tire, the broken jack.

The man looked in his seventies, with gray hair and reading glasses strapped around his neck. He asked, "Can't this wait until the morning?"

The reply caught him off guard—the man's response was a practical solution. Bray improvised quickly, "I'm sorry, I need to be in Albuquerque as soon as possible. My daughter has come down with COVID, and I need to take care of my grandchildren while she quarantines." The story sounded so plausible.

"I'm sorry. Okay, let me get my flashlight."

The man came out shining his light. He looked at Bray and then at Uly's hulking carcass. He walked to one of the rear compartments, then reached down and lifted the hatch.

Uly said, "Hold up, mister." Uly's arm lifted with the handgun.

The man shined the flashlight in Uly's face, then the hand with the gun. "What is this?"

Uly now did all the talking. "Just hold up right there, mister. Hand over your flashlight, then put both hands on the coach."

The man did as asked and then leaned against the motorcoach. His hands and legs were both spread like he figured Bray and Uly were undercover police, or FBI, or Immigration. To Bray, he looked and acted guilty.

"I have nothing to hide," the man said.

"Just stay there." Uly turned toward Bray and said, "Go look."

Bray walked up the stairs and into the coach. He looked right first and glimpsed the driver and passenger seats as big as La-Z-Boy recliners. To his left, no one sat on the couch or at the dinette table. He yelled, "Jo, Jo."

He heard something muffled from the back, human, but the sound was faint. Bray imagined Jo tied up and gagged. He moved toward the back carefully. He checked the bathroom and shower. No one. The door to the master bedroom was closed. He opened it slowly. Inside, he saw a walker with two little wheels on the front legs, just narrow enough to move through the coach.

A woman, clearly not Jo, lay almost completely under the covers, frog eyes peeking above. He knew it wasn't Jo because the woman's hair was completely white, almost yellow, and so thin he could see the liver spots staining her scalp. Her eyes focused on his movement, and from beneath the covers, Bray heard the muffled, "What do you want?"

Bray backed out. He said, "Nothing, I'm sorry. I thought you might be someone else." He didn't explain and just backed away.

Outside, the man was still leaning spread-eagle against the motorcoach, Uly still holding the gun in one hand, the flashlight in the other.

The man said, "Please don't hurt my wife."

Uly looked toward Bray, "So?"

Bray told the man, "I'm sorry, this was a big mistake. We thought you were someone else. Someone fitting your description and driving a Thor Outlaw abducted my wife. Again, I'm deeply sorry." Bray felt deflated and ashamed. The plan had gone so horribly wrong, and now they'd scared this old man and his handicapped wife. He just wanted to flee.

He said to Uly, "Let's go."

"It wasn't her?" He sounded dejected, like all the fun and excitement had turned tragic, which it had.

"No, let's go."

Uly dropped the flashlight, and they walked quickly back

toward their vans.

Bray started up the Travato. He wanted to leave right then, leave behind the embarrassment he felt. But his bowels now insisted otherwise, a buildup like a river behind a concrete dam, one that threatened to burst. He put the Travato into drive and tried again to keep the river of poop dammed, see if the feeling would pass. It wouldn't. Bray moved the shifter back into the park position, unbuckled his safety belt, and squeezed through the front seats to the toilet in back. As soon as his posterior flesh touched molded plastic, the river of poop violently broke through.

Almost relief, but the shame of the incident stayed with him. He thought the word, *shit.* That's what he felt like—and he was full of it.

Twenty minutes later, Bray caught up to Uly's slow-moving rig. They convoyed at the pace of the Xplorer for over two hours to get as far away from Taos as possible. They finally stopped at a Cracker Barrel restaurant just outside Albuquerque.

The time was near two in the morning, but both were still too jacked up on adrenaline to sleep. They stood outside and talked in whispers. Uly asked what had happened inside the motorcoach. Bray explained what he saw—a handicap walker and a scared old woman. He then said, "We can't do this again. We're no better than cops with a no-knock warrant."

"I thought it went pretty well even though we had the wrong Outlaw."

"Sure, like clockwork." Bray meant the comment to be sarcastic, but it came out vague and half-hearted.

Uly took it at face value. "I think we make a good team—like Starsky and Hutch."

12

Mansplaining

The motorcoach hadn't moved in two days. Jo knew they were parked forty miles from the nearest supermarket and town. The generator and two air conditioning units ran nonstop, and because no campground would allow a generator to run all night long, she was sure they were on desert federal land. Hugh had said he was going to Las Vegas to play in some gin rummy tournament, so Jo guessed they were in New Mexico or Arizona, but they could also be in Utah or already in Nevada. All this speculating did no good other than to know that if she could get away, she'd be forced to walk ten, twenty, thirty miles on her injured ankle that was still swollen to the size of a grapefruit, still bruised the color of eggplant.

Jo slept in her locked room, ate bad pre-packaged food, and played long games of gin rummy with Hugh. She won some games but lost most. The trick she knew was to keep track of the cards that passed through the discard pile. She had to remember what she'd discarded and then what he picked up and discarded. She was sure Hugh had a system, like card counters at blackjack tables. She asked him about it.

Hugh's face lit up like she'd just proposed marriage. He explained, "There is no trick. I think beginners try to memorize each card that passes through their hand, but in the end, that becomes confusing. It would be like knowing all the ingredients in making a pie but not understanding that the flour is for the crust and the fruit is for the filling—all you'd get is mush. So, what you want to do is imagine your opponent's hand based on the cards you're first dealt. Then, over time, you want to re-imagine that hand based on what has been discarded and picked up. Eventually, you zero in on possibilities, probabilities."

"Probabilities?"

"Statistical likelihoods, but let's leave that for another time." He dealt the cards.

She despised his condescending tone. It reminded her of Bray when he'd try to explain how the plumbing worked in the Travato. *Mansplaining.* Jo could scarcely listen to him without cringing, and she learned that understanding something like plumbing was easier or elicited less anxiety when she referenced a manual or watched a YouTube video.

She decided to change the subject—try to understand her captor. She asked, "How did you meet your wife?"

"Your discard."

Jo put a card down. "Were you childhood sweethearts?"

"God, no. I met her through my practice. I'm a doctor, a psychologist. We started playing cards, and I found that I enjoyed her company. Prior to that, I thought I'd never enjoy another person in my space. I was wrong."

"Through your practice? Did she work for you, or was she a client?"

"If you must know, Florence was seeing me because she

was trapped in a horrible marriage and didn't know how to get out of it."

"So, you were doing marriage counseling? Were you also seeing the husband?"

"Yes."

Jo looked up from her hand. Hugh sorted a few cards, then discarded. She asked, "Isn't that illegal to have a relationship with a client? A patient?"

"Not in Pennsylvania, not then." Hugh paused and placed his cards face-down on the table. She'd never seen him not holding his cards while in the middle of a game. "Listen, her husband was abusive. He was an insurance broker who showed up each night after drinking past his limit at local watering holes. He'd come home and yell at the kids for not getting straight As, or not scoring the winning goal, or whatever. Then he'd start in on Florence for keeping a messy house or overcooking a steak. I met him, of course. A grubby little man with a mustache like an upside-down horseshoe."

"A Fu Manchu."

"Yes, one of those. She threatened to divorce him, so he agreed to counseling. He was in our sessions for only six weeks. He used that time to complain about his wife, always looking to me to agree with him, like we were pals or something. He'd make her cry every time. It wasn't my job to take sides, and I didn't. Then, in one session, I told him that it might be better if I did one-on-one work with Florence, like I would make a special effort to make her a better wife. He seemed pleased to be out of the loop and maybe vindicated. My thought was to get her to open up without her husband around. Turned out she didn't want to talk about him, and, frankly, neither did I."

Jo put her hand down and massaged the wrist shackled to the table. She asked, "So, what did you talk about?"

"What she wanted to do with her life. One child was off to college already, and the other was graduating from high school. She wanted to travel more and go to the theater and movies. She even thought she'd like to join a bridge club. All her husband wanted to do was work and drink.

"You need to understand that Florence was special. With her husband out of the sessions, I found she had a quick wit and was quite funny. She read voraciously, and we could talk away a whole hour about the books she was reading. After a few more weeks, I suggested that we play a game of cards while talking. I wasn't the gin player I am now, and she beat me. One day I asked if she would like to see me socially for dinner at a restaurant. Well, that was that."

Jo tried to see it, the attraction. The port-wine birthmark was the least of his issues. The man smoked cigarettes, which disgusted her—she'd now made him switch on the kitchen overhead blower to vent out the fumes. His mustache was trimmed just past the edges of his mouth and slightly stained brown from nicotine, and his parted, ashy gray hair was cut unfashionably long and hung just over the top edges of his ears. It looked like he'd locked into that style in 1970 and just stuck with it. Then, the split-screen bifocals made him look five years older. She didn't see how anyone could be attracted to this man.

But she could see his charm. She could see that he knew how to manipulate a person; he'd been trying to manipulate her since the abduction.

She asked, "What happened to her husband?"

"Oh, Florence finally told him she wanted a divorce and that she was having an affair with me. I told her not to, but Florence wanted the truth out there for everyone to see. Personally, I think truth is more malleable—a function of outcomes and will. One person's truth can be another person's lie. If you understand that—the desired outcome—then it's a matter of knowing the tactics and the probabilities to reach your goal. The husband knew what outcome he desired—hired a good attorney, froze all their assets, and left Florence with a mortgaged house and little else. I sold my house and moved in with her."

There was that word again, *probabilities*, and she seized on it. "So, there's no truth? It's all what you perceive and what you want and the probabilities of getting it?"

"Sure, like winning at gin rummy. Tactics and probabilities of winning."

"Games are one thing; human lives are another. Your rationale sounds, well, psychopathic. I'm surprised your wife didn't see that. I'm surprised you even had a relationship."

Hugh smiled. "Even a psychopath needs love. Humans are one of the most social species of all mammals, and it's a myth that psychopaths feel no emotion or have no relationships. Have you seen *Silence of the Lambs*? Dr. Hannibal Lecter had a real, almost lover's bond with Clarice. And maybe she had a thing for him, too?"

Jo laughed nervously. The man knew he was a psychopath. She guessed most did. She ignored his question—she got it; he was Dr. Lecter, and she was Clarice. Jo asked, "What are the probabilities that you'll be arrested for kidnapping?"

"I think as slim as the possibility that you'll eventually beat me at gin. No one knows where you are. The authorities will not care unless there's a ransom note or body, and as you may have guessed, we're in the middle of a desert, miles from civilization—nowhere to escape to. So, play cards."

Jo picked up her ten cards. She couldn't remember if

Hugh had discarded or not. She wasn't thinking of the cards. "If there's nowhere to escape to, then maybe you can let me get some fresh air."

Hugh discarded. "I'm sorry, Josephine, that would reduce the probability of the outcome I desire."

———

Hugh started the Thor Outlaw and drove slowly out of the desert on the pitted dirt roads, careful not to get stuck—that would be a disaster. He'd told Jo over the speaker to hold tight. He turned west and headed toward Las Vegas and the Sam's Town Casino, where the Gin Rummy Association Open Tournament had been moved to after Bally's had been closed due to the pandemic. Sam's Town—some off-the-Strip local's casino he'd never been to or heard of.

By the afternoon, he was on a highway and passed through a larger town. He stopped at an Albertson's grocery store, parking as far from the entrance as possible. He switched on the generator so that any sound Jo made would be muffled. Posted on the automatic sliding doors of the supermarket was a sign requesting customers to keep six feet from each other and wear masks. Of course, this was a joke in rural New Mexico, and Hugh figured he'd look more conspicuous with a mask than without.

Jo had said she wanted to cook, and Hugh hadn't had a home-cooked meal in years. He filled the cart with an assortment of vegetables, a box of lettuce, a lemon, and garlic, and then went through the meat section and bought steaks. In the aisle, he picked out pasta he liked, a bag of long-grain rice, a can of tomatoes, olive oil, a can of baked beans, a baguette, and finally, a wedge of Colby cheese and more of his almond milk. Hugh didn't know what Jo liked to cook, and he didn't have any recipe in mind for what he wanted, so the items were mostly random and would have to do. He felt generous. In the last aisle, he picked up a six-pack of beer. Though he didn't drink himself, he'd watched her drink a can right before the abduction. Hugh chose Heineken, a brand he'd seen in a James Bond movie.

He got on I-40 near the Arizona border and then zigzagged on smaller roads north and west into Navajo reservation land. Camping on the reservation was illegal, but he'd researched an obscure place about twenty miles off the main road near an old uranium mine where people could camp undisturbed. The gravel road was solid and relatively easy for the motorcoach to navigate. After years of neglect, the mine was now a shell of concrete walls rising up from the rust-colored sand of the desert floor. Ruins from the Atomic Age.

Only one other camper was parked nearby, an ancient school bus that looked like it hadn't moved in months. One wheel was missing, with the bare axle resting on cinder blocks. Hugh parked behind a crumbling industrial wall that blocked any view of his motorcoach. He took his binoculars and left the coach to watch the bus. Lettering on the side spelled out "Brigham Young Bible School." Right off, he saw a young man and two women eating around a makeshift table that was once a spool for heavy-gauge wire. Despite the heat, both women were wearing ankle-length dresses with long sleeves. Both looked pregnant. Hugh figured the guy was a fanatic Mormon polygamist living off the grid, the kind of guy who was deeply suspicious of outsiders and wouldn't want to socialize.

Hugh thought about what it would be like to have two wives. It seemed it could go either way—double love or double trouble. Josephine seemed to be moving from trouble to something that might approach love. He knew it wouldn't get there, but possibly an understanding, or maybe even companionship.

Toward evening, he brought Josephine out from the back toy hauler room and sat her down at the dinette. He uncuffed her hands from behind her back, then re-cuffed them with her hands in front. He opened cupboards and the refrigerator and showed her what he'd bought. He said, "Why don't you make us a meal?"

Josephine stood and went through the food. She pulled out the pasta, the can of tomatoes, the garlic cloves, the baguette, and olive oil. From the refrigerator, she selected red and green peppers. She said, "You'll need to uncuff me so I can cook. You'll need to let me use a knife to slice the garlic and vegetables."

Hugh hadn't thought through all this. Florence had always cooked and, in fact, did not like him in her kitchen. He realized, though, that a certain amount of trust would go a long way toward getting Jo on his side. He kept trauma bonding in mind. She needed to be kept prisoner but also allowed some pleasures—the back and forth of punishment and rewards. Hugh touched the can of pepper spray clipped onto his front pants pocket, satisfied it was there and ready, then uncuffed her wrists. "You can use the steak knife in the drawer." Hugh moved further away to the door of the motorcoach and swiveled the front passenger seat so he could watch her.

She talked to him as she sliced vegetables and boiled pasta water. She asked, "How did your wife die?"

"Breast cancer. Unlike you, she just had a lumpectomy, but a year later, the cancer had metastasized. She's been gone now for over five years."

The lumpectomy was a lie; she'd died of other causes. But

the lie would resonate with Josephine and her cancer experience. He thought the story might create sympathy that would go toward her eventual thought of him as a good man.

"I'm sorry. That must have been terrible for you."

Then he told her some truth. "It took me a year to just begin to get over it. I didn't go out, watched too much television, and let the house go. At the end of that year, I threw out or gave away just about everything in that house and filled it again with meaningless items that wouldn't remind me of her. I wanted to create new memories to replace the old, but that didn't work, either."

"Did you try to date like other, normal people?"

He looked at her and felt anger build. "I'm not like other *normal* people. In fact, I hate the idea of normal people—birth, death, taxes. But, yes, I did have another . . ." He thought for a second to get the right word, a careful word. He finished, "relationship."

She slid half the packet of pasta into the boiling water, then began moving the strands around with a fork. "Tell me about that."

What was there to tell? He'd met another woman in a troubled relationship. The man she was with was just as mean and self-centered as Florence's first husband. This one had a goatee instead of a Fu Manchu. The woman was a successful lawyer but still had to get home to cook the meals and clean the house. Hugh thought her husband was jealous of her success—she also made more money than him—and he became bitter and cruel. Hugh again suggested that she do one-on-one work with him, and the husband was more than happy to bow out and let Hugh fix her—just like Florence's husband had done years earlier. They had an affair, but the relationship turned sour. Then, she sued him for malpractice, and he lost his license. It had all gone so horribly wrong. He was still bitter.

Hugh revealed none of this to Josephine; the story would lessen the likelihood of his desired outcome. He said, "Not much to say. I had a relationship and then I didn't. I guess we weren't really compatible."

Just thinking about what had happened after the affair put him in a foul mood—losing his practice, selling his home, and leaving Sewickley. He lit a cigarette and blew the smoke into the overhead fan. He sat quietly, smoked, and watched Josephine cook.

He forced himself to think about other things. The tournament, what he would do afterward. How could he ever let her go? He knew he couldn't.

Minutes later, Josephine tasted a strand from the boiling pasta. She said, "I think it's done." She lifted the pot by its handle, then suddenly swung it his way. The scalding water and pasta hit him in the face and chest. The attack startled him, and he couldn't react fast enough to what happened next.

In seconds, Josephine was out the door.

13

Just Another Day at the Office

The last thing she saw of Hugh was the cooked spaghetti sliding down his scalded face. The last thing she heard was his high-pitched nasally scream.

What she'd done was not premeditated. She had a steak knife in her hand, about four inches of serrated stainless steel, but Hugh sat eight feet from her and held the pepper spray. The actions of attacking someone with a knife were, even in her situation, almost impossible to comprehend—all that slashing, struggling, and blood. But she *had* considered it before and knew she could do it if it came to that. Nonetheless, if she tried, he'd be on her with the spray before she even got close. Then she was staring at a pot of boiling water. Jo didn't think; she just acted, and in one swoop of her arm, the water with the boiling hot pasta was in the air, flying toward him. As the scalding mixture started to burn his face, she was already halfway to the door. She pushed the button and the door opened, and before the two steps could mechanically slide out, she jumped. The landing sent a shock of pain through her injured ankle, and she collapsed to the ground.

She briefly looked around to get her bearings. The motorcoach was parked next to a cement wall of some industrial ruins. The land was flat desert dirt and unobstructed except for the small shrubs of Russian thistle that would one day turn into dried tumbleweeds and blow away. The sun was nearing the horizon, but she thought she had at least two hours of daylight left, which could be good or bad depending on whether you were trying to find someplace safe or trying not to be found. She stood and started hobbling.

Jo wore one hiking shoe on her good foot. Her other swollen foot was bare without a sock or supporting bandage. She hobbled down the only road that led from the parking spot. She took a step, put some weight on the toes of her injured foot, and then took another step. Each time the toes hit the desert floor, a shock of pain exploded in her ankle. She still wasn't sure if the injury was just a sprain or worse, and now it felt worse, like a fracture in one of the numerous little bones that make up a foot. But it was pain she could endure, and she kept hobbling. She knew he'd be searching for her soon.

There was no place to hide. She could try and take off into the open desert, but she had no food or water, and it could be twenty, thirty, or more miles before she hit another road, or a ranch, or a town. Her only chance was to follow the dirt road until it met with a larger paved road with traffic. She had no way of knowing how far that was. She kept hobbling. She started crying, maybe from the pain, or the hope of escape, or the futility of trying.

She heard the motorcoach driving up behind her. At first, she didn't turn around. Then Hugh slowed and the brakes made a hissing sound, like air escaping a balloon. Jo looked back and saw the looming vehicle. She kept hobbling and the coach kept following.

Hugh let her keep going. He hung back about twenty yards and just crept along. Her pain was now all-encompassing, moving up her leg, clouding her thoughts. Jo kept hobbling and Hugh let her.

She then saw the old school bus in the distance, a glow of light behind pulled drapes and lettering on the side that spelled out something, something, "Bible School." It seemed so far away, a spec in the distance, but she could smell the smoke from their wood stove. She changed direction and limped toward the bus, toward someone who could help.

Her left foot, her good foot, hit the berm at the edge of the road. She stumbled and put way too much weight on her swollen foot. She collapsed and then lay on the side of the road, screaming for help.

She crawled and screamed. The motorcoach stopped beside her. She looked ahead and kept screaming, "Help, help."

No one came running, and now Jo saw the light go out inside the bus. They did not care. A woman was screaming for help, and they did not care.

She heard the coach door open. If Hugh wanted to stop her, then he'd have to drag her back. Or he could kill her right there in the desert, in front of whoever was in the bus—the person or persons who wouldn't get involved. She didn't care.

Jo didn't look back but heard Hugh's footsteps. She finally looked up as the footsteps neared and then stopped. She looked up just as he depressed the button on his pepper spray canister. Jo held her hands in front of her face and tried to block the stream of spray, but he twisted and turned his arm so that the slippery goo coated her eyes and face. She couldn't see and her skin burned. The fumes seemed to suck the air from her lungs, and when she opened her mouth to scream, only a hiss emitted, a sound like a punctured tire.

This was his payback for what she'd done.

After the can was exhausted, he grabbed one wrist and dragged her toward the motorcoach. Her hip skidded along the dirt road's surface, grinding sand and gravel into the waistband of her pants.

While Hugh pulled, he whistled. The sound was soft, almost bird-like. He was enjoying the violence even though he'd surely been scalded moments before.

Hugh pulled at her arm from the bottom step of the coach. He commanded, "Get up."

Still, no one emerged from the school bus, and the wood smoke smell was gone, the fire doused.

Jo moved onto one knee and placed her hands on the bottom coach step. She pushed up and sat on it. He said, "Move." Jo stood, then hobbled up the steps. She was still blinded, feeling for the railing and then the edges of the couch and dinette. The pepper spray coated her face and hands. Her eyes watered, and the cascade of tears washed the stinging goo down her face and neck. Moving blindly through the coach, the pain increased, and she gasped for air. She found her way back to her room and fell against the bench seat. She heard the door shut and the latch close. She didn't dare touch her face—fearing she might spread it around or rub it in and cause more pain.

Jo felt for the gallon jug of water under the bench seat and lifted it out. She filled the basin in the porta potty. She splashed water on her face. The spray was gel-like, not soluble, and the water only made the stinging worse. She reached into one of the storage tubs and found a cake of soap. She soaped up her hands in the porta potty and scrubbed at her face. She rinsed the soap off with more water, and that helped. She lay down then and just waited. Minute by minute the pain subsided until she could open her eyes and see around her. She saw nothing at first, and for a moment, the lack of sight scared her, maybe lasting damage. Then she realized that the room was pitch-black, that no light from the moon or stars penetrated the skylight vent. She closed her eyes and just lay still.

She hadn't thought through anything. What did she expect when attempting an escape into the desert with an injured ankle and one shoe, no water, and no idea of where she was escaping *to*? How stupid could she be?

She remembered her cancer diagnosis given by a doctor who seemed to be reading from a script. The details of the cancer seemed to drift by, Bray asking the questions and scribbling notes. What went through her mind then was what she'd done to cause it. In her twenties, she smoked. Jo remembered that she loved to smoke, was thin with a great figure, and that men were attracted to her. It was a feeling of power—that she had control over things and people around her. She quit smoking soon after she met Bray and a few years before she had Rose, but what she thought about after the diagnosis was that her smoking had caused the cancer. And if it wasn't the actual smoke in her lungs that caused it, then it was simply the hubris of thinking she had any real power over the world. For years, off and on, she dealt with the guilt that what she'd done to herself and her family was her fault. That's what she felt now—it was her fault she'd been caught and assaulted and that, in some real way, she deserved it.

Then she remembered the tune Hugh whistled as he dragged her across the desert, "I've Been Working on the Railroad." She guessed, just another day at the office—no remorse as he meted out her punishment.

"Just to pass the time away."

14

Unauthorized Boundaries

They were friends with benefits. Margo had met Lucas six months prior on the beach in La Jolla. He was surfing with a few guys she knew—all lifeguards at Shores Beach. Lucas looked magnificent with his perfectly sculpted body, blond hair down to his shoulders, and blue eyes that matched hers. Right then, he invited Margo to have coffee with him at the Bird Rock. What they found in common was a passion for Instagram, and Lucas was an aspiring photographer. What they didn't have in common was a passion for each other. Margo thought Lucas was kind of a dope, and Lucas thought she was a spoiled rich kid. She knew because he'd said so, "What are you, one of those prissy trustafarians?"

On another level, they were both beautiful and young with insatiable sexual needs. Both wanted to be on top, dominant—both obstinate about their desires. Margo, in her sexual journey, was way past putting out to just please a guy, getting what *she* wanted as a byproduct—past being anyone's porn star chippy. What she craved now was the experience and the release, and she wanted it just so. She'd tell Lucas exactly how to use his tongue, hands, and body. But then Lucas had things he wanted and was not shy about explaining each position in tedious detail.

After a month of butting heads, they'd come to an agreement of sorts. Lucas would get more of what he wanted—be in control on Mondays, Wednesdays, and Fridays. Margo took Tuesdays, Thursdays, and Saturdays. Sunday was their official day of rest. One rule—everyone gets a happy ending.

Now, after five months on the road abiding by this schedule, each sex day was beginning to follow similar patterns, and the coaching and coaxing started to subside. Sex might have turned boring, but for Margo, at least, it was nowhere near that. And she wondered if they weren't starting to get along.

But still, Lucas was a dope. He could surf, ride a skateboard, and take great photos, but when it came to fixing anything on the van or posting on their Instagram account, he was next to useless—Margo had to follow up and finish whatever he started. Then, when it came to cooking meals, his one and only specialty was boiling water for packaged ramen. He couldn't even clean dishes correctly; the plates and utensils always still coated with a greasy film. How hard could it be to do dishes correctly?

And the fact was, she did have a trust fund, which indisputably put her in the category of trustafarian. The trust was established when Margo was fifteen, when her parents divorced. The money came from her dad's Internet company formed in the nineties when the information superhighway was just getting paved. He'd created a dating website called *uToo.com* after his favorite band, U2. The concept was that people could hook up based on their mutual love of similar music. For a few years, the site was huge, with almost five million subscribers. Then, he sold it to harmony.com for half a billion dollars. After the sale, interest in the *uToo* site sunk, similar to sites like Friendster, Merkat, and Yik Yak. By that time, Margo's daddy had walked away with his cash.

She had grown up in La Jolla and attended the prestigious Bishops Prep School. Afterward, Margo's now divorced parents got her into USC on a rowing scholarship even though she thought a cockswain was some adult toy. At USC, Margo majored in communication and started her first Instagram page called @mangomargo, which featured tips on how to dress, apply makeup, and date in college. She cultivated over forty thousand followers and a paying sponsorship from Blemish Rescue. Then she graduated and was no longer a college student, at which point COVID crushed her dating advice for good.

It was Lucas who said #vanlife was trending and that during the pandemic, escaping to the road was going to be huge. Lucas was no trustafarian, so the money needed for the campervan they purchased and customized all came from her. Lucas chose the actual van, a Mercedes Sprinter, but Margo made all the interior decisions and came up with the van's name, Fabvan, and Instagram handle @fabvanlife. Then, on the road, Lucas was supposed to pay for his share of the expenses. That was the deal—in theory—but it was just another source of animosity between them.

For the first month, they stayed near the beaches in California and had loads of fun. Lucas did his photography and surfed while Margo wrote posts, posed for photos, and built her following. Toward spring, they moved east through Joshua Tree and Death Valley. The desert had beautiful landscapes she'd never seen before, and spectacular sunsets featured in their photo backdrops. Then, in the mountains near Telluride, they took long hikes up to glaciers and hidden lakes. Along the way, Margo researched and posted things like outdoor cooking tricks, van hacks for easier life on the road, and ways to avoid blisters. Lucas's photos looked phenomenal, and their following increased exponentially. They discovered a whole world of people during the pandemic who were either already on the road or aspiring to buy a campervan to begin a new life journey.

They got as far as Omaha before realizing the Great Plains were a great big bore. That was when they turned around and headed back west, finding the campground where the woman, Jo, was abducted.

Their Instagram following was over ten thousand before the abduction, but after the Thor Outlaw posts and calls for leads, it grew to over fifteen thousand in just a few days. They decided to change things up and search for the missing woman.

———

Unknown to her, Margo had received one of the best leads on the whereabouts of the Thor Outlaw but wouldn't see it until the next day when she had cell phone reception. That day she and Lucas were beyond the reach of cell towers, twenty miles into the Mesa Verde National Park in southwestern Colorado. They planned a photo shoot at the thirteenth-century Anasazi cliff dwellings lining the steep arroyos that dropped from the mesa plains.

On the day of the shoot, she woke up before Lucas and lay on the platform bed in the van, feeling the sun's warmth streaming through the open doors. Surprisingly, Margo loved the small bed and the compactness of the campervan. She didn't mind that she had no shower and just a porta potty that slid from beneath the bed's platform. She found that she slept well in the tight space, looked forward to going to bed, and looked forward to her dreams. It was strange because back in La Jolla, she'd hated going to bed, anticipating the hours of tossing and turning before sleep came. She could not remember one dream from back in La Jolla. She thought maybe the van was like the comfort a dog took in sleeping in a kennel, some primal response to the threat of predators.

She remembered her dream from that night. It involved searching for the abducted woman, Jo. She and Lucas were in the van, Margo driving through the open desert. There were rocks and cacti, but the van floated above as if on a cushion of air. They came upon the ruins of a castle, and somehow, Margo knew it was where Jo was being held prisoner. Then, she was standing in front of a steel door with a lock that disappeared when touched. The door opened on its own. Jo was staring up from below. Margo took her by the hand and led her out. Then they both leapt from the ground and flew away in a small plane Margo could miraculously pilot. The dream was vibrant and fresh in her memory, as though it had occurred right before she awoke. Could a dream also be a premonition? She dwelt on that before rolling off the platform bed, lighting a burner, and filling the kettle for tea.

By late morning, the campervan was packed up, and they drove across the mesa to where the cliff dwellings faced the southern sky. The road funneled a line of RVs and passenger cars to a series of parking lots surrounding a visitor center and museum. Just inside, in the line for tickets to see the one accessible cliff dwelling, was a sign that said all tours were canceled because of COVID. Margo could see the dwelling across the arroyo but was not allowed in.

That did not fit with her plan.

She said to Lucas, "Let's go," then grabbed his hand and walked toward the cliffs. She added, "Put your mask on."

Lucas pulled her back. "What are you doing?"

"Just follow me." She pulled again, and this time Lucas followed.

Lucas wore a red bandana tied around his neck that he pulled up over his nose. Margo strapped on her mask, a tie-dyed cotton affair she'd purchased online through Etsy. Tourists, most with masks, stood just outside the roped-off area, taking photos of the ruins embedded in the cliffs. Margo led Lucas under the rope and walked in as though they belonged. No ranger was on duty to tell them otherwise.

Lucas stepped in front of her and stopped. "Margo, you can't just do this."

"Yes, I can. Get your camera ready." She stepped around him and kept going.

The long path to the dwellings descended down the arroyo and back up the other side. They kept walking. Margo could see the individual dwellings that lined the deep caverns of the rust-colored cliffs, seemingly one right on top of the other with narrow passageways and stairs that carved up the labyrinth.

For the photo shoot, Margo had picked out a flowing white cotton dress that billowed like drapery and hung off her shoulders just enough to show her delicate clavicle. With this, she wore mustard-colored cowboy boots with pointy toes and a wide-brimmed black bolero hat. The whole look was very Santa Fe, and the dress would contrast nicely with the dark rust color of the ruins. Margo slipped beneath a wood railing with a red and white sign, "Stop, Authorized Personal Only Beyond This Point."

Lucas, in an adamant whisper, a whisper-yell, said, "Margo!"

She kept walking as though she owned the place, like she was authorized personnel. She assumed Lucas would be sufficiently guilted, or perhaps bullied, into following without her having to say so. When she finally looked around, he was there. They ascended to the base of the ruins.

She climbed the stairs into one of the little rooms. Lucas was below with his camera, and he snapped photos when she emerged leaning through a carved window opening. He said, "Okay, let's go."

"Just a sec."

Did she think most people were lemmings, that she was special, and that rules didn't apply to her? In a word, *yes*. Margo knew who she was and what she was capable of doing. On her sixteenth birthday, her father bought her a Porsche convertible, and she became the kind of driver who always drove faster than the flow of traffic and rode the bumper of anyone in her path. She'd been pulled over plenty but avoided most citations with a cheap smile and a few coquettish words. Then college. She'd barely graduated from high school, but her parents had greased the wheels with someone at USC, and she'd been accepted, with a scholarship to boot, for a sport she'd never participated in.

The word *entitled* had always been there, like a scarlet L for "Loser" tattooed across her forehead. She'd been called entitled her whole life as though everything—money, cars, clothes, jewelry—were just given to her, and she'd done nothing to earn any of it.

Margo knew she was entitled. But she wouldn't let that entitlement go to waste.

Deep in the dwellings, she straddled a round turret-like

wall with her boot resting on the end of a log joist that held up the floor. Lucas kept shooting. Further down the wall was a ladder made of strapped-together sticks. Margo walked over, climbed a few rungs, and posed.

Then she stumbled. Her boot heel slid off a rung, and she reached out to stop herself from falling. She grabbed at the wall that now moved beneath her grip. A hand-hewed stone the size of a cinderblock fell, but she'd found her footing on the ladder by then. Lucas jumped to the side to avoid the stone that went crashing over the edge of the dwelling and down to the deep arroyo below. The sound it made as it tumbled was, in Margo's imagination, like a screaming burglar alarm.

From across the arroyo she heard, "Hey, get out of the dwellings, you're not allowed."

Margo looked around. There was no way up to the top of the mesa that she could see, and no way down. The only way out was the way they'd come, and now she could see the dimpled crown of a ranger hat coming her direction. Lucas stood where he was, trying to look invisible. Margo stepped down the ladder and walked toward the approaching man. She smiled as she got nearer and then went for the feigned ignorance. "We aren't supposed to be here?"

Lucas inched to the side, trying to move away from the ranger and let Margo take the brunt. That was okay with her; you couldn't be in the Instagram business without breaking a few rules.

The ranger wore wraparound sunglasses, the kind that looked aerodynamic and sporty. He took them off and hooked one temple piece over his ranger shirt pocket. He looked at Margo without answering the silly question. She thought he was about her age, maybe a few years older, and not bad-looking. She smiled again. "I guess we should leave."

Then he read her the riot act. She'd ignored the sign. She'd ignored the fact that no other visitors disregarded the sign. She'd defaced a sacred archaeological site. She faced a potential five-thousand-dollar fine in addition to a misdemeanor trespassing charge and possibly a felony charge for destruction of federal and Indigenous property.

Lucas had already slipped past the man, and Margo could see him becoming just one of the tourists watching the altercation. She said to the ranger, "Jeeze, I'm so sorry." She pouted her lips and looked down, affecting a semblance of shame.

The ranger said, "Let me guess, you're some Instagram wannabee?"

The pout turned into a steely set jaw. "I have fifty thousand followers. I'm hardly a wannabee." She knew the number was a lie when she said it, but she thought it really more of a half-truth. In college with @mangomargo, she did have that kind of following.

"I don't care if you have a million followers. I don't care if Melania Trump *liked* your posts." He used air quotes around *liked*. "You're trespassing on sacred grounds, and now you need to leave this national park."

The man seemed unreasonable. All she'd done was take a few photos. If the stone she toppled was that fragile and tippy, they should have secured it better. Margo did not distinguish in her mind if "they" meant the rangers or the Anasazi who built the dwellings more than eight hundred years earlier.

She said, "We have another day in the campground that we've already paid for."

"Not anymore."

With that, Margo walked back across the arroyo to the campervan where Lucas was hiding and peeking out through the side windows. The whole time, she felt the ranger following her, and when she opened the van door, she looked back to see him writing down the van's license plate number.

An hour later, they left the national park and turned toward Durango. On the highway, her phone connected to a cell tower, and she pulled over at the first exit. The DMs, texts, and emails flowed to the apps. She checked the updated count of her followers, and @fabvanlife was now at almost twenty thousand. The new followers were all tracking the posts about the abduction.

One DM said they'd seen a Thor Outlaw with the Thunder Canyon color scheme turn down a dirt road in New Mexico on the Navajo reservation. The person gave the coordinates that, when entered into the navigation system, showed Margo and Lucas were only four hours away, back in the opposite direction toward Cortez, then south.

Lucas sat quietly in the driver's seat and stared at his phone. He'd seen the lead, too. He said, "Why don't we just take a break and spend the night at a nice hotel in Durango."

"Lucas, quit being such a dope."

Lucas started the engine and put the campervan into drive. He said, "Fuck you, Margo."

Margo smiled to herself. If she wasn't agreeing, she wasn't paying, and Lucas had no cash for a hotel room in Durango.

He took a U-turn and headed toward Cortez.

15

Jo Smokes a Cigarette

The motorcoach stayed parked in the desert that night and the next day. At dinner time, Hugh finally opened the door after instructing Jo to lie face-down with hands behind her back. She did what he asked and didn't look at his face until after she was seated at the dinette, and then she stared. The scalding wasn't as bad as she'd thought. Both cheeks were a bright pinkish red that matched and blended with his birthmark stain. His glasses had protected his eyes. The bridge of his nose had turned a chestnut brown, and on the tip rose a whitish blister like a plantar wart. All in all, she thought the scalding looked more like a bad sunburn. She felt no pleasure over his injuries.

Hugh put two bowls of Chunky Beef Soup in the microwave. He placed a plastic spoon and paper napkin in front of her, along with slices of white bread. When the microwave sounded, he served her bowl first, saying with a voice laced with bitterness, "Enjoy."

They ate in silence.

Anger, though, wouldn't get in the way of his games. After

they finished, he said, "Okay, let's play cards." He dealt.

She played. It was something to do, something to comply with, and she did it without thought. The cards moved through her hands. She discarded an eight of diamonds and Hugh picked it up. Two discards later, Jo laid down another eight, and now he looked up at her, irritation showing in his clenched jaw. He said, "Pay attention." Hugh ginned and caught her with two face cards, ten points each, plus the twenty-five-point bonus. He didn't mark down the score and said, "Let's start over."

Then he asked, "Would you like a beer?"

Jo had never seen Hugh drink, and he'd never offered her a beer. She did want a beer and said, "Yes, please."

He stood up, retrieved a can of Heineken from the refrigerator, and placed it on the table. He sat without getting a beer for himself. Jo asked, "You're not having one?"

"I don't drink."

Few people started their adult lives without having a drink or two. She thought people quit because of control issues or alcoholism. She'd had plenty of friends who'd been pushed to quit over the years.

She asked, "Do you have a drinking problem?"

He looked at her. She could tell he still harbored anger from the night before, and maybe also for her disregard of the cards. "Why does everyone assume that because a person doesn't drink, they've had a drinking problem?"

Jo hadn't meant to antagonize him, and maybe she'd been insensitive to assume. But then again, it seemed so obvious that he'd quit drinking because of control issues—either he lost control when drinking or feared losing control. She thought probably the latter; Hugh was a man who needed to be acutely aware of his surroundings and willfully in command of any interaction. With gin rummy, he'd turned a game laced with chance into an exercise in memory, rules, and probabilities.

She said again, for the second time that evening, "I'm sorry." Then she asked, "Did you buy that beer just for me?"

He ignored her question. "Just play cards."

Jo opened the beer, took a sip, and played. She lost the next hand when Hugh went out with a knock. He'd only caught her with eight points. She finished the Heineken, and Hugh brought her a second one. He dealt another hand.

This time, she looked more closely at her cards. She had pairs of sixes and jacks plus three eights. She remembered what Hugh had said, "Try to imagine what hand the other player has." She did that and imagined the long string of cards left over from what she held. As the game progressed, she zeroed in on his possible hand, and it became clear to her the cards he might be holding. Among them, she thought, was a pair of twos, and she discarded the two in her hand to test her instinct. He picked it up.

She knew he was down to one, maybe two cards needed to gin, and she was certain that the single seven she held was a card he needed. Jo drew an ace she couldn't use but was convinced he held three aces—no other aces had moved through the pile or her hand. She was convinced Hugh would gin if she discarded either the seven or the ace.

She knocked.

Hugh laid out his hand. He did, in fact, have the three aces and the two sevens. He was left holding just an eight that would have allowed her to gin—he'd known that she needed that eight. Jo saw him look over at her cards. He saw the seven and ace. He smiled and said, "Nice play."

From his shirt pocket, Hugh pulled out his pack of cigarettes—Marlboro Lights—and tapped one out between his fingers. He lit the tip with a disposable BIC lighter, then stood up and turned on the overhead fan to vent the smoke. He sat back down.

Jo looked at the pack of cigarettes now lying on the table. She wasn't sure why, but now the smoke smelled good. She said, "Do you mind if I have one?" She didn't examine her request, equate it with cancer guilt, or her previous reaction to smoke. All she knew was that it brought back a sense memory of the time before she'd married and had a child. A time of confidence when she loved to smoke and loved the smell— loved the way it made her feel.

He tipped the pack in her direction, and she pulled one out. Jo put the cigarette into her mouth, and he lit it for her. The smoke hit her lungs and she held it there. She felt the need to cough but resisted the urge. The nicotine blanketed her nervous system and merged with the alcohol, already inhibiting the little chemical messengers in her brain. The feeling was both comforting and invigorating, like driving through winding backroads.

————

The next day, they played gin rummy at lunchtime. The tactic of imagining Hugh's hand thrust the game into a new realm for her. It was like first learning how to ride a motorcycle. The hard part was balancing the throttle and clutch so that when the clutch was released, the bike didn't just jerk forward and stall but smoothly drove off. It took her half a day to get the hang of that. When she did, she found second gear, and the bike accelerated with this deep feeling of power and freedom like she could be anywhere, anytime. Shifting gears, that's what learning to imagine Hugh's cards was like.

They played quick games to one hundred, and Jo started to win a few. She identified other pieces to the puzzle that concerned choices: the safest cards to discard, when to match cards of the same rank or follow a straight, when to abandon a pair of face cards, and whether to knock early or wait for the gin. Jo took mental note of each issue and resolved to flesh them out later when she returned to her room.

They hadn't said much to each other through the first few games, but then Hugh asked, "How long have you and Bray been married?"

She looked at him above her cards. He was looking down, the question seemingly nonchalant. "Twenty-eight years next June."

Hugh pulled out his pack of cigarettes and offered her one.

She took it and Hugh lit the end.

"I'm sure you miss him."

The sentiment felt incongruous coming from her abductor, who'd admitted he was, in fact, a true psychopath. So, he was probably just fucking with her head. She did not provide a response to his hypothetical statement.

He asked, "How did you meet?"

They'd met over a mutual love of motorcycles. Jo had learned how to ride from a grandfather who bought her a small dirt bike when she was fourteen. The deal was that she could only ride the motorcycle off-road while vacationing at her grandparents' lake cabin. When she turned twenty, Jo bought an old Triumph motorcycle from a friend. The Triumph was an English bike that looked cool. It was like the motorcycle Marlon Brando rode in *The Wild One*. The problem was that it broke down continually, and only one shop in town, the Blue Cat, could fix it. That's where she met Bray. The Blue Cat held a monthly rally where they opened their shop to customers, put out a boombox for music, and filled a cooler with cans of beer. Customers came and showed off their bikes. Jo had her Triumph and Bray had his prized 1969 BMW. He asked her out for coffee, and they started riding together.

What she told Hugh was, "We met at a party, then started dating."

"When I met Florence for the first time, I just knew. It wasn't love at first sight. I don't really believe in the concept of love; it's too often confused with raging hormones or some exalted idea of family. What I believe in is an intellectual attraction, the ability to be so close in thought that you become merged or enmeshed. I guess it's a sort of synergy, the concept that one plus one equals more than two. Florence and I were like that. I believe the two of us together were much better than each of us apart."

Hugh went back to studying his cards. "Do you think you and Bray have synergy?" He kept looking at his cards, sorting, re-sorting, picking up, and discarding. He acted casual as though the conversation wasn't breaking into uncharted, unwelcomed territories.

Jo was losing track of the game, and maybe that was his fucked-up idea of smart play. Maybe it was working. She thought of Bray. Once they'd decided to have just one child, he convinced her that they should both give up riding. She loved riding and loved riding with Bray. One summer, they'd even taken a two-week trip to western South Dakota and ridden the winding roads through the Black Hills. They carried everything they needed strapped to their bikes and camped in a tent each night. But she gave up riding for the sake of the family. She sold her bike, but Bray kept his, spending hours restoring parts and keeping it clean. He would fire up the engine but never take it out for a spin, and it sat there, lifeless. It was as if Bray killed the child within him for the sake of the new child being born. For Jo, that inner child was always there, and being a responsible mom felt like adult playacting. Did she and Bray have synergy? Did the two of them together make something special? She did love Bray in her own way. She knew what that love meant and could define it for herself, and it did have something to do with family, a commitment, and a sacred bond. She wanted it to mean more, a passion and oneness that said, "You complete me," but their love hadn't evolved that way. Bray was a different person after Rose was born.

She said, "Probably not, but I love him."

Hugh ginned. Jo looked up to see the twitch of his ash-gray mustache.

He dealt another hand. "Your discard."

Jo held her hand loosely and sorted the cards one at a time with a concentrated look that she hoped camouflaged the excitement of holding almost the *perfect hand*. She had two complete melds, a partial meld, and needed only two cards to gin. She took her time, maybe conveying that her hand was complicated and undeveloped.

She never finished that perfect hand. The generator was on, both air conditioners were screaming, and the windows were shuttered. She did not hear the campervan that drove up the dirt road and parked. She did not hear the two kids walk to the side of the motorcoach. All she heard was the loud bang on the door.

Hugh reached into an overhead compartment and pulled out a handgun, just a small thing. He released the clip and Jo could see the brass tip of a bullet. He pushed the clip back into the gun's handle.

He grabbed a towel from the bathroom and threw it on

top of the dinette. He said, "Keep that hand covered."

Jo placed her cards on the table and stretched the towel over her left hand and handcuffs. She said nothing.

Hugh slipped the gun into the back pocket of his khaki trousers. "Do something stupid and they're dead."

16
KOOKY SHIT

Margo and Lucas had reached the Navajo reservation by early evening and drove up the gravel road corresponding to the coordinates they'd been messaged.

Margo saw the old school bus—a schoolie—and told Lucas to pull over nearby. The sun was close to the horizon, but there was still more than an hour of daylight. They parked and Margo stepped from the passenger door with her tie-dyed mask covering her mouth and nose. She read the lettering on the side of the schoolie, "Brigham Young Bible School." Drapes on the inside covered all the windows, and a hole had been cut through the roof for the smokestack of a wood-fired stove. One tire was flat, and an axle had been jacked up so that it rested on a large chunk of concrete that someone must have dragged from the crumbling ruins of the industrial building in the distance. She knocked on the glass window, and from inside, a hand moved the mechanical lever that opened the folding door. A person stepped down and toward them wearing olive-green army surplus from head to toe.

Enveloping the person's head was a gas mask hood with two goggle eyes and a breathing apparatus like a large pig snout, like something from a *Mad Max* movie. A gloved hand then raised, like, *stop there*. A muffled voice said, "What is it you need?" Definitely a man. Behind him, at the top of the stairs, were two women or girls in chin-to-ankle *Little House on the Prairie* dresses. Margo couldn't tell their age because they wore the same gas mask hoods. Beyond a doubt, both were pregnant, their dresses let out in front with sewn-in material the shape of oversized footballs. He lowered his hand.

"I'm looking for an RV motorcoach that was supposed to be around here somewhere. Have you seen it?"

"We like to mind our own business." Now, he sounded like Darth Vader.

The man, the women, and the whole getup were so mind-blowing—*Little House on the Prairie* meets *Mad Max*—and Margo wondered how this might play into her Instagram account. "Do you mind if we take photos? I have this Instagram page with over twenty-thousand followers . . ." her explanation trailed off—it occurred to her that this man probably had no idea what Instagram was.

Inside, the two women scurried further back into the bus. The man said, "I *do* mind."

"What are you, like Mormons?"

"We're members of the Fundamentalist Church of Latter-Day Saints."

"So, why are you out here?"

The man's pants were patched and dusty, and the leather of his construction boots had worn down so she could see the steel of the steel toes. "To stay away from people like you."

"What do you mean, like me?" She always sensed other people putting her into some cliché of the pretty rich girl, which bugged her.

"If you hadn't noticed, the apocalypse is upon us. People like you bring the pestilence and disease that precedes the second coming of Jesus Christ." The man pointed his finger right at her like some preacher denouncing a sinner. "I would like you to leave now."

The mask and Darth Vader voice made the cultish talk all the more sinister. Margo thought it was *so* cool. Earlier that summer, she'd read something on the Internet about religious nuts. She remembered the catchphrase used and said it out loud as a question, "Hunker and bunker?"

The man thought for a moment, then repeated, "Hunker and bunker, waiting for the second coming which should come," he paused, "any time now."

"You have enough water and food to last 'til then?" Margo had in mind a swap of some kind. Food for photos.

"We'll manage and the Lord will provide."

Margo thought of what she and Lucas had in the van, stuff they could get by without. "I have two gallons of drinking water, a five-pound bag of rice, and three cans of diced tomatoes that I'll give you if I can take photos. The women, too." She tried to find the man's eyes through the dusty glass of the goggles. They were in there looking at her, twitching back and forth like some rodent. She added, "The Lord provides in mysterious ways," and thought he might consider that.

The man stood silent for minutes, thinking over the offer. Finally, he said, "We can't expose ourselves to the fetid air that surrounds your being."

Margo thought about the word *fetid*. She'd only heard it used once before, back in college, and that was to describe the stench of a frat-boy fart.

She told him, "Okay, keep your masks on."

The Mormon nodded, his bulky hooded mask flopping like a Muppet puppet. He said, "Be quick about it."

She returned to the campervan, opened the side door, and said to Lucas, "Quick, you need to take some shots of these freaks before the sun goes down. Hurry, this should be good." The two gallons of water were behind the driver's seat, and she grabbed them by their looped handles. She put the cans of food and their large unopened sack of rice in a plastic grocery bag.

Lucas watched as she pulled his camera from its case. "What are you doing?"

"Never mind, just move."

Minutes later, Margo was back at the school bus. She placed the water and bag of food at a safe distance from the man and then stepped away. The man stepped forward and retrieved the supplies. He handed them up to the women on the bus, then returned. "Okay, what now?"

Photography was where Lucas really shined, and right away, he said, "Let's start with photos inside."

The man walked into the bus, and Lucas followed with Margo right behind. She had to applaud the ladies; the place was clean and tidy, but otherwise, they hadn't evolved much from a prairie dugout. The stove was little more than a cut-up oil drum. Around the drum stood an assortment of chairs that'd probably been salvaged from street corners. Milk crates were stacked up to hold supplies, and on top and between them lay a salvaged wooden door, their kitchen countertop. A wire was strung to hang clothes, and beneath that, more milk crates to hold their miscellaneous belongings. On the floor in the far back was one single mattress big enough for the three of them. Margo guessed king size, and it just then occurred to her that both the women were most likely his wives. Pregnant wives, and she wondered if they did their procreation business separately or all mixed together in one big sacrosanct orgy.

Lucas snapped photos of the three Mormons in their gas mask hoods along with the bizarre backdrop. He urged the man to lie down on the mattress, then the two women on each side. Lucas shot more photos outside with the three posed beside the bus. He never asked Margo to pose with them, but then she knew a photo with her in it would look stupid and contrived, like *look at me with the freaks*. She let Lucas do his thing.

Finally, Lucas asked again about the motorcoach. He said, "Have you seen an RV near here? We're looking for this Thor Outlaw motorcoach."

And maybe because Lucas, a man, had asked him, or maybe because the guy had just lightened up, he said, "Oh, the Class A. Yeah, hiding behind that concrete wall over there." He pointed.

Margo couldn't see the motorcoach itself, but something about the wall and the building seemed familiar. Then, she remembered—these were the castle ruins she'd seen in her dream, where Jo was locked behind a steel door. The premonition. She knew in her gut Jo would be found somewhere behind the ruins. Then, if she stayed still and silent, she could hear the rumble of the motorcoach generator.

The man added again, "We like to mind our own business."

————

Margo and Lucas were back in the Fabvan and drove further down the road to the side of the ruins.

Lucas said, "What do we do?"

"Get your GoPro. We need to film this live."

He raised his voice, "Margo?"

"Lucas?"

"You can't just barge in there. This guy abducted a woman. He's like a rapist or something. You don't think he has a gun?"

"You just film, and I'll do the talking. We're just gonna be two kids who lost their way." She playacted using her cute little-girl voice, "Oh sir, we don't know where we are, and this dessert is *soooo* big." Margo pouted her lips with the sad look she'd acted out more than once in front of Lucas's camera. "Can you help us, *pleeease?*"

The performance made him smile. "Any sign of trouble, we run."

"Roger that."

Lucas drove and parked on the opposite side of the wall from the motorcoach. His GoPro Hero4 was the smallest they made, and Lucas had a mount that clipped onto the bill of his Patagonia trucker hat. The GoPro could easily be misconstrued as a harmless headlamp. Lucas switched it on and followed Margo.

She walked around the edge of the wall, right up to the front of the motorcoach, and stood still. She could see the glow of lights, but all the windows, including the enormous front windshield, were covered. She felt surprisingly calm. This was way beyond just doing Instagram posts. Exciting. It was like journalism, like a journalist heading into the heat of battle somewhere overseas, like Iraq or Iran (she could never remember which was which). Being at the battlefront was now Margo's job.

Margo knocked on the door. She waited, then knocked

again.

An older man, very unattractive, was at the top of the stairs—gray hair in some throwback seventies style, a bushy mustache, a badly sunburned face like meat cooked medium rare with the tip of his nose more blood-rare. He leaned forward, his hands behind his back. He said, "How can I help you?"

Lucas was behind her, his chin almost resting on Margo's shoulder. "I'm sorry, we seem to be lost. We were looking for a campground. Our app shows there's a place called Indian Springs. Do you know where that is?" She gave the look, not quite a pout, but one that suggested complete stupidity.

"No, there's no campground near here."

The man moved back into the motorcoach, done with the conversation. But before he could push some button that closed the door, Margo stepped in and walked up the stairs, Lucas right behind her.

She said again, "The app shows that this place is called Indian Springs Campground." She waived her phone back and forth, her proof, the ultimate source of information. She looked around and added, "I've never been in one of these Class A motorcoaches. Nice." Behind the man, a woman was sitting at a dinette table. She held a towel across her one hand as though it were cut or hurt, but she smiled and didn't seem to be in any pain.

The man glared at Margo now. "I didn't invite you in."

"I'm sorry." Then added, "Hi, I'm Margo." She smiled. "Permission to come aboard, Captain?"

The man ignored her stupid permission request. Then, behind him, the woman smiled and said, "Hi, Margo."

Margo had seen the photos of Jo on @vanlifevagabond and knew it was her, the abducted woman. "Hi, so where are you guys heading?" Margo looked at Jo, trying to play it cool, and watched for any sign that things weren't how they appeared.

Jo said, "Las Vegas."

The smile was pasted on her face—Margo thought phony, but it seemed half the people she met had phony smiles. "You like to play the slots? I love the slots."

The man interrupted, "No, we don't play slots." His tone showed disgust with the whole idea. "We play cards. Now, if you could, please leave us alone. We didn't park out here to receive guests, and there's no campground within miles. Feel free to find your own piece of desert. Camp wherever you like, but not here."

Margo took one last look at Jo, who sat still and continued to smile. She noticed a missing shoe, a swollen ankle, and a covered hand. She looked unkempt and dirty. The woman looked like an abductee, and for a moment, Margo was frightened.

She sensed the woman trying to think through the right thing to say. The words came out carefully, "We're just trying to be alone here and enjoy each other's company." Then she added, "We recently became engaged to be married."

The words seemed forced and, again, phony, but maybe this abduction business was simply a made-up Instagram story, or maybe Jo ran away with this guy and didn't want to tell her husband in advance. The fact that she was disheveled didn't necessarily mean anything; most people out camping were somewhat dirty. Then, the ankle—not that uncommon for an ankle to twist on a rock-strewn hike. Furthermore, the Internet was full of bullshit people and their bullshit made-up stories— she'd made up a few herself. Now, it felt like it was all none of her business. Whatever these people wanted to do with their sordid lives had nothing to do with her. It was obvious this woman wasn't being held against her will.

"Congratulations," Margo said, then added, "We'll let you guys enjoy your privacy."

The creepy man with the sunburnt face smiled at her, yellowish teeth all crammed together like a closet full of mismatched shoes. She guessed he had money; why else would anyone marry him? But maybe they were just two peas in a pod—him with his burnt face and Jo with her dirty face and swollen ankle; maybe they were into kinky stuff. It wasn't Margo's thing. She didn't like her sex rough, none of that ass and titty slapping, and certainly no chains or whips. But that kind of thing was all over the Internet; she had to assume there existed a pervy subculture as big as the population of Texas, or at least Arizona. Leave them to their predilections. Whatever.

Margo smiled back at the two, then she and Lucas exited the motorcoach.

The thought suddenly hit her on their drive back to the main road. *What about the dream, the ruins, the premonition?*

As a kid, she'd believed in ghosts and aliens and horoscope readings. Even though her parents never went to church, she thought there had to be a God. She'd been a believer and continued to want to believe. But as she grew up, her innate cynicism took over, and all those ghost and God stories started to look, well, hokey—like Mormon golden plates or Scientology's Galactic Confederacy. Could dreams be premonitions? She'd wanted to think so; she wanted to be that child who still believed in Santa Claus. But her grown-up mind wouldn't give in.

She ultimately didn't believe any of that kooky shit.

17

The Here and Now

Jo had seen Hugh touch the handle of his gun as he talked to the young woman, the girl. He stepped back, and the girl boldly stepped in and climbed the stairs. She got to the top, looked in Jo's direction, and said she'd never been in a Class A before. Something about the girl was familiar: beautiful blue eyes, perfect nose, straight blonde hair that fell past her shoulders, breasts. That was it, the perfect breasts that could fit into a champagne coupe. The Instagrammers. The Instagrammer guy stood right behind her, looking over her shoulder. His blond hair was tucked into a Patagonia cap with some gizmo on its bill like a headlamp. Though it was no headlamp. Jo knew the GoPro line because she'd experimented with them at her wedding photography job. The guy was shooting video. She figured Hugh didn't have a clue.

Jo wanted to let them know she was okay and hoped she could signal something about that to the girl—Margo was her name.

She'd wondered what Bray was doing to find her, what he

was going through day by day, not knowing if she was still alive. Bray had probably gone to the local police, who'd taken in his whole story with a grain of salt—they'd seen countless jilted husbands. He would've put the word out on the Internet to other RVers that she was missing. But she had no idea what Bray knew. Somehow, though, he'd enlisted the help of these fellow Instagrammers, and they'd tracked her down.

She wondered what Bray had said to their daughter, Rose. Or if he told her anything. Rose was twenty-six, an assistant in an insurance office, married to a man in Milwaukee who repaired cable TV and Wi-Fi equipment, and they'd had their first child, a boy, Jo's grandson, Tyler. During the pandemic, Rose worked from home and cared for the child. Her husband was deemed an essential worker—everyone, *everyone*, needed Internet service—and he worked out of a truck ten hours a day. Bray would be loath to tell her, upset her, but eventually, he would feel he had to. Rose wouldn't be able to do anything but worry, which Jo didn't want.

When the girl said her name was Margo, Jo offered her own name, and she could see Hugh stiffen. Then she'd said they were going to Las Vegas. Dumb, in retrospect.

Jo could see Hugh wrap his hand around the grip of his gun and see the gun slide from the back pocket of his pants. The slots comment put him off for a moment, the thought that he'd play a game purely based on chance, but it also pissed him off further. He was going to kill both of those kids. That's when she stepped in and defused the powder keg. She told Margo and the boy that they'd just become engaged to be married. Hugh's hand relaxed.

The motorcoach took off a few hours later after the sun had gone down, hours after the two kids had left. Hugh told her she could sit up front if she wanted, and Jo said she did.

He uncuffed her from the dinette, led her up between the two seats of the cab, and re-cuffed her one wrist to the loop of the seat belt. He did not have a can of pepper spray. She thought about reaching over to somehow cause an accident that would lead to a police call, but the distance between them in the wide cab was further than she could reach.

Hugh drove the coach out slowly with his headlights off, finding his way by the glow from a half moon. They passed the school bus camper off in the distance with the inhabitants' lantern light sifting through the drapes—the assholes could have helped her. The motorcoach passed no one else. When he turned onto a paved highway, Hugh switched on the headlights.

Jo sat back in the living room-sized passenger seat and stared ahead. The two-lane road was straight, and she could see the edges of the desert lap over the older blacktop.

He asked, "What did you mean by the two of us being engaged? What was that all about?"

"I thought you were going to kill those two kids."

"I would have. I think those snoopy kids were looking for you. I've seen them somewhere before."

"At the campground where you abducted me."

"Yes, they were taking photos of each other, hundreds of them. What do people do with all those photos? I have a few snapshots of Florence that I enjoy looking at, but many I've since left for the garbage man. Now I see people taking photos constantly, some with long sticks used to photograph themselves. And it's all digital, right? Nothing's ever printed?"

"No, you're right. Almost all the photos are digital and stored in the cloud."

He took his eyes off the road and looked at her briefly. "What cloud?"

That was a good question—*what was the cloud anyway?* Images were captured in a non-tangible medium—millions, trillions of them—then banked in a virtual safe…somewhere. She knew that the bank, the vault, was a real thing, some air-conditioned facility with rows and rows of solid-state drives cabled together. All those drives were called "the cloud" as though, *poof,* the photos drifted into the atmosphere where anyone could reach up and just pull one down. How did all that look to a Luddite like Hugh? Maybe like some magic act, but most likely, he'd see the ridiculousness of it all, that somehow people thought they'd live on forever in digital images, their virtual souls rising up like balloons to rest forever in The Cloud. She thought Hugh was not a man who would ever exist in the cloud, that what he wanted was all here and now, tangible like a snapshot in a photo album, tangible like Jo sitting right next to him.

It occurred to her then that Hugh saw no future beyond the gin rummy tournament in Las Vegas. She did not know what that meant for her.

She'd almost forgotten the cloud question and now answered slowly, remembering what Hugh had said days before about metaphors. "The cloud is an interconnected bank of computer servers that store data. I think someone coined the term so that people could understand the complicated processes in one simple metaphorical image, like how you said that electricity behaves like flowing water."

Jo saw his smile. Her answer obviously pleased him.

That was just before he coughed.

18

The Rumaki Method

Bray had already called his daughter Rose to tell her about the abduction. That was before the Instagram video showed Jo alive, stating she was engaged to be married—or rather re-married. Thank God, Rose didn't follow Instagram. The call and conversation had not gone well.

His relationship with Rose was complicated. She'd grown up an only child with Bray doting on her like his prized BMW; he wanted her to be perfect. But she wasn't a machined engine made of cast aluminum, and in retrospect, Bray thought maybe he'd pushed his daughter too hard, too soon. The Suzuki violin lessons began when Rose was five, giving her a treat after each practice session like some dog-training reward. When she turned ten, the violin was somehow smashed at a Duluth concert. When he said that it was okay, insurance would buy her a new one, Rose admitted, "I smashed it on purpose. I don't want to play anymore." A year later, he signed her up for the school's chess and debate clubs. He thought participating in the clubs would help Rose become a better critical thinker and place her in safe friend groups. Bray said he would buy her a Game Boy if she just gave the clubs a try. Jo referred to his overbearing approach—his aggressive pushing of his daughter followed by treats or rewards—as his *rumaki* method, a chestnut of aggression wrapped in pleasurable fatty bacon. The reality was that, deep down, he knew what he was doing when he did it, but he couldn't help himself. Rose dropped out of both clubs, but not before getting her Game Boy. By the time Rose was in high school, she'd begun to tell him straight to his face, "Fuck off, Dad."

The kid did well on her SATs regardless and was accepted into St. Olaf College with a substantial merit scholarship. Now, she was married with a small child, worked a part-time job at an insurance agency, and had a husband who repaired electronic equipment. Her job as a seventeen-dollar-an-hour clerical assistant did not require a college degree. He'd said something about it once, that maybe she was underemployed. She'd given him that look, then said, "Fuck off, Dad."

He called her in St. Louis. They exchanged pleasantries before Rose cut to the chase, "Dad, why are you calling?"

He wanted to say, "Does there have to be a reason?" But he knew there was one and just said it, "I think your mother's been abducted."

"What do you mean, *you think*?"

"I mean, your mother has been abducted. We were in western Nebraska at this campground. I'd gone to buy firewood . . ."

Rose cut him off, "So, Mom has disappeared, or left? Do you know where she went?"

"You don't understand, she's not missing. Well, what I mean to say is that she *is* missing but missing because she's been abducted by another man."

"So, who's this other man? Do you know him?"

"Of course, I don't know him."

"But you, for sure, know she's been abducted."

The conversation felt like it was going round and round, circling the drain. He tried another tack. "I know that he's older, like in his seventies, and drives a Class A motorcoach with Pennsylvania plates. When I came back with the firewood, she was gone."

"How do you know she went with this particular guy?"

"A lady with a basset hound saw her go into this motorcoach, and then they drove off." He did not know why he mentioned the basset hound but knew he'd regret it.

"Lady with a basset hound, huh?"

He chose to ignore the sarcasm. "There was also this Instagram couple who were taking photos. The coach is in the background of one of them."

"Okay, Dad, you think mom's been abducted. A fifty-eight-year-old woman has been abducted by an old man in his seventies. Have you talked to the police?"

"Of course."

"Well?"

"I filed a report, but they don't seem to care, and now I've crossed state lines. They're no help at all."

"You remember when Mom just took off one day on your precious BMW?"

Bray was dreading where the conversation was going. He'd had a fight with Jo years ago. She was working for a wedding photography company and doing well, and they liked her. She wanted to leave the company and its benefits to start her own photography business. He told her calmly that starting her own business was laudable but she might want to think of what's best for the family (that chestnut of aggression), and if she just stuck with the company, then maybe they could take a two-week vacation to Florida (the bacon wrapping). Jo took off on his precious and valuable BMW, and didn't return for a week. Jo never did start her own business, which, in retrospect, was smart because it would have been shuttered during the pandemic. Bray had reminded Jo of that just recently, a comment she hadn't appreciated. "Yes, I remember, but it's not like that."

"Did you and Mom have a fight?"

"No."

"So, what do you want *me* to do? We're in a pandemic. I have a job, *and* I have to take care of Tyler, *and* Rick is working around the clock. Oh, and by the way, I'm pregnant again."

"Well, congratulations!"

"Yeah, great. We're thinking of naming her or him Corona. So, you can see that I'm a little preoccupied."

"Really, Corona?" It seemed like such a bad idea. He'd quit drinking the Mexican beer ever since a rumor circulated concerning trace amounts of urine.

"Dad, it's a joke. COVID, the *corona*virus? So, what do you expect me to do?"

"Nothing. I don't expect you to do anything." When he said those words, he knew they sounded guilt-laden, aggressive.

He chose new words to soften their implication. "Just an FYI, and congratulations again on the baby." His Rumaki Method.

"Well, let me know when she shows back up."

"I will."

That was how his conversation with Rose had gone, and then came the video. The first thing he thought of when he saw that Jo was okay, that she was healthy and apparently going to Las Vegas (and illegally getting re-married), was to let Rose know. But he was scared of his own daughter and knew she hadn't believed the whole abduction business in the first place. He'd have to listen to her condescending tone.

Bray decided instead to just text her, "Mom is okay." That was all he said. If she wanted to know specifics, she could call or text him. Bray was hoping she wouldn't; he didn't want Rose to see the video and open up that whole can of worms about her mother being engaged.

He received a text back minutes later, "That's great."

Phew.

19

Final Exit

Jo sat up front through the night. Few people were out on these lesser highways, and without the ambient light from towns or streetlamps, the stars looked like glitter tossed across deep black velvet. Hugh had stopped once to make a thermos of instant coffee. He gave her a cupful with one ice cube and then smiled. Hugh sat behind the motorcoach's huge steering wheel, moving it in slight degrees with the touch of one hand at six o'clock.

Jo wanted to know how his wife had eventually died from the metastasized breast cancer. A recurrence always loomed in the back of her mind like a sensitive tooth that might blossom into decay. A recurrence was a death sentence. Metastatic breast cancer could be fought off for a few years—the average was three—but the disease almost always won. She'd cultivated friends during the hours spent sitting in chemo chairs for infusions, and two had subsequently died. Death didn't come like an aneurysm or massive heart attack; it inched along gradually, painfully, with an overwhelming fatigue. She'd delivered meals to their families and attended small gatherings in support, but over the years, she'd shed many of those friends still alive. Jo felt the guilt of abandoning them but also knew that it was easier to repress the anxiety of a possible recurrence if she wasn't reminded by others. Those friends weren't hard to shed, and she sensed her need to separate was mutual. But the thought of a recurrence loomed, and like everyone, she guessed, Jo felt a sadness at the prospect of dying alone in a hospital surrounded by strangers. And she didn't think her life was yet fulfilled.

"Did your wife die at home?"

Hugh didn't answer the question immediately. Thinking or composing. "I imagine everyone that's had cancer remembers where and when they first felt the lump like I guess everyone remembers where they were when JFK died, or when the twin towers were attacked. You?"

"I was in the shower at our condo in Minneapolis. The day was normal for Minnesota in October—overcast, a light rain, damp. I felt the lump while soaping up in the shower, but I didn't put two and two together at the time. Then, the one detail I remember was that the shampoo bottle was empty and that I unscrewed the cap to fill it with warm water to dilute the remaining soap. I remember that I needed to buy more shampoo. I felt the lump again while toweling off and knew something was wrong. Seems trivial and stupid."

"Florence and I were at our home playing gin rummy. We lived outside Pittsburgh in a suburban neighborhood called Sewickley. I know, sounds like a combination of the two words, sewer and sickly, but supposedly the name means 'sweet water in some American Indian dialect. Florence had lived in Sewickley before her divorce. The house was hers after the settlement, and she made it ours over the years. As a rule,

I don't care about my surroundings. My office had been furnished based on some idea I had of how a psychologist's office should appear, with random reproductions of innocuous oil paintings, professional diplomas, a couch to sit or lie on, a coffee table with Kleenex and hard candy, a winged back chair, and a shelf of academic books that I knew gave the place an air of decorum and expertise. I bought my first home because it came completely furnished and decorated—my pre-established persona. When I moved in with Florence, it, too, came pre-established. Florence, though, discovered what little I knew or liked in terms of outward appearances and imbued the house with what she learned. Little things like color. I'd always been attracted to silver-gray—my Audi and many of my suits were that color. She put in drapes of that color and also a new bedspread. In one of the few boxes of personal belongings, she found photos of my deceased mother and aunt and ones of me growing up. She framed a few and hung them next to *her* personal photos. So, you see, we had our home together, a home that she made. The lump was discovered while we were playing our favorite game, gin rummy. I distinctly remember that her gray-streaked hair was down around her face, and she looked beautiful. She scratched at her chest absentmindedly, then found the lump an hour later while undressing for bed.

"We had another motorcoach then, a Fleetwood Bounder, that we used for two weeks each winter to vacation in Florida, then occasionally for gin games around the East Coast and twice all the way to Las Vegas for the American Gin Rummy Open Tournament. We traveled more after Florence had her lumpectomy and chemotherapy treatment—she felt the need to do more and see more. And I was content to leave my practice for months at a time and travel with her. Three years after finding the lump, Florence had a recurrence. This time, the cancer had metastasized into her hip bone. I bought this motorcoach with the toy hauler back end because eventually Florence couldn't climb stairs, let alone walk without extreme pain. I could lower the back gate, and she could drive her little three-wheeled scooter right up and in. From there, it was a few steps to the bedroom. We only used this motorcoach for one summer before she was too weak to travel. Then she died."

Toy hauler—her prison cell for toys—his toy box. Jo asked again, "Did she die at home?"

"Yes, she died at home. Have you heard of the book *Final Exit*?"

Jo knew of the book that detailed assisted suicide and had seen the author's story on a *Frontline* episode. He'd helped his wife, who was dying of cancer, commit suicide. He founded the Hemlock Society. "Of course. Derek something."

"Derek Humphry. I read his book and followed the instructions. I stockpiled Florence's narcotics and was able to get other prescriptions needed for the 'cocktail.' I gave it to her one morning, mixed in a bowl of yogurt. I said nothing. She died peacefully in her bed."

"You said nothing? You mean she didn't know?"

"No, I didn't think she'd want to. Florence still had these silly Catholic ideas about God and heaven and dying. She would've objected to suicide. At the same time, dying can be such a dreadful and exhausting experience. My aunt, who helped raise me, died slowly of lung disease. She was a smoker who developed emphysema. At first, it was just an oxygen tank with tubes to her nose, then years of doing nothing but staring at a TV set, eating, and sleeping. Then, the wheezing and weight loss, then another two years of dementia until my mother put her in a nursing home where she died another two years later. No thank you. I can't imagine anyone would want to go through that process unless they either didn't have the willpower to take their own lives, or waited too long to carry it out themselves, or had deep religious convictions. Florence had those deep convictions, so I just took that reason to live—if you can call it that—off the table."

"That's not assisted suicide, that's murder."

"And with her beliefs, she's not going to hell. I respected her beliefs."

Jo let the conversation end there. Was what he'd done right or wrong? Would she want Bray to slip her the pills so she wouldn't have to make that decision herself? She certainly didn't want to die a slow, prolonged, and painful death. Then, she might not have the willpower to do it herself or just wait too long. On the surface, what Hugh had done seemed entirely compassionate. But she knew his rationale was the same used in Nazi Germany to euthanize infants born with disabilities or anyone else deemed to not be part of their master race. Compassion and the evil of self-interest were slivers away.

Jo saw road signs: Kayenta Monument, Tsegi, Hog Heaven, then Tuba City. The highway sign said EAST 160. A side road had a highway marker in the shape of the state of Arizona. Past Tuba City, she started seeing tourist signs for the Grand Canyon.

Hugh pulled off State Highway 64 just past the entrance to Kaibab National Forest when the sky was beginning to lighten in the east behind them. A mile in on a gravel road, they stopped at a remote boondocking campsite with no other RVs around that she could see. Hugh uncuffed Jo from the front seat and led her back to her prison cell, the toy box. Jo heard the generator crank on, then the loud drone of the air conditioners.

Before falling asleep, she thought about what Hugh had said and done. She wondered how close to self-interest his supposed compassion really was.

———

Jo watched Hugh light up a cigarette, inhale, then cough. He coughed again, like trying to jar loose a fishbone lodged in the back of his throat. He tipped the pack toward her, and she reached over with her free hand to pinch one out. Hugh lit the end with his disposable lighter.

He explained tournament rules, "Players cut the cards to see who deals. Each player is dealt just ten cards. The twenty-first card is turned face up to determine the number of points available to knock later in the hand. The non-dealer then picks the top card from the deck. Play continues until one player either gins or knocks. All this, you know. On the tournament's first day, the games are played to two hundred points, with players selected randomly. To make it to the next day, you must win ten games before losing seven. Then, over the next two days, a series of three-hundred-point games are played in a round-robin—everyone plays each other once. The winner is the player who wins the most games."

"So, what does the winner get?"

"It's a five-thousand cash buy-in. The top five players in the finals all walk away with prize money. The winner takes home fifty thousand dollars. I've won four times and have always brought home at least fifteen thousand."

"Okay." Who knew there was so much money in gin rummy.

"So today, let's play as though it's the first day of the AGRA Open Tournament."

"Let me guess, American Gin Rummy Association."

Hugh ignored her and continued, "We'll play games of two hundred. Since it's just the two of us, we'll play until one of us wins ten games."

Jo tried to think through what winning ten games would entail. Assuming she or Hugh lost a few, they'd be playing maybe fifteen or more games. A game up to two hundred points could take a half hour or more. So, she was looking at playing gin rummy for the next eight hours. It was past two o'clock in the afternoon so they'd be playing well past ten, assuming she took the time to eat and go to the bathroom.

Until then, Hugh had used blank pieces of paper to keep score. Now, he had a scoring journal, a plastic-bound booklet with a black pigskin pattern. He turned to the first blank scoring page and wrote their names and the date on the appropriate lines.

He dealt, and Jo drew the top card from the deck.

She looked at her eleven cards and sorted the possible melds. Jo had no need for the ten-point king of diamonds and discarded it straight off. Hugh ignored the king and drew a card from the deck. The tournament commenced.

Jo lost the first game and then the second. She asked Hugh for another cigarette and a Heineken if he still had one. He gave her both, and she smoked one and sipped the other. She tried to calm herself and not consciously monitor the discards against what she held in her hand—let her mind relax and drift. She knew instinctively that her subconscious was more perceptive than her conscious mind. It was like the memorization of names at a wedding she was photographing. She'd be introduced to the wedding party, but it wasn't until she scribbled out a flow chart with their connections and allowed that image to enter her subconscious that she could instantly recall their names. She'd let the mechanics of card play seep into her subconscious mind and then imagine what cards he held. And what she imagined was a hand of thirty or more melded cards or combinations with a range of opportunities. Then, slowly, as the discards piled up, Jo narrowed down the possible hand he might have. Toward the end of the first hand of the third game, she held onto a five of clubs. She'd not altered the image of two fives and the four of clubs she initially imagined in Hugh's hand. When she finally ginned, she discarded the five face-down. He did have the three-way combination, none of which he could lay off against her hand. She scored thirty-nine points.

She won the next two games and lost the sixth.

Hugh won the seventh game. He now had four wins to her three.

Hugh had talked about probabilities but never explained how they worked. She assumed there was a whole list of cards played or held that gave a player a statistical advantage. But what key statistics carried the greatest weight? Three came to her. The first was so obvious but seemed the most important—as the game progressed, discards became less safe, more "wild," as Hugh would say. So the implication was to play aggressively through the first five or so discards and focus on making melds—don't worry that your opponent might need a discard and don't worry about shedding points. The second wasn't so obvious but might give her an edge—if faced with throwing a wild card that you know your opponent needs, it's more advantageous to throw one that adds to an existing meld rather than a card that completes a new one. Then, the last went hand-in-hand with playing aggressively in the game's early stages—if the knock card was a seven or more, play to the knock; if six or less, play to the gin. Obvious but insightful enough to give her an initial strategy. Of course, Hugh would know all this, too, but she saw an advantage in knowing that Hugh didn't know what she knew.

Jo won the next two games played for two hundred points each, and they were tied at five games apiece. Then Hugh won the two after that. Three more losses and she'd be out. They stopped for dinner. Jo drank a second beer and the game continued.

The next few games would determine the winner, and she started to win. She kept track of the cards that passed through the discard pile without having to consciously *think*. She visualized each of his hands and began to whittle down the possibilities from thirty or so to the likely ten; it took her around fifteen discards to get there. She began to trust her second sense when Hugh would likely gin or knock.

In the seventh game, the knock card was an eight, and Jo knew instinctively that Hugh would go for the knock. She didn't have a good enough hand to hold out for the gin, so she held onto any card she could lay off against Hugh's knock and any wild cards with a low rank. Hugh knocked early with seven deadwood points. After Jo laid off two of her un-melded cards, her point total was only five. She'd undercut his knock. She scored the difference, two points, plus a twenty-five-point bonus. The tournament was now tied at seven games. Hugh said nothing.

Then she began to understand Hugh's unconscious body language, like a mother-in-law's crossed arms at a wedding or the subtle smirk of the best man during a toast. It was all there, the anxiety and thoughts displayed at critical times of the game—looking at his cards more closely if he was going to gin, looking up more when about to knock. For Jo, this was a revelation. She lost the next game but won the following two.

All she needed was one more two-hundred-point win to take the tournament. And in some corner of her mind, she held out the unlikely possibility that if she won, he'd keep his word and really let her go.

She and Hugh had filled an ashtray with cigarette butts, and they continued to smoke. Jo drank another beer, and Hugh brewed hot tea for himself. She looked at her watch. It was past midnight; they'd been playing for over ten hours. She'd become absorbed in the game, and the time had gone by without her being aware.

Hugh was not a man who liked to lose. The hands went back and forth with her now one hundred and seventy-three points to his one hundred and eighty. The next hand could likely give her the win. After Hugh's discard, his sixth in the game, Jo held two three-card melds of the same rank and knew she could only make the fourth in one of them. She held a straight and a single card, a two. She knew he had a two, but she'd imagined both a pair of twos and a two-three straight. The smart decision would be to knock.

Hugh looked closely at his cards. Jo thought he was going for the gin, and now the knock seemed all that more tempting. She drew a card from the deck, another card she imagined he needed, and now she had to decide which to discard—either might give him the game. She could still knock, should knock, but she wanted the gin and the tournament win and decided not to. She played the two, hoping he held the two-three straight. He quickly picked it up, a smile on his face. "Gin."

She knew what she'd done was more than simply aggressive and impatient; it was an act of hubris—the kind she'd seen in Hugh and despised. Now she'd learned an easy lesson—wait, play aggressively only when her planned strategy called for it. On a more practical level, if given any opportunity to knock, she should knock—multiple small wins were better than no win at all.

Then she wondered, "Would you have really let me go if I'd won?"

Without hesitation, he said, "You'd know I was lying if I said yes."

"But you understand that you can't hold me forever. You'll have to let me go eventually," she paused, thought, and added, "or kill me."

Hugh stood and then moved to the white leather couch across from the dinette. He lit another cigarette but did not offer her one. He said, "I'll let you go . . . in time."

"What does that mean?"

"After the tournament in Las Vegas. I'll let you go after that."

She'd been naïve to think that if she won, he'd let her go. She didn't think he ever would. That realization had been so obvious. Hugh could never remain a free man if he let her go. He had to know that the police would find him. She thought about the suicide cocktail he'd made for his wife without her knowledge. He could do the same to her. She wanted to say, "I don't believe you," but what she said was, "I can wait."

She thought the response would appease him, but what he said then startled her, "If you try to escape again, I'll simply kill you and get it over with."

20

A Damsel in Distress

Margo and Lucas drove west toward Lake Powell after finding Jo and posting the video of her seemingly safe and newly engaged. (She thought Jo was already married, but who knew?) Now, their pursuit of the supposedly abducted woman seemed like such an embarrassment, a waste.

The weather had been hot and dry, with temperatures well into the nineties since they'd left the high country near Durango. Throughout the southwest that month, a heat wave pushed temperatures into the hundreds; the afternoon temps in Phoenix were above one hundred and fifteen. Wildfires were burning all over California, and the wind blew acrid smoke eastward. The Fabvan's windows were rolled up with the air conditioning on high. Lucas drove and followed Highway 160 through small towns like Kayenta and Tsegi, with Navajo tourist shops selling handmade rugs, jewelry, and frybread tacos. The landscape stretched endlessly with scrub desert and small outcroppings of wind-carved stone, the arid reservation land given to the American Indians by the conquering white

European settlers—Margo's forbearers likely among them. She had no cell service and resigned herself to silently watch the tumbleweeds tumble and the mileage markers flash by.

Just past noon, they reached Page, Arizona, where they found cell service. By midafternoon, they'd bought groceries at a Safeway, then driven west to Lone Rock Beach on Lake Powell.

Margo had read on the Internet that the beach was a popular destination in the summer months for those escaping the heat of Phoenix. The cost was only fourteen dollars a night, and the camping dispersed, meaning you could camp anywhere—an RV free-for-all—and swimming was strictly at your own risk.

The sand beach was as big as the old San Diego Stadium parking lot. But instead of blacktop and painted lines, the beach had sand roads that switchbacked between camping spots and the occasional pit toilet. Very few RVs occupied those spots. Most were parked near the waterfront, far from the toilets, and within feet of the lake. Hundreds of campers in every imaginable contraption: converted school buses, vans, trailer campers, pickup campers, teardrops, tents on the beach, and tents-perched-on-top SUVs. And like when the Chargers still played at the stadium, these people were all tailgating, many with pop-up canopies and all with coolers nearly the size of coffins.

Just off the beach floated kayaks, paddle boards, and inflatable water toys. In the distance, near the namesake Lone Rock, circled wakeboard boats that threw up surf-sized waves. Interspersed were jet skis that zigzagged back and forth like water bugs. Old folks, parents, young adults, and kids were in the water, on the shore, under the canopies, on lounge chairs, and in the boats. Not one person was wearing a mask or keeping a safe distance, and no way all those kids were hiking the one hundred yards uphill to reach a toilet. Margo saw a cluster of infants in saggy diapers playing with muddy sand in a few inches of water. The scene was one giant super-spreader event where you could pick up COVID, E. coli, or both.

Lucas pulled into one of the hundreds of vacant camping spots away from the beach. Margo cranked out their awning for sun protection and set up camp chairs. What she hadn't initially seen was a whole other group of campers parked further away from the beach and close to the sand dunes that stretched beyond them like the Sahara Desert. These people were ATV enthusiasts with dirt bikes, four-wheelers, three-wheelers, jeeps, and dune buggies. And all those vehicles were making a whine of noise as they careened up and down the hills of sand.

The noise was everywhere, coming from the ATVs, the jet skis, the wakeboard boats, outdoor stereo systems, and the hundreds of generators keeping the RV air conditioners humming, the food and beverages cold, and the music loud.

Lucas took off toward the beach with his camera.

Margo settled into her camp chair with a White Claw and thought about what to do next. The issue was that their accumulation of Instagram followers had stalled since the last post about the woman, Jo, who was now seemingly safe. Margo needed something to generate new interest and excitement. She'd come to this beach with that in mind, but now wasn't sure. This combination of loud partying and gas-guzzling just wasn't her scene.

She'd originally posted a brand statement that read, "Exploring the Fabulous and Tranquil Lifestyle of Van Living." Margo had already gone off-brand by following the abduction story, but she justified that as a solidarity thing among the campervan community. Across the lake's shoreline, Margo counted the number of actual campervans. She thought twenty or more, but many seemed to be towing trailers, and real #vanlife enthusiasts didn't do trailers. The #vanlife lifestyle was all about traveling to remote places to be close to nature. Jet skis or wakeboard boats pulled behind a van didn't travel well on remote and rutted dirt roads, and you needed more than a trailhead lot to turn those rigs around. No, these were weekend tourists from the city who were not seeking tranquility. The beach scene on Lake Powell was anything but on-brand.

Lucas was already down by the beach taking photos of the scene—ones that would likely never be posted. He focused his zoom lens on a kid sitting in a beach chair watching watercraft careen across the lake. Then, he took more shots of the vacationers as they drank beer, listened to music, and played in the water. It might've seemed voyeuristic, but she thought what Lucas was doing had more to do with art. The fact was, if he wanted voyeuristic photos, all he had to do was shoot her half naked for the millionth time.

Then Margo watched in almost slow motion as a jet ski careened close to shore. She knew those things looked like harmless toys. In reality, they were powerful and heavy, with the big ones weighing more than a thousand pounds. The one coming toward the beach was big. The driver, most likely some drunk kid, didn't seem to know what he was doing and didn't turn away as he neared the beach. In his path was a woman lounging further offshore in a blow-up raft, the kind with a backrest and beverage holders. Margo expected the kid to ease off the throttle or turn away, but he kept going. The woman, maybe napping, did not look up as the jet ski neared. It hit her without slowing, the jet ski launching as if crossing a small wake. Then the woman was gone, and now only shreds of plastic raft floated above the water. The kid on the jet ski, oblivious to what he'd done, or too drunk or scared to stop, just kept going, now losing himself in the hive of other jet skis out toward the Lone Rock.

On the beach, others had seen the incident along with Lucas, and now ten or so were running, then swimming with tired strokes toward where the woman had last been seen. In the race to save the woman, a few were left behind.

Lucas was a trained lifeguard who had worked at Shores Beach for three seasons. He dropped his camera and ran into the shallow water. Then he leapt and, with his powerful front crawl, quickly put the others behind him. He was first to the wreckage of the raft. Lucas dove and he was down for what seemed like minutes. Then his head broke water. He looked around and then dove again. When he came up the second time, the woman was with him and locked into his arm. He kept her head above water as he swam with a side stroke back to shore, the woman unconscious and unmoving.

Margo was at the shore when Lucas pulled the lifeless woman into shallow water. Others were there to help carry her onto the beach. Margo saw the cuts across the woman's forehead and across her chest where her bathing suit top had been ripped off, exposing stark-white breasts.

They all just watched as Lucas gave the woman chest compressions, then mouth-to-mouth, and chest compressions again, repeating the process over and over. In the background, Margo heard the siren of an ambulance. She was next to Lucas when the woman finally responded, water gurgling from her mouth, then coughing. There was no clapping or cheers, but a universal sigh of relief seemed to be released, like breaths held too long.

Someone nearby covered her exposed chest with a beach towel.

The kid on the jet ski pulled up to shore. Up close, he looked more of an adult in his early thirties, now wide-eyed and scared. The jet ski was still idling when he jumped off and staggered—drunk or stoned or both—toward the crowd. He said, "I didn't see her," which was obvious to everyone. Some stepped toward him, and again, he said, "I didn't see her." He tried to walk toward the injured woman, but the crowd wouldn't part. Then he was surrounded, held in place by a wall of bodies as the ambulance arrived and took the woman away.

Lucas had retrieved his camera and was taking photos of the mob scene. Margo guessed twenty people were standing around, mostly men. Margo saw the drunk/stoned man's head with curly ginger hair. His arms and hands were raised and gesturing in some vain attempt to hold off the inevitable. She saw a fist in the air, then another, and another. The red curls disappeared and reappeared among bare feet and ankles, like a football in a rugby scrum. And then—more like soccer—the head was kicked.

Minutes later, another siren announced the presence of police. Lucas then photographed the officers taking away the now battered and bloody man who'd almost killed a woman.

———

The beach and dunes scene never settled down. That night, Margo lay in the campervan bed with the reflection of bonfires dancing across the windows and the congealed mush of competing music accosting her ears. She thought only of Lucas, her traveling companion who'd saved a woman from drowning and then shifted around to photograph the mob scene. The whole episode made her have second thoughts about who he really was. He seemed so . . . heroic. And what did it matter if he couldn't turn a wrench to fix the van or cook more than dehydrated ramen? He was brave and beautiful, and not just the kind that was Instagramable. He wasn't just the dope she thought he was. Then she wondered if seeing Lucas in this new light was, in fact, shallow, like she was this damsel in distress falling in love with her knight in shining armor. Whatever . . . It just didn't matter.

In retrospect, what really mattered was that she hadn't taken any video of the beach rescue. It was so unlike her. After the ginger-haired guy had finally been taken away, she looked down and saw her cell phone clutched in the disembodied palm of her hand, like it was someone else's appendage and gadget. She'd totally forgotten to lift it up and press that little red button. The video wouldn't have necessarily been on-brand, but the life-saving action would've created the excitement she was looking for. It could have reignited her stalled Instagram page. So stupid.

She needed *something*.

Margo took up her phone, opened the Instagram app, and looked again at @vanlifevagabond, but the page had been silent for days.

21

How to Win at Gin

The motorcoach moved again the next morning. Jo was not shackled to the seatbelt, but the handgun she'd seen earlier was now holstered on his hip. They stopped only once for fuel, and it was clear to her that he'd use it if she tried to escape.

They drove south on Highway 64 to Williams, Arizona, where Hugh pulled off into the parking lot of a Walmart Superstore. He had Jo move back into the toy box. When he unlatched the door thirty minutes later, he held out a black plastic walking boot. "You'll need this for the next few days to move around more easily."

The boot was two-piece, calf high, with wide Velcro straps to sandwich her ankle. The price tag was still attached: $39.99. She just looked at the thing and tried to figure out why he'd buy her a tool to allow her to walk and potentially escape. But even in a boot, it wasn't as though she could run. She looked out into the hallway of the coach and saw bags of groceries on the floor of the small kitchenette. Of course, he wanted her to be able to move around so she could cook. No doubt he was just as tired of the cans of Chunky Soup and Dinty Moore Beef Stew.

She slipped her swollen foot into the boot, pulled the Velcro straps tight, and hobbled into the coach to put away the groceries. Again, the items were random with no clear idea of a menu. Afterward, she sat in the front seat as Hugh drove south through the flat scrub desert. He smoked, and his intermittent cough from the day before continued.

They drove past small ranch towns, impoverished with trailers and single-level homes surrounded by wire fencing and yards cluttered with rusting junk. The thought occurred to her that the accumulation and coveting of unneeded stuff crossed economic boundaries—that a rusted-out Model T could be just as emotionally valuable as one in mint condition and, like Bray's precious motorcycle, just as useless. At a place called Skull Valley, they waited for twenty minutes while a herd of sheep crossed the road. Further on, just past a town called Hope, they passed a sign that read, "You're Now Beyond Hope," which seemed prophetic. Hugh turned off the main road beyond Hope and drove north. Thirty or forty miles in, the blacktop abruptly stopped, and the motorcoach bumped along a dirt road until they reached a padlocked iron gate. He stepped out and retrieved a key from a combination lockbox. He unlocked the gate and drove through.

"What is this place?" Jo asked.

"An entire ghost town I rented on Airbnb. It's called Dustwater Ranch, though it was never a ranch. It's an old copper mine. No one will bother us here."

Hugh locked the gate after they'd driven through. It was another half hour along the pitted road through the desert before they stopped.

By the time they arrived, the sun was going down. They

did not leave the coach and ate older cans of Chunky Beef Soup before playing gin rummy. He easily beat her, and she figured her almost-win the day before was just a brief streak of luck, a fluke.

Before Hugh sent Jo back to the toy box, he gave her two books she hadn't seen before. He said, "There are tactics you need to learn, like combinations, speculating, fishing, buying time, inducing, and a few others."

Lying in bed, she leafed through each one. Both were entitled *How to Win at Gin Rummy*. One was a hardbound book with its dust jacket long lost, copyright 1959. The other was newer, with a 1994 copyright and a subtitle, *A Simple Guide to Odds & Winning Plays*. The books were short, with sections on rules she already knew. He'd assumed she'd want to read the books, and maybe because she was bored, or maybe because she did want to get better at the game, Jo started reading. She finished the older book that night before going to sleep.

She slept in late, the morning sun throwing a beam of light through the overhead vent that illuminated a seam of pink insulation. The door to the interior of the motorcoach was already open. She still hadn't changed her clothes since the abduction, still sleeping in them each night. She sat up on the side of the bed to strap on the walking boot.

Hugh was not in the coach. The outside door was open, and she walked down the stairs to where he sat at a collapsible card table shuffling a deck of cards. The roll-out awning had been extended to provide shade, and an outdoor carpet covered the desert floor. He said, "Good morning, Josephine."

She said, "Good morning."

"Would you like some coffee?"

She said she would and then sat down at the other side of the card table. Minutes later, he brought out two cups of coffee, and they played cards, another tournament up to ten games.

They took a break at noon, and Jo made sandwiches.

They took another break around three o'clock, and Jo walked on her booted foot through the ghost town. Right away, she recognized the grid pattern of streets with the charred remnants of house foundations, where a fire had consumed them all. In the distance was a home still standing, and she walked in that direction. Closer up, she could see that it was once grand with clapboard siding and Victorian details—she guessed it might've been the mine owner's home. All the paint had peeled off long ago, and every window and door was missing. A creepy sign in front with a skull and crossbones warned people to stay out. She passed a hand pump that looked still in working condition, but again, a sign warned, "Caution Non-potable Water." The ruins of some processing plant were further away but well within limping distance. The walls had collapsed with rusted iron beams and caldrons standing above broken red brick, like the shelled remnants of a battlefield. Behind the plant loomed a ten-story mountain of slag devoid of any vegetation. Scattered beyond were the mine pits themselves, just shoulder-width caves in the ground, and she wondered about the desperate people who'd swung the picks and shovels. She stood before one mine, now closed off with cross-hatched rebar. Another skull and crossbones sign read, "STAY OUT! STAY ALIVE!"

She circled back past empty and windowless barracks made of cement and impregnable to fire, then a line of barracks that had been restored. She twisted the handle of a locked door, then looked through a window. Inside were rows of unmade cots. She wondered who rented out barracks in a ghost town, and she imagined a movie studio or some religious cult.

She figured, because of the pandemic, Hugh had gotten the place cheap.

Jo circled back to the motorcoach and sat at the card table. Hugh dealt. After a few hands that she lost, he started in on his lessons:

"Unmatched low cards are always less of a liability then unmatched high cards."

"Don't pick up a discard unless it completes a meld. Otherwise, that's speculating. Exceptions are if it's early in the hand or you want your opponent to think you have a meld."

"Prefer to knock early in the game if you can. As the game goes on, the odds increase that your opponent will gin or knock. But don't be predictable; a player who knocks at the first chance usually loses in the long run."

"Think of your knock cards as a third meld and build it accordingly. Hold on to aces—if you don't need them, your opponent will."

"If you can't knock or gin, a ploy to get an opponent to knock is to discard a low-rank card—an ace or a two. This works especially well if you have other cards to lay off."

"If you're down significantly in points, it's a good time to be aggressive—take the gamble and go for the gin."

There were many more, some she'd already read about in the book.

She asked him the point of giving her all these lessons, and he said, "If you're a better player, you make me a better player."

Hugh beat her by five games.

Afterward, she made a dinner of lettuce with ranch dressing, hamburgers cooked on a frying pan, and canned baked beans. Hugh did the dishes, and Jo retreated to her room and read the second *How to Win at Gin Rummy* book.

Jo fell behind early in their tournament the next day, losing three games in a row. Then she started to win. It was the simple realization that Hugh followed all the rules in the book, rarely breaking any. He avoided speculating, so when he picked up any discard, she knew it likely completed a meld. He kept a tight hand of low cards to knock as quickly as possible. He obsessively kept any wild card that might help her, sometimes to the detriment of ginning himself. He purged his face cards early, even if they were paired in combinations. Jo found she could reliably imagine his hand after just twelve discards with this insight into his play. And she was able to take advantage of his more conservative play by being aggressive herself— holding onto face cards, speculating early in the game, and going for the gin. By the end of that day, he still beat her, but only by two games.

They smoked while they played, filling up an ashtray by the time they'd finished. Hugh continued to cough intermittently, and Jo suggested he might want to cut back on the cigarettes. He ignored her.

On their last day at the ghost town, she beat him ten games to his seven. It was all there—his predictable defensive play, his body language (what the book referred to as "tells"), and her vision of his cards. She now knew when to knock and when to play for the gin. The few times he broke his rules, she knew instinctively, like she knew her own husband's moods. In the end, when she laid down a final knock card that took him for twelve points, she felt pride and even a flash of excitement, a feeling like seeing her child's first A-filled report card.

She did not expect to be released. She didn't even ask.

———

That night, she made dinner again, and they ate outside at the card table under the awning. They ate in silence. But she watched him, and what she saw was exhaustion; the man could barely keep his eyes open. Then he winced with some unknown pain.

She asked, "Are you okay?"

Hugh closed his eyes. "I'm fine, just this headache."

His ailment came to her in a flash. "I think you have COVID."

22

Circle of Trust

Bray had all but got down on one knee. Actually, he was standing, his arms spread, hands open in a welcoming, Jesus-like posture. He said, "Will you be part of my circle of trust?"

Uly did not know what that meant and said, "Excuse me?"

Bray's arms slowly descended to his sides. "A COVID circle of trust. It had just been Jo and me; not even our daughter was let in—her husband was in like a hundred homes every day repairing TVs. Jo's not here anymore, but I want us to be able to share meals and not have to wear masks."

Uly thought this explanation sounded so sad and pathetic, but on another level, what Bray was asking seemed touching. He was really asking if Uly would be his friend now that his wife had gone off with another man. And, of course, he said, "Sure, I will." Though in the back of his mind, he thought the cynical words, *I do*.

They'd decided to move further west into Arizona from New Mexico, maybe within a day's drive of Las Vegas should there be any new developments with Jo. Bray searched one of his camping apps and found federal land outside Sedona, located in cool high country and free. They had been there two days, camping side-by-side in the desert of rust-colored dirt. The spot was beautiful, with wind-carved rock steeples in the distance and the desert interspersed with mesquite, juniper, and other shrubs. A drawback was that he and Bray weren't the only ones who knew about the place. Lanes of dirt roads crisscrossed the desert and gave access to another thirty vehicles or so. Most were the usual campervans, pull-behinds, school buses, and class A, B, and C rigs. One SUV nearby had a tent perched on its roof, and Uly imagined the torturous task of having to leave the tent in the middle of the night and navigate the narrow ladder just to take a piss. A few of the vehicles appeared broken down and were surrounded by piles of accumulated junk—they looked like the inhabitants had settled in to ride out the pandemic.

Now that he was part of Bray's circle of trust, they proceeded to cook and eat together. Then, one night while eating, Bray said, "Have you seen all the trash around this place? I think we should organize our neighbors to do a clean-up."

To that, Uly answered, "Sorry, I can't even reach down to tie my own shoes." He patted his enormous stomach, then added, "But you go for it."

Bray gave him a serious look, one Uly had seen before, and said, "Weight is one of the most common risk factors for COVID hospitalization. No offense, but it's treatable."

Uly was not overly self-conscious about his weight; it just seemed part of him, like fingers and toes. He said, "Yeah, I get it. No offense taken."

Then Bray held out his fist for a reciprocal bump. Uly

did not like fist-bumping, high-fiving, or even handshaking, but he didn't want to offend Bray—the guy was just so earnest. Uly bumped fists.

Bray left their campsite early the next morning, and intermittently throughout the day. Uly could see him with his wide-brimmed sun hat lead a group of three or four others through the desert with their buckets and pails, stooping to pick up trash like children on an Easter egg hunt. It made him wince in pain just watching. When Bray finally returned in the afternoon, his bucket was filled with, among other detritus, hundreds of cigarette butts—little cocoons of cancer.

————

That night after dinner, Uly looked again at the @fabvanlife video. In retrospect, he thought the whole abduction and then engagement story seemed so weird; like, who could make this shit up? He and Bray were outside in their camp chairs, sitting side-by-side with Uly's computer between them and connected to Bray's hotspot.

The video was shot from behind the girl, just over her shoulder. They had a clear picture of the man—older, with gray hair just over his ears, a gray mustache, and a severely sunburned face. The camera panned the inside of the coach: white leather, huge front seats, and a kitchen with granite countertops. Bray's wife sat calmly at the dinette table. She said they were going to Las Vegas. Why Vegas? There was a pause, maybe some tension, and then Jo said she was engaged to be married. On the surface, it seemed Jo had just left Bray for another man. It happened all the time, and that story trope was older than the Bible, old as humankind. Uly imagined the first Neanderthal bludgeoning a woman and dragging her by the hair back to his cave after having just sliced the throat of another suitor.

He said to Bray, "Sorry, dude."

Uly's own marriage had failed a few years before. He'd left her and moved out, but his leaving was a preemptive strike against Bunny's emotional weapons of destruction. He told her through a text message, which he thought saved them both the ugliness of a face-to-face confrontation. In reality, his message was just the crossing of the T—Bunny hadn't talked to him in weeks. Months later, he wondered if another man had been involved. He didn't think so, but then he didn't know for sure.

Right then, Uly had a thought. He asked, "Did you look at her phone records?"

"Yes, when she was abducted, her phone was left behind. We've both had the same password for as long as we've had cell phones. I couldn't find any calls to people I didn't recognize. Jo did not know this guy."

"Let's look at the video again."

Uly moved back the time slide on the screen. It did seem strange that she'd offered up all that information. He wouldn't be so forthcoming if two kids barged into his campervan. Then he said the obvious, "Who gets engaged to be married when they still have a husband back home and no divorce papers?"

"Exactly."

Uly played the footage one more time. A minute later, he hit pause and pinched his two fingers to deftly zoom in. What interested him was the towel over Jo's hand. That towel and hand never moved, like it was lame. But why the towel? What was it covering? Uly hit play again. When Jo said they'd gotten engaged, her right hand touched her left wrist through the towel, gently massaging it. As she massaged her wrist, she spread the towel's fabric to outline something. Uly paused the video, zoomed in, and turned the screen toward Bray. He said, "What do you think that is?"

He watched Bray start the video, rewind, and watch for the towel and any movement. "She doesn't move that hand."

"Maybe she can't. Maybe it's secured to the table somehow, handcuffed even."

Bray sat back and took a drink from his beer. "She's being held against her will. I told you."

Uly smiled. Uly was a regular smiler—he smiled when something was funny, smiled when he saw a car accident, and smiled if he thought something was interesting. A happy smile, sad smile, ironic smile, intrigued smile—they all looked the same on his extremely large, bearded face. His smile had driven his wife crazy—*why are you smiling?* He smiled now because what he once considered a lark—traveling around with this guy to find his abducted wife—was now a true mission, a very Bronson-like quest.

This brought up the next question, "Why Las Vegas?"

"They're obviously not getting married there."

"I get that, but still, why Vegas?"

"I have no idea. We've never been, and it's not the kind of place we ever liked."

Uly never understood that response. What's not to like? Great entertainment—like ten Cirque du Soleil shows—best restaurants and chefs in the world, all-you-can-eat buffets, sex and drugs if you're into that sort of thing, pretty great weather, the desert, the mountains, Lake Mead with Hoover Dam, and gambling if you're into that sort of thing. Plus, it had all the other stuff Americans wanted—suburbs, shopping malls, schools, Costco, and now professional sports. Uly had lived there for over twenty years and loved it. Maybe Jo and Bray didn't like Vegas, but supposedly, the guy with the Outlaw did, and he was headed there. And when, in the video, Margo said something about slots, the guy got all in the bag. Cards. "The guy said he was going to Las Vegas to play cards."

"What? Like blackjack or poker?"

"I don't know. The guy's already passed nearly a dozen casinos through Colorado and New Mexico. He could have played blackjack or poker at any one of them. My guess is a tournament."

"Let's assume he's taking Jo to Las Vegas to play cards. Where do you think he'd stay?"

RV parks dotted Las Vegas, but most catered to permanent residents, RVers who spent all year in the same spot, like trailer parks. They weren't the kind of places you just pulled into for the night. Now, if you were coming to Vegas for a few days to gamble or participate in a tournament on the Strip, a place where you could pull up in a forty-foot motorcoach and have access to water, electricity, and sewer, there was one very likely choice. He said, "Circus Circus Casino."

"We can head there tomorrow."

Uly was heading back to Las Vegas. He wasn't sure if he was excited about that or not.

23

The Bubble of Love

From Lake Powell, Margo and Lucas drove south for two days through Flagstaff and Phoenix to a town called Casa Grande. Margo had read about a collection of futuristic and dilapidated industrial domes she thought might be suitable for an Instagram shoot. But if she was honest with herself, it felt as though they were just going through the motions after the falloff from the abduction thread. And now they were actually losing followers.

By the time they reached the dome, the temperatures at midday were well over a hundred and ten degrees, a fact they hadn't considered. They did not have a rooftop air conditioner or a generator to run it.

Margo said, "Let's just shoot this and get out." They parked on the side of the road and left the Fabvan's motor running, the AC on high.

She could see the domes in the distance rising from the barren desert. Then, just off the road, a sign read, "No Trespassing." But there was no fence to keep them out, no one around, and obvious from the colorful graffiti covering the domes that few people had heeded the notice.

The backstory on the domes was that they were initially planned in the late seventies to house a computer factory but were never completed. From a distance, with the graffiti, they looked like bath bubbles with a rainbow sheen. One larger stand-alone dome appeared to hover above the desert like a gigantic flying saucer. Most of the graffiti was the crude tagging kind, but some stood out with whimsical designs that showed artistic merit. The concrete shells were all crumbling, exposing a brownish spray-on insulation where kids had carved their initials along with crude, sometimes offensive, images.

Margo wondered what it meant for a kid, most likely a boy, to carve a huge penis? Was it pride or wishful thinking? Or was it just the freedom of offensive expression? She asked Lucas.

He said, "When I was like twelve, I drew penises everywhere—penned in textbooks, carved on desks, spray-painted on walls. I think it had to do with repression. Like, no adult talks about sex, but you find your dad's hidden dirty mags filled with it, and you just want to shout 'cock' or 'dick' or something. But then a picture lasts longer." He laughed, then added, "Maybe that's why I like photography."

Margo smiled. "Do you still have a compulsion to take dirty pictures?"

They were walking through the flying saucer dome. Parts of the ceiling were missing, and beams of sunlight poured onto the concrete floor like the reflections off a disco ball. He said, "Why don't you strip down and we can find out."

What then ensued was the kind of dirty sex Lucas might have found in his dad's magazines, and literally dirty sex because they floundered about all sweaty in the filth of the place. It felt like pornography, though more like a book a couple might hide *together*, like some Kama Sutra thing. Margo—all dirty, sweaty, and naked—liked it.

Only later did she realize that it was Sunday, which had once been their one day of rest.

————

That night, back near Flagstaff, she read a new post from Bray. He'd used all 1,000 characters allowed in an Instagram post to explain what might have been going on in the motorcoach— the gist being that Jo *had been* abducted, that if you looked at her covered hand, you could see Jo pulling the cloth tight to outline her shackled wrist, and that she couldn't be engaged to be married if she was still married to him. Jo was being held against her will, and she was telling them that they were going to Las Vegas to play cards somewhere.

She showed Lucas the post. He then opened his iPad and pulled up the video taken three days before. Margo leaned over as he paused the image of the woman stretching the towel tight over her wrist. He zoomed in. Margo thought she could see the top ridge of a handcuff and possibly the outline of a chain.

She said, "Well, fuck."

Lucas said, "I don't know. The lady said they were engaged to be married. I think she'd have said something different if she was actually abducted. Maybe the towel was just hiding a disfigurement. You know, like a club foot."

"Really, a club foot?"

"Maybe her hand was cold. That's why she covered it with the towel. You know, like a blanket."

"Don't be a dope, Lucas. It's the fucking desert in the middle of summer."

"Don't call me a dope."

Now she felt bad. "I'm sorry." She was genuinely sorry.

Lucas ignored the apology. "Then what? Was she really abducted? We had a chance to save that woman and did nothing?"

Margo took the laptop from Lucas. She played the video again from the beginning and pointed out what she saw and thought. "Look, her hand never moves—it can't. Look at the guy. He's definitely pissed off. Then, just before Jo says they're engaged to be married, the man reaches behind his back. Why? It's awkward. Something's in his back pocket. What?"

Lucas said it, "A gun."

"A gun."

She continued, "Now, look at his hand after Jo says that they were engaged. The man's arm relaxes, and his hand moves to his side. It's like she said it to get the guy to back off. She's for sure being held against her will. I know it."

Lucas leaned back, dejected. "And I did nothing."

"We didn't know. How could we?"

Lucas just shook his head.

Then Margo had another thought. Her Instagram account had been losing followers since the last time she'd posted about the abduction. If she pursued the story again, her following would resume growing. She realized the idea was selfish, but her mind had a will of its own.

She said, "I'll repost the video with a new message."

"We should drive to Las Vegas tomorrow."

Margo was excited. Despite the sweaty and dirty sex in the dome, the shoot had felt routine and boring. That old Instagram thread of the fabulous #vanlife lifestyle and their blah, blah, blah brand statement now seemed trivial.

She gave Lucas a wet kiss on the mouth, then sang out,

"Viva Las Vegas!"

24

Then Came Uly – Episode #1

Uly drove the Xplorer fifty-five miles per hour through the desert toward Las Vegas. He guessed the temperature was a hundred degrees out, hotter on the highway's black asphalt. The windows were closed, and the air conditioner was on high. He still sweated through his white, or near white, T-shirt, and his underwear was damp and sticky from his ass that broiled against the vinyl seat. The air conditioner never did work well, and he needed a one-ten outlet for the roof unit to power on. Uly considered just turning the thing off and opening the window for the hot, dry breeze but decided against it. About thirty miles from the city, he passed a bright green sign, "Rest Area," and pulled off. The exit ramp funneled into a dirt parking lot the size of a football field. A few big rigs were parked side-by-side with their diesels running. Otherwise, nothing—no picnic benches, dog runs, shade of any kind, or bathrooms. So, this was what they called a rest area in Nevada.

Uly found a frosted chocolate Pop-Tart in the back kitchenette cupboard and ate most of the two pastries in the foil packet. The rest he hand-fed to Calypso in her glovebox nest. What he noticed about the mouse was that she rarely moved from the glovebox and was starting to get fat. He wondered if he was feeding her too much and worried that the mouse wasn't getting any exercise. He thought maybe he'd get her a small cage or fish tank and one of those rodent treadmills.

Uly checked in with Bray. He'd been more thorough in his search while traveling from Arizona to Las Vegas. DMs had come in with supposed sightings: the campground on the south rim of the Grand Canyon, in the desert near Sedona, on the federal lands of Kaibab National Forest, and along Route 66 in Peach Springs. Bray hadn't seen a Thor Outlaw with a Thunder Canyon color scheme, and it would take him another few hours of driving to get to Las Vegas. In a grave tone, Bray had said, "I'll leave no stone unturned," like Uly imagined Lincoln might've sounded at Gettysburg.

Uly said, "Okay, whatever. I'll meet you at Circus Circus this afternoon." Overall, he thought Bray was well-meaning but fussy, like an old lady at the Safeway who scrutinized a receipt before taking out her checkbook.

Before leaving the rest area, he stepped out onto the parking lot and pissed in the dirt with his back to traffic.

Uly drove on to Las Vegas, past Nellis Airforce Base where a fighter jet landed just to his left, past downtown where the old Union Plaza Casino still presided over Glitter Gulch, and past Sahara Avenue where he should have exited if he'd wanted to go directly to Circus Circus. He drove all the way south to Tropicana toward the end of the Strip. Out of nostalgia, Uly wanted to drive by the apartment where he'd first lived when he moved to Las Vegas in 1987. Tropicana then was a main thoroughfare bordered by open lots of desert where residents dumped garbage in the middle of the night, and feral dogs and cats scoured the refuse for scraps of food. Now, it was lined with hotels, casinos, and condos all the way to McCarran Airport. He took a left on Paradise Road, then another quick left on East Naples Drive. The complex of studio apartments was still there, and they still offered a move-in special, but now the building was painted in Caribbean blue with murals of whales and dolphins and whatnot. When he moved in, the place didn't have a name he was aware of. It was The Krib now, the one-room studio apartments advertised as lofts. Their image had changed, though he suspected the apartments were still full of hookers and drug addicts. Uly lived there for over five years, until he moved in with Bunny and her son.

Her son, Uly's stepson, now owned the bar he and Bunny had bought years before; the bar Uly had pretty much run into the ground. The place was located further out on Tropicana and originally called The Lunch Box. And maybe the earlier proprietors had once served lunch back in the sixties, but when he and Bunny owned it, they just served booze and bags of chips. He always knew the bar's name was stupid, but he'd been too cheap to change the signage. His stepson, Jack, had renamed it Jackhammer's.

Uly had no intention of dropping by and reliving old and painful memories. He and Jack had never been close, the kid was always closer to his biological dad. From the first day they'd met, Jack had built an emotional wall that wouldn't be crossed. Uly guessed the kid resented him like any stepchild would, saddled with a new man banging their mom. Jack was smart, though, and a good worker. He'd grown up working in the bar and was running it by the time he was twenty-one. Jack repeatedly told him to get some slot machines near the front door and poker machines in the bar top. Uly resisted, maybe because he was too cheap, but he wanted the kind of bar East Coast expats could frequent, watch a Patriots or Ravens game and shoot the shit. Once the kid finally bought out Uly's share of the bar (it wasn't worth much by then), he changed the name, got his gaming license, and put in the slot and poker machines. He guessed the kid was making a killing.

Uly turned around where Naples dead-ended at a garbage dumpster, went back onto Tropicana, and drove to the Strip. He turned north at the MGM Grand with its gold Leo the Lion statue. There was little to no traffic, normally unheard of at any time of the day or night. The Strip, Las Vegas Boulevard, was usually crowded with taxis, Ubers, Californians, motorcycles, rental cars, exotics like Lamborghinis and three-wheeled Slingshots, sightseeing buses, and those box trucks toting billboard signs like "Girls, Girls, Girls." The Strip was a corridor locals had always avoided like they avoided, well, tourists. Now, with the tourists holed up during the pandemic, the homeless had taken over, and Uly passed ladies pushing shopping carts filled with their stuff, men hunched in the nooks and crannies of buildings drinking, smoking, snorting, huffing, and God knows what else. He knew they'd always been there with their signs and cups and dogs, scrounging for change to get through one more day, but now the multitude of homeless stuck out with the absence of, he guessed, normal people.

Some casinos looked closed, but the big ones like MGM, Bellagio, and Caesars were open. He knew from Facebook posts that the ones still open were trying to attract *anyone*, and room rates were as low as they'd ever been. He'd read that you could get a room at the Bellagio for fifty bucks. Circus Circus was probably offering rooms for half that. Tourists weren't flying, and people with real money were hunkered down on a beach or mountain somewhere, so the casinos were attracting the riffraff, mostly from Southern California. Uly saw a few groups of people with neck, arm, and chest tats walking the Strip carrying forty-ouncers of malt liquor, plastic novelty cups that could hold a gallon of toxic slurpy, and smoking weed—now legal. Then, strangely, really old people riding Medicare scooters. These folks were prime victims of the virus and dying by the thousands while hooked up to octopus-like ventilators. Some wore masks, but most were maskless. He guessed they just didn't care, or ignored the pandemic commotion altogether.

Uly drove past The Mirage, constructed right after he'd moved to Vegas, then past Treasure Island, the Venetian, Wynn, and the Peppermill Restaurant and Fireside Lounge. He took a left on Circus Circus Drive, a right on Sammy Davis Jr. Drive, another right on Ringmaster Drive, finally pulling up next to a pink and white striped circus tent-looking thing with a sign that read, "Registration," where he paid forty-one dollars per night for his less than thirty-foot RV. He paid for just one night, leaving the option open the next day for an air-conditioned room with a king-sized bed in their nearby hotel that would probably cost fifteen dollars less.

The RV park was one big parking lot with water, electricity, and sewer hookups. It looked more like a drive-in theater than a place to camp. About half the spots were empty.

Uly had number 153, as close to the showers and bathrooms as possible. The whole line of spots from 130 to 168, between Dumbo Drive and Topsy Street, were reserved for Class B RVs under thirty feet, and they were mostly taken by other campervans. Then, across Topsy Street near Blinko Lane, spots were reserved for the bigger rigs—Class A RVs and the fifth-wheel trailers up to forty feet pulled by heavy-duty pickups. Strangely, the demarcation of Topsy Street separated the tribes—the campervans with Biden and Bernie bumper stickers from the big rigs with Trump stickers and American flags. The bathrooms were smack-dab in the middle, but no self-respecting Class A or fifth-wheel owner would deign to use one. Uly parked, hooked up the electricity, turned on his rooftop A/C unit, and then went for the showers. He stunk.

When he walked back to his van, an older man stood out front wearing Teva sandals, shorts with too many pockets, and a tan drip-dry shirt with the sleeves rolled up and secured with those button tabs that somehow reminded Uly of the old sock garters his dad had worn. The man wore a blue surgical mask. He said, "You must be Uly," and put out his fist for a bump.

Uly ignored the fist and stood ten feet back; he was not wearing a mask. "How do you know who I am?"

"We all know who you are. Just about all of us on Dumbo Drive have been following the Instagram posts. You've been featured in them. Margo and Lucas are here from fabvanlife, but we haven't seen Bray from vanlifevagabonds. We're all here to help."

Uly thought that the only time he'd ever been recognized was by the hostess at the Tropicana buffet when, from a distance of fifty yards, she'd seen him coming once again to eat. He said, "Thanks," then added, "Bray should be here later."

"Just to let you know, two Thor Outlaws are in the park. We've been watching and don't think either is where Jo's being held. None of the occupants look like the man in the video. Neither rig has Pennsylvania plates."

Uly said, "Okay." He thought he should say something else, maybe some comments on the Outlaw's likely whereabouts, but all he could add to okay was, again, "Thanks."

"We're gathering for a socially-distant happy hour at five near the tree. If you can make it, that would be great. We're all wondering how we can help in the search."

"A tree?" Uly looked around. He could not see a tree or remember passing one on his way in.

"At the end of the row, near the fence on Carousel Boulevard." The man pointed, "There."

Uly could just barely make out the top of something green. He wondered if it was a real tree or one of those fake trees designed to camouflage a cell tower. He said, "Sure."

————

Uly saw Bray's Winnebago Travato with the vintage BMW motorcycle pull in later in the afternoon and park a few spots away. Uly phoned him rather than walk the thirty or forty feet. He brought Bray up to speed—the Outlaw had not been seen, people were here to help, a happy hour at five. Bray had no new information from his search across Arizona.

Just before five, Uly stopped by Bray's van and the two walked together toward the tree. Both carried camp chairs. Near the campervan group, they passed a cluster of Class A and fifth-wheel owners across Topsy Street standing around a big propane grill and sipping navy-blue cans of Bud Light. Half the group were wearing red and white MAGA caps. None were wearing a face mask. Uly saw one guy turn toward them and hoist his beer in greeting. The guy looked middle-aged, too young to be retired, and wore a sage-green T-shirt with lettering that spelled out, "Welcome to America, Now Speak English." Both Uly and Bray wore masks, and Uly knew that the guy's greeting was really a fuck you to who he probably thought were a couple of liberal sheep. Uly nodded in the man's direction anyway.

The temperature was still in the nineties, and most of the men and women at the happy hour sat in camp chairs arranged in a circle, wearing shorts, T-shirts, masks, and floppy sun hats. Uly did not like showing his thick and hairy pale legs in public and, instead of shorts, wore an ancient pair of baggy sweatpants with a logo of the bygone Baltimore Colts, his hometown team years before. He guessed the pants were over forty years old and now stretched beyond their original size. It surprised him that they hadn't disintegrated completely. His V-neck T-shirt was clean and voluminous. What little blond and gray hair he still had was neatly combed over his bald crown, and his completely gray beard was trimmed to the length of two fingers. He greeted everyone with a nod, his ubiquitous smile hidden behind a blue surgical mask. He said, "Hey," then unfolded his wide camp chair on the pavement near the tree, an acceptable distance from the others.

A man wearing a mask screen-printed with "Vote" walked up to Uly and Bray and offered beers. Uly said, "Thanks." He looked at the label, *Hopathon* by a local brewer called Hop Nuts. He took a sip and said, "This is good."

Bray said, "Nice hops, slightly fruity."

The man said, "It's a local West Coast IPA. I think it's as good as it gets in Las Vegas."

A woman walked up wearing an N95 mask that clouded her perfectly round tortoise-shell glasses with every breath. Loudly, so everyone could hear, she said, "So, Bray, what's the plan? Everyone wants to know."

Bray stood up from his camp chair and walked over to the tree. Closer now, Uly thought the tree was a variety of ash that needed no maintenance whatsoever. Over the years, kids with their little pocketknives had carved various initials, dates, hearts, and genitalia. He remembered doing something similar when he was a dumb kid stoned on weed, though the wood had been the top of a picnic table, and what he carved was a cartoonish hand with its middle finger extended.

Bray was now in the center of the group and more than ten feet from the nearest person. He pulled down his mask so everyone could hear. He looked confident as if his special purpose in life was organizing volunteers.

"I want to thank everyone who drove here to help in this search." From there, he gave a speech, describing his wife and the kind of person she was—generous, loving, wouldn't hurt a fly. Then, the abduction and what he knew of the Thor Outlaw. He said that the police in Nebraska would not help or get involved, nor would any other law enforcement agencies. He said, "They don't care about us," which brought the campervan community together under one united purpose. He asked, "Are Margo and Lucas here?"

From the back of the group, Margo said, "We're here."

"Maybe you could stand up and give us a firsthand description of the man who abducted Jo."

Uly saw the couple stand. They were by far the youngest in the group. He'd been following them on Instagram since before the abduction, and now, up close, they were as attractive in person as in their photos—like celebrities. Uly sensed a hushed silence that might have existed before but now felt tangible, like the subtle feeling of air pressure dropping.

Margo left her tie-dyed mask on with her voice slightly muffled. "Well, you've probably all seen the video." Uly heard a murmur of affirmations. "The guy is, well, like that. You know, old, I mean older, you know, with a mustache and, like, khaki pants."

She was pretty but no public speaker.

Then, a crushed can of Bud Light crashed onto Topsy Street, thrown by one of the Class A Trumpers. Margo stopped talking.

Someone from the campervan group said under his breath, "Litterer."

Another said, "Trash," and Uly wasn't sure the person was referring to the can or the people across the street.

Lucas stepped forward. He walked through the group and onto Topsy Street. He bent over and picked up the can. Uly could see him look at the group of Trumpers.

The one with the "Welcome to America" T-shirt said, just loud enough for everyone to hear, "Pussy."

Total silence. Not the hushed silence from before, but the kind of silence where Uly could hear the muffled sound of traffic a quarter mile away. Then the one Trumper tending the propane grill flipped a hamburger, and the sizzle of meat was like a soundtrack that amplified the tension. Lucas stood with the crushed can of Bud Light in his hand while the campervan group remained quiet.

Lucas cocked his arm back with the can. The arm sprung forward, the hand releasing the projectile. It was a good, practiced throw from a guy who obviously grew up playing baseball, and it was aimed straight at the man with the "Welcome to America" T-shirt, straight at the Welcome Man's head. Lucas missed by inches when the man jerked to the side. The can landed on the large right boob of a woman behind him.

She said, "Motherfucker."

The Welcome Man now stepped onto Topsy Street. He stood just over six feet tall and beefy like a guy who spent time in the gym. His short hair was neatly combed with the sides recently razored—a man who still saw a barber during the pandemic.

Lucas looked like a small child in comparison.

Uly stood and walked slowly forward to stand in front of Lucas. Uly heard someone say from behind, "I'll find security." Others were whispering into phones after calling 911. He knew still others were standing with their phones up high and filming the altercation.

The Welcome Man said, "What are you going to do about it, fat man?"

With Trump at the helm, Uly and the whole country had witnessed a degradation in civility. Name-calling, once the tactic of schoolyard bullies, was now acceptable adult behavior in some circles. Las Vegas had always been a tough town with tourists bent on drinking too much, smoking too much weed, and snorting cocaine or crystal meth. The saying, *What happens in Vegas, stays in Vegas,* was now the mantra of every asshole in America. It was only a year ago that Uly had walked down the Strip, and some woman said to a friend, loud enough for him to hear, "Look at that gross fatty." He'd stopped, turned, and given the two his most shaming look, but the woman just laughed and kept walking. What kind of person does that? Uly realized it was the kind of person who now stood in front of him.

The Welcome Man was waiting for Uly's next move.

Uly outweighed the man by over one hundred pounds, and not all his weight was fat. He'd lived in Vegas for a long time, had dealt with bullies, had dealt with drunk assholes in the bar. He knew you didn't wait to get hit. As quickly as a five-hundred-pound alligator moves to take down a small deer, he crossed the few feet to the Welcome Man and slapped him with an open hand. The Welcome Man fell to the ground.

The guy tending the grill and flipping burgers said, "Get him, Spitball."

The Welcome Man had a funny nickname—Spitball.

Spitball stood slowly, his face bright crimson where he'd been slapped. He stepped forward, and Uly stood his ground. Lucas moved back. Uly gave Spitball the time he needed to figure out his next move, but Uly would not let the guy hit him with a fist. He'd use his tremendous weight to tackle him in one linebacker rush.

Before that happened, security showed up.

The golf cart came speeding down Topsy Street as fast as a golf cart could. No siren blared, but an LED bar on the hood of the cart flashed like a state patrol cruiser. Spitball looked in their direction, and Uly immediately sensed that the altercation was now over.

The golf cart came to a stop. Spitball was the first to speak. He touched his now slightly swollen cheek and said in almost a child's whiney voice, "He hit me. I didn't do anything," which was technically true if you didn't count the littering. And with the current administration in Washington, calling people names was now more-or-less accepted.

One of the security officers stood from the golf cart. He looked twelve years old and was dressed in a cop outfit with a walkie-talkie microphone hooked to his shirt beneath his hairless chin. Handcuffs and a can of mace hung on one side of his utility belt, and on the other was a holstered Taser with its bright yellow handle. He looked at Uly and said, "Is that true?"

"Yes, after he called my friend here a pussy."

The security officer, the boy, ignored the pussy comment (again, calling people names was now acceptable behavior) and said to Uly, "You need to leave." Then added in his best command voice, "Now."

Uly considered himself a nice guy, one of those gentle giants people talk about. He thought of himself as someone who helped others, like Jim Bronson. He was helping Bray find his wife and had just helped Lucas after the boy had been verbally assaulted.

But he did have this thing with authority. He didn't like being told what to do by bosses, his stepson, or this prepubescent security guard at Circus Circus. In the past, he'd been a smart-ass to authority figures, always saying something he thought funny but which was really just stupid and flippant. He knew it was a personality flaw but couldn't help himself. He said something stupid now—something connected to the whole Circus Circus theme.

He looked at the kid in the cop outfit and said, "You ass clown."

As soon as the words left his mouth, Uly knew he was no better than the man who had called Lucas a pussy.

The kid, the security guard, reached for his plastic Taser, flipped up the safety latch, and withdrew the gun. He pointed the gun at the very large target of Uly's chest and fired. All this before Uly could say he was sorry for calling the kid an ass clown.

The electrodes sunk into his skin like fish hooks and released a surge of electricity. He felt a tingling sensation like when, as a kid, he'd accidentally stuck his finger into a light bulb socket. He felt slightly dazed but did not fall to the ground. Uly didn't fall until the other officer—he remembered a woman—unholstered her Taser and followed suit.

He squirmed on Topsy Street like a hooked bass at the bottom of a fishing boat.

Uly was handcuffed and escorted to the back of the golf cart, where he was strapped in with an extra-long lap belt—not the first fat man arrested.

The cart did a three-point turn on Topsy Street, and as they sped away, Uly saw Spitball and the other Trumpers wave goodbye. He saw the campervan group under the ash tree, standing still and aghast. Bray was in front of the group with his cell phone raised and still recording the incident. Uly heard him yell, "I'll get you out." Others in the group were also taking videos of the action, and Uly knew he'd be a #vanlife celebrity within hours.

The cart sped off the RV park, then down a ramp leading to the bowels of the main casino. It stopped outside double doors with a sign that read "Security." The two officers led him inside.

It was another three hours before he was released into the custody of Bray, who vouched for his better behavior. In that time, he was fingerprinted and photographed like a booked criminal, then held in an actual prison cell with a locked door that had a center sliding gate to slip in trays of food. He did not stay long enough to get a meal. On one wall was a cot, and on the back wall was a stainless-steel combination sink and toilet. Before his release, an older man with a neatly trimmed mustache read him some legalese from a notecard. The gist was that he'd been permanently banned from ever entering the Circus Circus Casino again. In the parlance of Las Vegans, he'd been *eighty-sixed.* The same guy escorted them out onto Las Vegas Boulevard. Uly gave Bray his keys to pull the campervan around the front.

Afterward, Uly booked a cheap hotel room nearby.

Later, as he lay in bed, the day's events looped through his mind. He thought he'd done the right thing, standing up to the tyranny and bullying sweeping the nation. But then he remembered an episode of *Then Came Bronson* where Jim Bronson stood up for a woman against her overly jealous and abusive boyfriend. Uly remembered there was a subtlety to Bronson's words and actions. He didn't just overtly take her side and call the boyfriend a bully. He'd actually distanced himself from the woman to avoid worsening the jealousy. He then saddled up to the boyfriend by competing with him in an enduro motorcycle race. The boyfriend was as competitive as he was jealous, and Bronson beat the man with an ego-crushing victory. But Bronson didn't gloat. With very few actual words spoken, he showed the boyfriend that his anger and paranoia were unfounded. The couple reunited, Uly guessed, in a more supportive and understanding relationship. That's what Uly figured he'd done wrong. Bronson would have never slapped the man. He would have figured out a way to allow the man to reflect on his own actions without himself resorting to violence. Bronson would have never called the young security officer an ass clown—a kid just trying to do his job.

Uly thought he wasn't too old to learn to do the right thing and help people. He just needed to be more like Bronson.

———

The first thing the next morning, Uly checked on Calypso. He'd forgotten about her after the altercation and forgotten she'd stayed in the oven-hot campervan that evening while he slept in air-conditioned comfort. He unlocked the passenger door and reached in to open the glovebox. Uly half expected a decomposing corpse, but what he found was Calypso surrounded by six tiny blind babies all nestled at Calypso's paps like little piggies. How stupid could he have been? A nest, a fat mouse?

Part of him felt like a proud father, but the rest knew the campervan would be infested with hungry little mice in a few days.

He thought about what Bronson would do and then acted.

From his toolbox, he pulled out a Philips-head screwdriver. He then removed the sheet metal screws that fastened the interior of the glovebox to the dashboard. The box, made of compressed cardboard, pulled out in one piece with Calypso and her babies still nested and undisturbed. He carefully took the glovebox to the side of the hotel, to a hidden and shaded spot between an electrical transformer and the hotel's outside wall, and near the dumpsters. He gently set the box down with the open end facing the hotel. It seemed like a nice spot for a mouse to raise a family—close to the dumpster's refuse and near the hotel's air-conditioned rooms. He hoped they would discover a way in.

In parting, he said, "Farewell, Calypso!"

25

The Cards Dealt

Jo sat next to Hugh as he drove from the ghost town in Arizona to Las Vegas.

Hugh was sick. On the three-hour drive, his lungs labored in and out with a heavy wheezing noise, and he coughed intermittently to clear gunk from deep in his chest that he spit into a paper napkin. He drove hunched over the steering wheel, his elbows resting on the hard plastic rim. Hugh didn't wear a mask and she didn't have one for herself. Jo was certain Hugh was sick with COVID and was sure she'd also become infected. The average incubation period took something like five days. She waited for symptoms to appear.

Hugh had said that the AGRA Gin Rummy tournament was being held at a local casino called Sam's Town.

Jo had never been to Las Vegas. She'd wanted to, but Bray was always against it. She'd seen the casinos and resorts in photos, Las Vegas Boulevard lined with themed buildings: Paris, Venice, Rome, New York, Egypt, the Caribbean, and medieval Europe. Gambling seemed exciting, though she'd never even played the lottery or bought pull tabs. Then she liked the idea of all those entertainers in one place, shows to watch every night, and famous restaurants created by celebrity chefs. A Disneyland for adults. Sure, she loved the mountains in the West and the lakes of Minnesota, but why limit yourself to nature? Bray was a snob in that regard and looked down his nose at anyone interested in Sin City. Jo could see the lit-up skyline in the distance and was mesmerized.

But when the motorcoach reached the city's outskirts, Hugh turned away from the signs pointing to The Strip. Now, instead of themed casinos, they passed the schools, supermarkets, mini-storage facilities, banks, malls, and gas stations of an unimaginative place called Henderson. Hugh followed a four-lane road, Boulder Highway, and in the distance, Jo could see the huge red and gold sign of Sam's Town Hotel and Casino. Up close, an enormous building the size of a big-city convention center was sectioned off to look like an old-timey Western town with its false storefronts. Honestly, she'd seen the real thing in small towns all over Colorado and the Southwest, and she was more interested in experiencing a fake Paris or Rome.

They took a left into the Sam's Town KOA—Kampgrounds of America. The name was licensed to independent operators, and the brand usually suggested high prices, full hookups, campers cheek-to-jowl, a cheap swimming pool, and too many kids—definitely not cool for the #vanlife community. Before Hugh left to register, he asked Jo to go back into her room. He shut the door and closed the outside latch. Thirty minutes later, the motorcoach was parked, and she listened to Hugh hook up the electricity, water, and sewer.

The next morning, Jo heard the door latch slide open, but

Hugh didn't enter or use the intercom. She waited on the bench seat, thinking that anything could happen—pepper sprayed or shot—if she walked unshackled into the main living area of the coach. She put on her walking boot and waited. Finally, she thought, *to hell with it,* and opened the door. Hugh wasn't standing in the hallway or at the dinette table.

Jo knew, at that moment, she could just walk away.

She hobbled to the front of the coach and pressed the button that opened the door. The two bottom steps mechanically slid out. Only days before, she'd sat on that bottom step with the gel of pepper spray burning her face and eyes. He'd been whistling.

Beyond the steps was a parking lot filled with other RVs. She heard a cough from the back of the coach, his bedroom. She knew she needed to take the coach steps down to freedom—to flee. But she didn't.

Now she heard him coughing continuously, deeply, hacking up phlegm that might give him temporary relief. He was harmless now, a toothless old man.

She walked back and knocked on his bedroom door. Hugh said, "Come in."

She'd been in the room before—the gin rummy-themed rug, the side tables with stationary lamps, a white leather lounge chair for watching the wall-mounted flat-screen TV. Hugh lay in the bed covered by a gray-blue comforter that his wife Florence probably bought him years before. His breathing was labored, and his brow was sweaty from fever. The man was very sick.

He said, "The tournament starts today."

Hugh's eyes were straining against their sockets, his mouth wide open with a pink tongue pushing against his lower lip to move as much air in and out as possible.

She said, "Try sitting up."

His body inched up against the pillows. He coughed and spat into a Kleenex from a box sitting next to his thigh. He said, "You go."

"What?"

He spoke in spasms of words. "I won't be able to play . . . in this condition. The tournament starts today. You go." He gasped air, then continued, "I've seen you play. You have perfect instincts. I know. You can visualize the cards . . . that's most important. Get through the qualifiers . . . and I'll coach you from there."

"Why?"

Hugh coughed and spat again. "I'm done. You can go. I know what I did . . . in the minds of others . . . was wrong. I don't care. It's done. I did it of my own free will. You can go back to your Bray . . . go back to your tiny van. But then you'll think . . . I had an opportunity. I could have won."

Hugh continued, "You know . . . there's a quote from Nehru of India. 'The card hand that's dealt represents determinism . . .'" Hugh paused to get his breath. ". . . 'The way you play it is free will.' . . . This is the situation you find yourself in."

"So, what's that fortune cookie sentiment supposed to mean?"

"I'm the hand you were dealt. In this game, the luck . . . or I should say bad luck . . . of you being abducted . . . is just a small part. And that's over. Now . . . the way you decide to move forward . . . is your exercise of free will." The man looked spent and could barely talk. He added two last words, "Take it."

Jo sat down on the lounge chair and looked at the man, now wasting away and pathetic. *Free will.* What did that even mean? He'd abducted her, kept her prisoner, and caused pain. Anger clawed at her insides. She now had the freedom to exercise her own free will. She could handcuff this man and leave him in the RV to literally rot.

Another emotion resided within her. It wasn't empathy—she would never really understand his motivation. Certainly not sympathy—Hugh was not sympathetic on any level. She guessed what she felt was similar to when Hugh first told her a dog needed help—a kind of generosity. But that wasn't it either. Compassion she guessed, like the compassion she felt years ago for a kid who stole her car. She'd pressed charges and then learned months later that he'd been sentenced to three years in prison. He was only seventeen, and she felt that compassion and maybe regret. She knew she hated Hugh; she had to, but she also didn't want to see the man die—or even be let down.

Also, she'd learned to like the game of gin rummy, and there was some freedom in that.

She asked, "How?"

"There's five thousand dollars . . . in my bedside table drawer. Take it. Five thousand is the buy-in. Registration . . . is at ten." Hugh looked in the direction of his bedside table. "Take it."

Jo walked to the side of the bed and opened the drawer. Next to his handgun was a stack of hundred-dollar bills held together by a rubber band. She looked at the handgun and saw the details of its trigger, grip, and muzzle. Then she took the money.

26

Spot the Difference

Jo changed into a sleeveless knee-length lime-green dress Hugh had bought. The dress's Walmart tag still dangled near the shoulder, and she yanked it off like a Band-Aid. She strapped on her walking boot. Before she left for the tournament, Jo brought Hugh a large glass of water. He was sleeping, and she set it on the nightstand table next to the box of Kleenex.

Jo limped through the KOA carrying the five thousand dollars in a small plastic grocery bag she'd dug out of the trash. Despite the pandemic, the RV park was almost completely occupied, with rigs of all kinds filling the Costco-sized lot. She thought the temperature was mid-nineties, and having the sun on her shoulders and face felt good. A sign with a directional arrow Read "CASINO" and she followed that past a three-story parking garage. From the outside, Sam's Town was as big as most suburban malls, and maybe it was a shopping mall of sorts because the first thing she passed was a movie theater complex with eighteen screens. The casino entrance was just past Calamity Jane's Ice Cream Parlor, and inside the automatic doors was a Purell dispenser and a security guard in a cowboy hat who offered her a blue paper mask. She thanked him and strapped it on.

The jangly sound of slot machines was like stepping out from a sealed office building and onto a busy city street, and for a second, she felt overwhelmed and discombobulated until she focused on one sign overhead with directions. She followed the arrow that pointed toward the hotel registration. Despite the cacophony of machines that sent a wave of excitement through her skin, few people were actually playing the slots or other table games she passed. Some wore masks, but the majority were maskless, and most of the maskless—senior citizens, she thought—were smoking. Jo smelled the stale smoke mixed with the soured beer soaked into the carpet, then hints of cheap perfume. She kept walking and passed a sign, "Firelight Buffet," and beneath that, "Closed." She made it to the registration counter and queued up on one of the floor stickers with an outline of two men's shoe soles that said, "Please Keep Social Distance, Stand Here." She kept moving to the next sticker as the line progressed, and finally, a woman motioned for her to step up. Jo asked for directions to the AGRA gin rummy tournament. The woman paused before answering, consulting her computer screen. She repeated, "A-G-R-A," then, "That would be the Sagebrush Room." She pointed down a lane between more rows of slot machines. She said, "Go past the TGI Fridays, up the escalator, and past Shelper's Western Wear." Jo kept limping through the casino, seemingly as big as the Mall of America.

Two men sat beneath a banner, "Welcome To The 2020 Agra Open Tournament." Both were older, in their seventies—Hugh's age—and wore kelly-green polo shirts with AGRA logos. With their faces masked, it took Jo a minute to realize they were identical twins. Then, like some *Spot the Difference* photo, her mind went quickly to see how many she could find. Both wore identical, aviator-shaped prescription glasses, both had matching wedding rings, and both sported inexpensive hair pieces made with synthetic strands of brown hair, thick like fishing line. She'd always guessed that men who wore toupees did so as a result of the trauma endured while losing their hair at an unusually early age. That, she guessed, or run-of-the-mill vanity. A difference she noticed was one had eyebrows dyed to match his hairpiece, while the other seemed to have no eyebrows at all. The other difference, hard to find, was one nametag read "Don," while the other's "Dan."

The one with the eyebrows, Don, asked, "Name?"

"Josephine Osterhockenberger."

The man looked up. "How do you spell that?" And while Jo slowly recited each letter the way she'd done it thousands of times (the name could be broken down into three perfectly acceptable last names—Oster, Hocken, and Berger), the man thumbed through a file box. "I don't have you here."

"Do I have to be listed there?"

Don said, "No, you can register now if you'd like. It's the AGRA Open, so open to all."

"Thank you," Jo said and took the blank card handed to her. She stepped over to a small registration table set up with two water glasses of pens—one with "Clean," while the other read "Dirty." She used a clean pen to fill out the form, placed the used pen into the dirty jar, and then stepped back to the registration table.

Dan, the brother with no eyebrows, asked, "Do you have a ranking?"

"No."

"Okay, the buy-in is five hundred dollars. Cash. There's a

top prize of ten thousand dollars."

"I was told the buy-in was five *thousand* dollars."

"That's the high roller buy-in for ranked players."

Jo looked beyond the two brothers. She could see others in the Sagebrush Room starting to sit down at square tables, each tented with a numbered plaque. Someone stood behind her now, waiting. She said, "How much is the top prize for the high rollers?"

Dan, the one with no eyebrows, said, "Fifty thousand is the top prize, thirty for second, fifteen for third, and seventy-five hundred each for fourth, fifth, and sixth."

"Is it a rule that you have to be ranked?"

"Well, no."

Jo reached into the plastic grocery bag and lifted out the five thousand dollars. She unbound the stack, then counted out the fifty one-hundred-dollar bills, laying each on the table. The brother with eyebrows lifted the bills and counted them again. When he was finished, Dan said, "You sure? This is a lot of money to gamble away."

"I was told gin rummy was a game of skill, not chance."

"That's if you're skillful." His mouth contorted into a thin-lipped smile.

Don chimed in, "You'll be playing against ranked professionals like Melvin Selkirk and Hugh Croft. The Mountain is here. He and others will eat you alive."

"The Mountain?"

"Timide Montagne, or Tim, but we call him The Mountain. He's a three-time champion."

The guy behind her in line said, "Go ahead and take her buy-in already."

Don looked at Jo, now both dyed eyebrows raised in a questioning expression, allowing her one more chance to back out.

She said nothing.

Dan slid the cash into a steel lockbox. "It's your money."

Jo looked past the entrance for a man who might look like a mountain, but then she realized that the name might not have any connection to the man's stature—the French *Montagne* meant mountain. She saw throngs of men standing in groups and some starting to sit at tables. "Are there any women in the high roller group?"

Dan and Don looked at each other. Finally, in unison, they said, "Sandy."

Dan said, "Sandy Webb. But I don't think she's ever made it to the top money."

Jo was given a player's number, fifty-six, and an eight-by-five scorecard.

Don said, "If you can win ten games before losing seven, you move on to the finals. Good luck." Or was it Dan?

Jo limped in her walking boot through the doors of the Sagebrush Room and looked around. The square tables were lined up in neat rows, corner to corner, to the back of the conference room. Games hadn't started, but some participants were already seated. Others stood around a banquet table set up with drinks. All wore masks that were occasionally lifted to sip coffee, drink water, or suck a Diet Pepsi through a straw. Just about all were men. Behind the drinks table were two tournament bracket charts. The smaller of the two was listed "High Rollers," and one side showed each participant's number and name. Number one was Hugh Croft. Number two was Tim Montagne. The last five numbers, from fifty-five to sixty, were blank. Jo could see that her first game would be against player number twelve—the Melvin Selkirk the twins had mentioned—at table forty-six. She found the table at the back of the room and sat down.

———

Melvin Selkirk slowly approached the table using a cane with four stubby crab-like legs. He stood over the table, looked at Jo, and then lifted his left hand in greeting. He spoke through a black cotton mask, "Usually, we shake hands before each game, but unfortunately, that is no longer permissible. Melvin Selkirk."

"Hi. Jo." She did not mention her unfortunate last name.

Melvin sat across from her and reached for a fresh deck of cards. Above his mask, the man wore thick glasses in black frames that fogged with each breath. His hair was thin and almost translucent, and the loose skin of his face looked like it could slough off his skull at any moment. Jo guessed his age in the mid to late eighties.

He slid the edge of his thumbnail through the dime-sized seal on the pack and withdrew the cards, leaving the two jokers behind. He shuffled neatly with both stacks flat on the table, flipping the opposing corners with the edge of his thumbs.

Jo said, "This is my first tournament. I'm not entirely sure how it goes."

Melvin looked up. "Your first and you've chosen to drop five thousand on the high roller group? I assume you know the rules of the *game?*" He emphasized the word game as though it were some golden idol he worshipped.

"Of course, I know how to play. I just don't know all the specific rules, like who deals first."

"We cut." Melvin lifted a stack of cards from the pile and showed Jo an eight.

Jo did the same and showed a ten. He said, "Your deal.

Ten cards to each player, then turn the next one face-side up to show the knock card. Then I draw the top card from the deck. We play to two hundred points." She knew all this, but maybe her perceived—and real—lack of experience would work to her advantage.

Jo took the cards and began her shuffle. The fresh cards were stiff and sifted together in clumps. Then, she couldn't bend the cards into a bridge to merge them together. Hugh had always shuffled, her one wrist usually shackled to the eye bolt in the dinette table.

Melvin said, "Let me show you," and held out his hand palm up. She gave him the cards. He showed what he'd done before with the corners flicking together and then a simple push to get them merged. He handed the cards back to Jo.

He said in a condescending tone, "I'd shuffle and deal, but that would be against the rules, so you'll just have to learn."

Jo shuffled like she'd been shown, dealt, and turned over the last card, a jack. She could knock with anything less than ten points. Then, as soon as play started, Melvin began to fidget. He flicked each discard with his thumb as he theatrically lifted it up, then set it down. When he touched the top card of the deck, he first slid it back and forth as though it might be stuck to the one beneath. Then he did something with his lips and mouth behind the mask that Jo thankfully couldn't see. She guessed his strategy was to show so many physical quirks that no one quirk would be a "tell" that gave away his position.

Melvin won the first hand, then lost the next two. By that time, his one good leg and foot had started shaking and tapping, and the whole cacophony of quirks created a huge distraction so that by the fourth game, she began to lose her ability to keep track of the cards and visualize his hand. And again, with the sucking and licking noise behind the mask. It was more than she could take. She excused herself to go to the bathroom. Locked in the stall, Jo wadded up pieces of toilet paper into two stems like cigarette butts. She stuffed each into her ears. She filled a paper cup with black coffee on her return and then joined Melvin. He said, "Welcome back."

Jo looked at him and replied, "What?"

He said again, louder, "Welcome back. My deal."

The makeshift earplugs helped, and his fidgeting became just background noise, like an ambulance on a city street or Bray's snoring. She could focus on her cards, which ones had been played, and the possible hand of her opponent. Initially, Jo only knew the ten cards dealt plus the knock card, so the hand she imagined Melvin holding included thirty-one cards, mostly arranged in her head as melds of the same kind. Then, as cards were picked up and discarded, his hand was whittled down to fewer possibilities until, after ten plays, she understood the wild cards that would help him and the likelihood that he would gin or knock before she did. Jo quickly understood that his playing was overly aggressive, and she thought it was because he underestimated her skill. She played defensively—as Hugh had to her—and won consistently.

Jo lost only one more hand before reaching the winning two hundred points. By then, Melvin was nearly hyperventilating, his fogged eyeglasses pushed up over his forehead so he could see. Then, against the tournament rules, he pulled his mask down to breathe more air through his nostrils. She did not complain.

After she'd won the game, Melvin thrust out his right hand, shook his fingers, and said, "Give me your card. The rules are that I sign your player's scorecard." Jo handed over the card, and he signed it without saying a word or looking up to meet Jo's eyes. He then turned and hobbled slowly away with his four-legged cane bracing his one bad leg.

Jo limped back to the registration desk where the twin brother with dyed eyebrows, Don, recorded her scorecard, gave her a new one, and told her the table number where her next game would take place. His brother Dan added, "Congratulations. It seems you haven't been eaten alive yet!"

Jo replied, "Not yet."

27

What a Douchebag

The day after Lucas had been assaulted, and that brave, very large man had stood up for him, Margo learned that one of the owners in the campervan group, a woman who went by the online handle of Crazycat, had seen a Thor Outlaw at the Sam's Town KOA, a casino for locals far off the strip. A woman who matched Jo's description—graying hair, medium height and weight—was seen leaving the motorcoach by herself, unescorted, and without a gun to her head. What clinched it was that the Thor Outlaw had Pennsylvania plates. Margo, Lucas, and the others, including Bray, packed up to move.

Compared to Circus Circus, the KOA was crowded. The only available spots were along Calamity Jane Drive, which backed against the stucco wall that divided the park from Boulder Highway, where trucks, muscle cars, and Harleys screamed toward Boulder City and Arizona at all hours of the day and night. The park had a few trees but was otherwise indistinguishable from the RV park they'd just left.

The campervan group met at happy hour beside a tiny dog

run the size of the drained pool nearby. Margo and Lucas were there early and watched as ladies came by with their poodles, cockapoos, Pomeranians—little pets that fit nicely into RVs—and waited while their dogs ran in circles, peed, and then pooped. Each pile was neatly picked up using plastic bags from a dispenser near a garbage receptacle with a sign showing a dog pooping and the message, "Pick it up or it will be returned to its rightful owner." One large dog, like a cross between a hound and a Great Dane—a dog that might require a horse trailer for travel—was across the run in four strides chasing a smaller dog one-sixteenth its size. Margo turned away when the mastodon finally squatted, too grossed out to look. By that time, the meeting had started.

Crazycat stood in front of the group, maybe twenty in attendance, with a park map. Crazycat was Black, the only one in the group, and possibly the only person of color Margo had seen in an RV park, period. She stood about five-foot tall, five-foot-five if you included her afro. To Margo, nothing about her screamed crazy, other than she was possibly crazy to stay in an RV park half-filled with racist Trumpers.

When she finally spoke, her accent was British or Australian or something, which explained a lot.

Crazycat pointed out where the Outlaw was parked, closer to the casino on Rootin' Tootin' Drive at spot number 593, and Margo wondered if over five hundred spots really existed. It seemed unimaginable, but the map held up by Crazycat looked like an elaborate Chinese checkerboard.

Bray then stood up to organize the group. He divided them into teams to watch the motorcoach and rotate every two hours. No one was to do anything other than watch. The abductor was considered armed and dangerous, and Bray did not want anyone to get hurt on his account. There was nodding in the group while beers were consumed. Someone had prepared a cheese tray with each cube speared through with toothpicks. Members of the group went up one at a time, keeping their six-foot distance.

Margo did not like cheese trays and did not like taking directions from Bray, who she thought was a real douchebag. While his heavyset friend had saved poor Lucas, Bray, like almost everyone else, just lifted his phone to video the encounter. Regardless, she offered to take the first watch with Lucas. Bray asked for each person's phone number so he could create a group text.

Margo sat with Lucas on a bench with a view of the Thor Outlaw. Nearby was the swimming pool that was closed and drained due to the pandemic. They kept an eye on the motorcoach but also the two teen skateboarders who had taken advantage of the drained pool. One skateboarder stood at the lip and then dropped down along the deep-end wall. He came up the opposite side, then grinded his board along the coping. The other followed but shot up two feet above the coping, clutched the bottom of the board, and twisted in a one-eighty to skate back down. The trick failed at the last moment when the kid lost his footing, and he went knee first into the downward slope of the pool, sliding on padded knees to the bottom. Lucas said loud enough for the kid to hear, "Slam!"

Then, a woman sitting nearby whispered, "Where is that boy's mother?" Margo thought the mother was likely deep in the casino, half drunk, and a hundred dollars down.

Margo looked closely at the kid as he lifted his board and walked back to the pool's edge through the shallow end. She could see the intense concentration on his face, as though skateboarding was more than just tricks. Lucas was looking too, and Margo could see the same serious expression—that maybe he was remembering something from home, something nostalgic. Seemingly reading her mind, Lucas said, "Maybe we should drive back to La Jolla after this, take a break for a while."

She let that comment sit without immediately responding. What came to her mind was the realization that she was happy. They'd been having fun traveling the West, doing the Instagram thing, and chasing down the abducted woman. She wanted to continue and felt let down. But maybe they did need a break to just test things. It was like with one of her boyfriends in high school. Margo had gone out with a guy named Reed, whom she truly adored. But then, after a few months, she doubted herself and wondered if he was all she'd imagined him to be. Then, to test her doubts, she broke up with him and dated another guy named Hunter. Hunter was a dud in comparison. She tried to get back with Reed, but by then, he'd moved on to someone named Charmayne or Champagne. Maybe going back home would be a way to see if what she and Lucas had was something real, that maybe Lucas needed to go out with a Hunter—so to speak. Margo said, "Hey, sure, if you want."

———

A half hour later, she and Lucas saw Jo come down the path from the casino. Margo recognized her from when they'd barged into the motorcoach. Jo walked with confidence, looking straight ahead and seemingly with purpose. She casually opened the door of the unlocked motorcoach and stepped in.

Jo did not look or act like someone who'd been abducted, and now Margo started to second-guess (or was it third-guess?)

her thoughts as to whether or not the woman had really been taken against her will. It was all so confusing. Margo texted the group, "Jo came from the casino and entered the coach. No sign of man."

Bray texted back, "Stand down and stand by," like this was some military exercise.

To Lucas, she said, "What a douchebag."

28

Jo Gets the Real Dope on Hugh

Hugh was sitting on the leather couch when she walked up the stairs into the motorcoach. He had a full water glass and was eating a bowl of Fiber One despite it being late afternoon. Jo could hear that his breathing was less labored and thought that maybe he was over the hump and getting better.

He asked, "How did it go?"

Jo unstrapped her blue face mask. Whatever he had, she most likely had it now. She paused before answering. The day had been long and stressful, and she'd played over a hundred hands of gin rummy against only men. They were the type of clubby guys who assumed a kind of condescension in the face of a woman they'd never seen before, guys who thought it generous to point out any perceived mistakes and offer helpful tips. *Mansplainers.* Most played too aggressively, like Melvin Selkirk, confident they could easily beat the novice woman. She used their arrogance against them—gave away nothing they could use and held cards that could be laid off in a knock. She'd beaten nearly all of the men. "I qualified."

Hugh smiled, beamed. "Fantastic. Let me see your results."

The scores of each game were online, and Jo helped Hugh access them on his smartphone. He studied the results like a parent with a child's report card.

"You beat Selkirk in your first game. Marvelous. He's so distracting."

"I stuffed toilet paper in my ears and stopped looking at him. By the way, do you have earplugs?"

"Yes, I'll get them for you later. He thinks all that fidgeting keeps him from showing anything, but what he doesn't know is that he has one significant tell—he sorts the cards in his hand from lowest to highest. When you play him again, use it."

Hugh kept looking. "You lost to The Mountain. You wouldn't be the first. I've lost to him many times before. How did that go?"

Jo had played The Mountain in the fifth game. The man was anything but what his name implied. The Mountain was, in fact, diminutive. Jo didn't think he was small enough to classify as a dwarf or little person, but he was close to it, like a jockey. The Mountain had walked up to the card table with a thick padded seat, like a booster chair for a four-year-old, and then hopped up to meet her at eye level. The man wore turquoise rings on every slim finger, a gold nugget wristwatch heavy enough to build muscle, and a gambler-style cowboy hat pulled low to his eyebrows. Throughout the game, he gave no words of advice or condescending tips. He said nothing and gave nothing away, and what he did say was in a high-pitched French accent. She thought The Mountain was among the few players who took her seriously. "He squeaked that one out. I think the score was two-hundred-six to one-hundred-sixty-seven. So who is he?"

"Lives in town and works for one of the Cirque du Soleil shows now, but used to be a professional stand-in for child actors."

"There's such a thing?"

"From what I've heard, it's very restrictive to have a child on set, let alone two—child labor laws, school, and all that. So, apparently, the better approach is to hire a small person. Anyway, he'll have qualified for the finals to be played over the next two days. So will fourteen others. Now, the rules change somewhat. Tomorrow, you'll play ten games, then five the next. Everyone plays everyone once, so you'll play Selkirk and The Mountain again and a few others you haven't faced yet. Each game now goes to three hundred points. Luck will play a part, but at this level, very, very little."

"How is the winner determined?"

"Games won. Whoever wins the most games wins the tournament. One year, The Mountain won the tournament without losing a game. I've never done that. Typically, the winner can lose only two games."

Jo sat down at the dinette. The metal eyebolt still extended from the table, and she touched the cold steel and felt its smooth edges. She'd been shackled to it that first week of the abduction, eating microwaved food and playing cards. It seemed like last month or last year. Who was she now? She didn't know or maybe didn't care. In a twisted way, she'd already moved on. The tournament was now all she thought about—the excitement of winning.

———

She lay in the back room with the door unlatched. Jo was now free to do whatever she wanted, and what she wanted was rest for the next day.

In the middle of the night, she woke to Hugh coughing. She put in the earplugs he'd given her and went back to sleep. When she woke in the morning, Hugh was still sleeping, and she left the motorcoach an hour later without waking him.

Don and Dan were at the registration desk, both now with yellow AGRA polo shirts. Dan, the one without eyebrows, was using Lysol wipes to clean the BIC pens from the water glass labeled "Dirty" and then place them carefully without human touch into the other water glass labeled "Clean." Don, the one with eyebrows, said, "Congratulations, Josephine, you're now ranked."

"You can call me Jo. What do you mean, ranked?"

"You get ten points for each win in the qualifiers and two hundred points for making it to the next round. So, your point rank is three hundred."

"What do most of these high rollers have?"

Dan looked down at a list of competitors. He said, "The next lowest is fifteen thousand, three hundred and forty. The Mountain has just over forty thousand. A man named Hugh Croft has the highest with close to sixty thousand, but he didn't make it this year."

Don's blue mask had slipped down below his nose, and Jo could see his unshaven gray hairs that did not match the color of his toupee. "Points themselves won't give a player any advantage. It's just for show and tell. So, good luck!"

Jo took her scorecard and went directly to the assigned table. She sat and waited for her opponent to show up before the tournament officially began.

Ten minutes later, a woman sat down. She said, "You must be Josephine. I'm Sandy."

For a moment, Jo was startled. She'd heard there was another woman, but they hadn't crossed paths. Sandy was older but stunning. Her hair was colored blonde, long and pulled back from her face with a barrette. Her earrings were diamonds, and she wore two long strands of pearls over a midnight-blue dress with a square neckline. Jo wore the same dress from the day before and hadn't worn makeup since God knows when. She felt like a schlub in comparison. Jo said, "I'd heard there was one other woman."

Sandy shuffled the cards with manicured nails that matched the color of her lipstick. "I don't know why it's such a boys' club. You won't find the same at bridge tournaments, and even poker games seem to have more gals competing. Sometimes, I like the attention of being one of the few women, but other times I feel like a lone exotic fish in a very small aquarium."

Jo laughed. She cut the cards first and showed a two. Sandy cut a face card, then dealt.

They played almost casually and talked. Sandy had learned gin rummy as a child, but it was her husband who introduced her to tournaments. He was a doctor, fifteen years older, and they planned each year's vacations around going to tournaments. She said, "What am I going to do, sit on a beach for ten hours a day? I'd go mad." She'd been a widow now for three years and explained how her husband had tragically died while flying a small airplane he owned. She used the phrase "augered in." Jo imagined the twisting plunge of an ice auger and thought it a striking visual metaphor. She laughed, then apologized for laughing. Sandy said, "Don't be. It was devastating, but I'm certainly glad I wasn't his co-pilot at the time." Then she asked, "How did you find us? I've heard that you're an excellent player but new to tournaments."

Jo had never been good at outright lying. When she was a child, her mother always knew and could just read the lie on her face. She'd never needed to lie as an adult. She never cheated on Bray or misused a credit card or drank copiously in private—none of those things. But withholding bits of information was as natural as combing her hair. She said, "Do you know a man named Hugh Croft?"

"Yes, he taught you?"

"Yes, we met at a campground. We were both traveling in RVs. We spent a good deal of time together just playing. He told me about this tournament and encouraged me to enter." Saying that, she almost believed its intimations.

"My husband and I used to play Hugh and Florence, his late wife, in the partner's tournament. Sad about her."

"She died of cancer?"

"Maybe, but she was in remission. The last time I saw her, she was in a wheelchair—recuperating from hip surgery but happy as a clam. Then I heard she'd taken her own life. Pills. I can't imagine her situation was that dire. We talked two or three times a year, and I think we were friendly enough so that I'd have known."

Jo let that knowledge settle, and she concentrated on the game. While they'd talked, Sandy built up a forty-point lead. Jo had been playing more casually, and now she needed to *focus*. Toward the middle of the game, Jo figured out two things about Sandy. She optimistically held on to face cards too long and tensed her shoulders when close to a gin. Jo was able to take advantage of that twice and knock first. Once, she caught Sandy holding eighteen points.

During their final hand, Jo asked if Hugh seemed odd in any way.

"Well, Hugh was always doting on Florence and overly

controlling. He ordered for her at restaurants and often corrected her grammar in public. It could be uncomfortable at times. You could tell he adored her, but he also never let Florence out of his sight. It was like he kept her prisoner, and I got the feeling he was okay with her confinement to a wheelchair after the hip replacement. Quite honestly, I think she was ready to leave him. My husband was a psychiatrist, and Hugh was a *psychologist*, and there was an underlying combination of envy and defensiveness on his part. You know, like a medical doctor and a chiropractor. Hugh felt he knew as much about the drugs psychiatrists prescribed as my husband, and he'd try to one-up him on that level. My husband hated all that, thought Hugh was a bit of a know-it-all. And he felt Hugh maybe knew *too* much, that possibly the suicide wasn't quite how it appeared."

Jo was positioned to gin and held only a four that she knew Sandy needed. Jo drew a king from the deck and discarded it.

Hugh had told her he'd given his wife pills in some kind of mercy killing after the cancer had metastasized. But what Sandy suggested rang true. Jo said, "So, he possibly killed her?"

"That's what my husband thought. I personally haven't a clue, but I've no reason to believe Florence was ever deeply depressed. Then again, you never know. And to be clear, it's all speculation and gossip."

Jo smiled. She wasn't a big gossiper, but she'd heard and passed on plenty in her business as a wedding photographer. What she knew about gossip was that much of it was true or at least held a kernel of truth. She realized Hugh had probably made up the story about Florence's recurrence to make it more palatable or understandable to her—and to make himself look compassionate. It seemed probable that he killed his wife because she'd decided to leave him.

Jo picked up Sandy's discard and casually said, "Gin," then laid down her cards. "And game."

———

Jo won her next six games before playing Melvin Selkirk again. The man hobbled over on his four-posted cane and sat down. His mask had already been pulled beneath his nose. He looked at her without saying a word and then unwrapped a new pack of cards. He began to shuffle, and she counted the number of times. When he stopped at five, she said, "If it's okay, I'd like to do my own shuffle." She knew it was in the rules that she could do a reshuffle and knew from *How To Win at Gin* that, statistically, it took seven shuffles to randomize a deck. He loudly slapped the cards down before her. She shuffled three times. Afterward, Melvin shuffled twice more. He won the cut and dealt.

His quirky fidgeting and noisemaking commenced, and Jo inserted her earbuds, two stubs of bright orange foam. Melvin watched her do it and said nothing.

Hugh had told her about the man's tell, that he held his cards in rank order. The knowledge turned out to be game-changing and almost like cheating. She knew when he held face cards early in the game and the approximate rank of any card he picked from the deck. She knew his strategy in three discards and could visualize his hand in seven. She beat him mercilessly.

After she won the twelfth hand, and the game, he abruptly stood up and hobbled off. When Jo complained to Dan and Don afterward—Selkirk never signed her scorecard—Dan said, "He does that sometimes," then signed the card himself.

She saw The Mountain throughout the day, each time sitting up straight in his booster seat and looking intently at his cards. His style was the polar opposite of Selkirk's and probably a lot easier to accomplish without all that lip-smacking and fidgeting. She wondered if the finger rings were worn for distraction, like fishing lures, but knew his short stature was a distraction in itself. Hugh had said he worked for Cirque du Soleil. Rings were probably a thing among circus people.

She won the rest of her games that day without playing The Mountain and left with a perfect score.

———

Hugh was back in bed when Jo arrived at the motorcoach. He'd relapsed and his breathing was again labored.

She said, "You need a doctor."

Hugh ignored her and asked, "How did it go?"

"I won all ten games."

She opened up the scores on his smartphone, and he quickly scanned the results. It was hard for Hugh to smile, but Jo could see the excitement in his eyes. "You beat Sally . . . but . . . she isn't as good . . . as she thinks. You beat Selkirk . . . badly. He . . . had to be . . . furious." Hugh made a wide-mouthed smile as he sucked air. "You'll play The Mountain . . . . tomorrow . . . for prize money."

"Is there anything you can tell me about him?"

"Only that he's good . . . and he'll not underestimate you."

His water glass sat empty, and she went to refill it. She said, "Do you need some aspirin?"

"Yes. Take the key to the medicine cabinet. The aspirin bottle is on the bottom shelf." He pulled a ring of keys from his pants pocket and set it down on the table. With his finger, he singled out the smaller cabinet key.

Jo limped into the bathroom and filled the glass from the tap. Opposite the sink, she unlocked and opened a cabinet the size of a small closet to search for aspirin. What she saw then were prescription drug containers, twenty or more that lined each shelf. A few she knew were for ailments like constipation, cold relief, and stomach pain, but others were narcotics like Xanax, Percocet, and fentanyl. Other drugs had names she didn't recognize, like Polixin and Abilify. The cabinet contained enough pharmaceuticals to kill a dozen wives.

Hugh had abducted her, and if he wanted to resume playing in gin rummy tournaments, he would need her dead and silent. Jo knew she should flee, just walk out of the coach and keep walking until she found a security officer at the casino. But then the thought of leaving the tournament now when she was so close to winning seemed inconceivable. It was only one more day, and Hugh wouldn't do anything while living vicariously through her success. And he couldn't do much to her while sick with COVID. She decided to stay in the toy box and finish the tournament. Only five more games were to be played the next morning, with the prize money awarded that afternoon.

Jo found the bottle of aspirin and shook two into her hand.

29

Facing the Diminutive Mountain

Dan handed Jo a scorecard with the table number listed for her first game of the last day. He said, "You'll play The Mountain in your third game."

Don asked, "So, this really is your first tournament, right?"

"Yes." She sensed Don looking at her from the neck down. Jo felt self-conscious. She'd worn the same lime-green dress for three days now and still hadn't taken a shower since the abduction. Though she couldn't smell it herself, she probably stunk. Jo pushed the edges of her hair back behind her ears, then smoothed out the fabric over her torso. She added, "This is my first."

Dan looked up. "Where did you learn?"

She didn't see any reason to withhold. "Hugh Croft."

"Well, you learned from the best. Where is he anyway? I've never seen him miss an Open."

"He got sick with the virus and couldn't make it."

Dan asked, "Is he doing okay?"

Jo wasn't sure. When she left the coach that morning, Hugh was still in bed. He'd sat up when she came in. She thought his breathing had gotten worse and told him to call a doctor. He said, "Okay," and that one word seemed to draw out his last bit of strength. Jo knew he wouldn't call a doctor, that he wasn't finished with Jo or the tournament or whatever he planned to do next. But he wouldn't do anything until the tournament was over. She said, "I'll check on you after the last game, and before the awards." He squeezed out one more, "Okay," and then coughed up phlegm that he spat into a tissue. He looked down at the tissue-enfolded phlegm, a hunk of moss-green goo. She knew he had a stash of antibiotics in the medicine cabinet and assumed he'd already taken a dose.

She answered Dan's question, "He's still sick."

Don said, "I'm sorry. I hope he gets better soon."

Dan added, "He'll be proud you've gotten this far."

Jo said, "Thanks," and walked into the Sagebrush Room.

Her opponent was already seated and waiting—another older white man, this one with a tightly clenched jaw. And as the game progressed, the man's clenched jaw turned into a grinding of teeth. By the fifth hand, Jo could hear the man grinding harder when he had a painful decision to make, like which one of the un-melded cards he could safely discard. Then he'd hold his breath after discarding until Jo picked it up or drew from the deck. She imagined his teeth behind the mask, ground to little stubs like tiny-sized Chiclets. She beat him in twelve hands with fifty points to spare. The man did not say one word the whole time, which suited Jo fine.

She won her next game, then sat waiting for The Mountain.

He came with his booster seat seconds before Dan or Don announced the commencement of the third game. In addition to his turquoise finger rings and cowboy hat, the man now wore an ascot tucked into an open-collared pink shirt.

As she shuffled the stiff new cards, Jo asked him a question. "I hear you work for the circus in town. Can I ask what you do?"

The Mountain looked up from his cards and said in his French accent, "It's the Cirque du Soleil. Not a circus." He pronounced "circus" using his best mock-American accent. "I'm, in fact, one of the dancers. I play a lizard." *Leezald.*

Jo smiled behind her mask and said, "I'm sure you do it well."

He forced a smile "*Oui!*"

Jo cut the cards to reveal a seven. The Mountain cut a king and dealt.

He played aggressively, moving toward the gin in almost every hand. Because of the twenty-five-point bonus, Jo knew that one gin hand was worth three knock hands, but she decided to play defensively and wait it out. He ginned four times against Jo's one gin and five knocks. Halfway through the game, Jo was down thirty-eight points to his one-hundred-eighty-five. She needed to catch up.

Jo felt the cards fall her way with a few completed melds and several combinations. She began to play aggressively. She held on to possible melds of face cards early in the game and threw off lower-ranked cards that might help in a knock but might also risk her gin. She ginned the next two hands and was just shy of two hundred points. He knocked the next hand, and now both were tied at one hundred ninety-nine.

Jo called a break.

The bathroom was empty, with all eight stall doors opened inward. Jo sat on the toilet for minutes after she finished, just thinking. One hundred and one points remained. She only needed three gin hands to win. She needed, though, to be sensitive to the cards dealt. If the cards turned bad, she needed to react quickly and defensively, or he'd eat her alive. She washed her hands thoroughly and splashed cold water on her face before returning to the conference room.

When she approached The Mountain, a cluster of people were now surrounding the table, Don and Dan among them. They saw her coming and a few stepped aside to let her pass. Their game now had an audience.

She sat down across from The Mountain, who looked up but did not meet her eyes. It felt like he focused on one spot in the middle of her forehead, one blemish or wrinkle. It made her self-conscious, like she'd missed something when washing her face—or she was just getting old and pruneish. Then he cracked his slender knuckles, and that offended her on some level, like a belch or a fart. But it was not the kind of bodily function that would necessitate an apology. He was just trying to rattle her cage . . . again.

She resolved to beat the little man.

The Mountain dealt the first hand, and Jo felt the cards continue to fall her way. She ginned the next two hands to put her up sixty-eight points and thought she could win with one more gin. She heard whispering from the audience that had now grown in size. She distinctly heard, "She might beat him." Jo suppressed a smile.

After ten discards into the next hand, she was able to really know his cards and knew he was playing for the knock. She held two un-melded cards that added up to well over the knock card of eight, so she had no choice but to continue drawing from the deck. Then he did knock and caught her with twelve points. He knocked again early in the next game. Then he ginned, and they were nearly tied. The next winning gin hand would take the game.

Trying to draw his attention from the cards, Jo asked, "What is it like . . . being such a small man?" It was an impertinent question, but she added, "I imagine it's like being a woman."

"How do you mean?"

"It's a men's club, and so far, they've all looked down on me as though I'm small."

He thought for a moment, then leaned over and spoke quietly, "Yes, I very much understand. But I don't think small. I like to think big—big watch, big hat, big rings." He smiled and held up his fingers, then continued. "It's not *talking* big that I refer to. People use the term Napoleon Complex for one who's small and talks big. Yes? Though I understand that Napoleon was very much normal in size at that time. No, I have big thoughts and big dreams. I'm a fine actor and dancer, and an excellent gin rummy player. My size gives me a slight edge against taller, overconfident men who are plentiful in this room. Your femininity gives you a similar edge that I'm sure you've witnessed. But you, too, can think big."

"Do you think I'm an excellent player?" Part of her thought she'd asked the question in jest, and part knew she didn't.

He spoke honestly. "Yes, you're nearly *voyante*—how you say, clairvoyant. But that's not enough. I'm very much better."

It was The Mountain's deal, but he'd stopped shuffling. Jo asked, "How so?"

"Because you, like others, think I'm small. See, you think you know my strategies because you unwittingly think I have limited, small ideas. But you need to understand that I spoon-feed you the strategies you think you know, then react when you play your counter strategy. Intuitively, you might play a defensive style when you think I'm playing aggressively, and I would probably continue to play aggressively, but in a way that understands your defensive game. Does that make sense to you?"

"No. And I don't think you're small."

"But, of course you do—didn't you just ask me what it was like to be a small man?"

Now, she was deeply confused. "I still don't understand."

"That's, of course, why I'm a better gin player than you."

The man was arrogant. Possibly more arrogant than the other men she'd played, but she sensed he was not overconfident. The little man knew exactly what he was capable of. She asked, "So, what do I do?"

"Think big! Try to see beyond your current situation and do something unexpected. It's hard to comprehend, I know, but you will get to that place."

Their last hand was simple—the knock card an ace, and they'd have to play until one of them ginned. Her dealt hand was good—one complete meld and two possibles—and over the successive discards, she began to visualize his hand. By the tenth discard, Jo was certain he would gin with either of the two un-melded cards she held—a six of clubs or a two of diamonds. On the thirteenth discard, Jo drew from the deck. The nine matched the two in her hand, and the inevitable decision had to be made. She discarded the six.

He picked it up and called, "Gin." He laid down his hand. He did have a two, but it was melded with a straight. She'd chosen the wrong card to discard. Hugh would have said that she'd been outplayed.

The audience applauded politely.

The Mountain held out his small hand to shake, a breach of pandemic protocol, but she took it. He said, "You played well." *Pla-dad oo-ell.*

Jo won both the next game and the final game without the accompaniment of an audience. Those spectators had followed The Mountain, who finished undefeated.

Second place came with the prize money of thirty thousand dollars to be awarded that afternoon. Jo had never won actual money at anything. She felt elated and wanted to tell Hugh right then.

She limped out of the Sagebrush Room, past Dan and Don, who were now feverishly compiling scores, down the escalator, past the TGI Fridays, and through the side doors that led to the RV park.

Immediately outside, she ran into Bray. He was wearing his favorite T-shirt, the one with the imprint "Hoptimistic."

He pulled down his mask and said, "Jo?"

She looked at him. She'd been gone for only two weeks, but it seemed longer, and Bray seemed almost a stranger to her now. He stood there, his eyes wide, his mouth open and teeth apart as though ready to say something else—once *she* said something.

It wasn't what she wanted. Right then, she couldn't say what she did want, but it wasn't Bray.

Jo dodged past her stunned husband and walked quickly toward the RV park.

She heard Bray behind her say again, "Jo." But he didn't follow.

30

Judge Judy Makes Her Ruling

Hugh lay in his bed, focusing on each breath, the air moving through his trachea like a thick malt through a thin straw. Coughing helped when he could dislodge the yellow-green phlegm from deep at the bottom of his lungs. Then, for fifteen minutes or so, he could breathe more easily until the phlegm began to settle again, and his lungs began to feel small, the size of walnuts. In addition, he knew he had a high fever, which brought on oppressive fatigue. He barely got up to walk to the bathroom or refill his water glass. The fever produced chills, and he used the bedside remote control to turn off the air conditioning even though it was still in the nineties outside. What he really wanted for the chills and his lungs was a warm bath, but the motorcoach only had a shower, and he felt too weak to stand for that long. He lay in bed with the satellite television playing a marathon screening of *Judge Judy* episodes. It was difficult to simply follow the back and forth of each petty argument.

He had a whole medicine cabinet full of drugs he'd

accumulated over the years—enough opioids to supply an addict for months, psychotropic drugs to help with depression or even schizophrenia, and a wide selection of antibiotics. He collected drugs like some people collected rare bottles of bourbon they never drank. Or maybe it was a hoarding thing like people who bought toilet paper at the first news of the pandemic. Whatever. He'd bought the costly drugs mostly online with forged prescriptions, and the medications made him feel secure, as though he could control any behavioral or physical issues that arose—for him or anyone else. He never went to hospitals and wouldn't now. He'd taken antibiotics two days prior for the possibility of pneumonia, but they didn't seem to help. The one drug he thought *would* help was prednisone, a steroid to reduce the inflammation in his lungs, but he did not have that very common drug.

His thoughts drifted to Josephine, who was just outside his door, probably sitting at the dinette table and waiting to return to the casino for the awards ceremony. She'd lost to The Mountain but had finished second overall. He was proud of her and thought she'd be more proud of herself, but Josephine seemed rattled or sad. She asked him again to see a doctor. He said he would, but was sure Josephine knew that was a lie.

Josephine's instincts with the game were nearly perfect, much better than those of Florence, who had rarely excelled outside of playing as partners. He'd known it the first time he watched her through the binoculars—saw it in her eyes. She was an observer and smart with an almost telepathic insight. At first, he'd only wanted someone to play cards with, assuage his boredom, and sharpen his skills, but her excellence at the tournament was unexpected. He imagined her games with Selkirk, the weird bastard being one-upped by a newbie player, a woman no less. He imagined her sitting across from The

Mountain, the man's small stature, rings, and other clothing accessories a distraction like buzzing flies.

Games had always been at the center of Hugh's life, and their importance was something he'd explored. He suspected every psychologist delved into their own psyche to find the early causes of personality traits, and Hugh was no different. He knew his fascination with games had started when his grandmother and grandfather died in a car accident, and he and his mother went to live with her aunt. They moved from a small town outside Charlotte to Richmond, where they knew no one. Hugh was four at the time and hadn't yet started school. His unwed mother was just nineteen with no job or husband or high school diploma. It was there that the first game started. The game was called Imagine That. The aunt said, "Hugh, we're going to play a game called Imagine That. The idea is to imagine that your mother is really your sister, and wouldn't it be fun to have an older sister?" The game taught him that he was good at deception. He learned to lie fluently like a child learns their first language.

That was his earliest memory of playing a game, one conceived to cover up an unwanted pregnancy and a bastard child. But then regular board and card games became central to his new home. Like everyone else, they had a black and white television, and they watched the sitcoms of the day and Ed Sullivan on Sunday nights, but more time was spent playing Parcheesi, Monopoly, checkers, and even chess. The first card game he learned was Go Fish, but the second game was a simple version of gin where you play one hand until someone ginned. As he got older, they played a version called Five Hundred, where much of the game was played with an open hand, each person playing off the other's melds. He didn't learn actual gin rummy until college, when each point was worth a dime, and games could go on all night.

Even his profession of psychology turned into a game of sorts—find the dysfunction, understand the roots of that dysfunction, and then work to change the dysfunctional behaviors. He knew if he could subtly control the discourse through precise questioning, he could control the outcome or at least push the client toward that outcome. He'd done it with Florence's husband, asking him about his wife's personality faults and what he thought were the causes so when Hugh asked to work with Florence alone, the man was ecstatic to be released of any culpability. Then Hugh turned his marriage into a game of sorts. He could enjoy and prolong his marriage if he could control the options Flo had to involve herself in things that could be distractions. It's why he never wanted her children to visit or for them to own pets. He'd mostly won at that game.

He looked up at the television. A man in his thirties, a nice kid with neatly combed hair, stood before Judge Judy. He wore a white short-sleeved permanent-press shirt, a loose-fitting tie, and no sports coat. He was complaining about the bills his girlfriend had left him when she moved out. She'd taken his credit card and ordered many things online that he hadn't known about, and now she refused to pay him back. Judge Judy asked to see the list and pointed out a few seemingly frivolous items: a leather jacket—two hundred and fifty-three dollars, iPhone Airpods Pro—two hundred and forty-nine dollars, Chanel Chance perfume—eighty-two dollars. Judge Judy looked up at the woman standing in the courtroom. "I buy my fragrance at Walgreens. I think it's called Eternity, and pay half that, and it *lasts* an eternity." The bailiff laughed at that comment along with everyone else in the courtroom except for the accused woman. She stood there with her arms crossed, wearing the just-discussed leather jacket and likely the Chanel perfume. Judge Judy asked her why she needed eighty-two-dollar perfume. The woman ignored the question and reiterated that her ex-boyfriend had given her permission to use the credit card. Hugh decided right then that he hated this woman, and he thought it was because of the way she stood, all smart and acting cocky toward Judge Judy like it was her word against her boyfriend's. It brought to mind Florence and her contemptible divorce lawyer.

The anger welled up in him, and his mind raced to how he could hypothetically kill the woman on TV without anyone knowing. He sipped some water and tried to calm down. He didn't like to let his thoughts run away like that, and he'd disciplined himself over the years to think more evenly. He instinctively knew that it was the virus causing this lack of self-control.

He heard a knock on the door but ignored it. Then someone opened the door that Jo had left unlocked.

31

Then Came Uly – Episode #2

Uly opened the door of the Outlaw. He was holding his handgun, the Colt snub-nosed .32 revolver he'd bought ages ago from a pawnbroker on Sahara near the Strip. He'd bought it just days after being robbed at the bar by a kid in a ski mask who got away with the bills in his register, about five hundred dollars. He'd never fired the thing but kept it clean and in working order. The cold metal was something to touch, and he wondered if feeling it was genetic and atavistic like holding his penis. It was a fucked-up thought that he put out of his mind as he walked up the stairs and into the motorcoach. Uly had the small gun sagging in the front pocket of his sweatpants. He wasn't going to kill anyone, but his father had always said, *forewarned is forearmed*—so he was armed. He'd listen to Jo and the man, the abductor, as Jim Bronson would. Talk to both with measured and nonconfrontational words. Get Jo out of there.

It wasn't supposed to go like that. Jo was seen earlier leaving the motorcoach and walking into the casino. They'd had a simple plan. Bray would stay by the casino entrance and wait for his wife to walk out. He'd make sure that she didn't go back to the motorcoach, and he'd find out what was going on. If she *had* been abducted, they'd call the police. But when Jo walked from the casino, she didn't stop after seeing Bray. She bolted right past him and entered the Thor Outlaw.

The twenty or so people in the campervan group met right after that in the pool area and listened to Bray's plan. The skateboarders had not yet arrived, so it was quiet as Bray talked. His plan was to descend on the motorcoach as a group, call out the man inside, explain to him why abducting his wife had been wrong and unlawful, and that he should seek professional help. Bray had already researched a local helpline for those in a mental health crisis.

Uly stood near the front while Bray spoke and said, "Like an intervention?"

"It's possible that we could reason with him."

The obvious came up, and Crazycat, with her British or whatever accent, was the one who said it out loud, "This guy could be dangerous. He could have a gun." *This goy could be dangerous. E coowd av a guun.*

Someone else said, "We should call the police."

A man with wraparound sunglasses and a tan sun hat with side flaps said, "The police won't come unless there's a disturbance or some evidence of foul play. They'll just tell us to go home."

Uly had brought his gun and considered keeping that to himself, but then, in all fairness, these people were entitled to know and maybe walk away. He said, "I have my handgun. I won't use it, but just in case . . ."

Uly thought there'd be gasps of horror, but another man in the back said, "I've got a gun, too."

Then, a woman beside him said, "I've got bear spray." She was no more than five feet tall and nearly seventy. It then occurred to Uly that people who lived nomadic lives in campervans might be concerned for their safety.

Another woman he couldn't see said, "I've got a gun, also."

Bray stood in front of the group, silent and stunned. He took off his sun hat and scratched his head. "I'm a pacifist and believe in nonviolence. I think we can all just leave the guns and bear spray in our campervans. I don't want anyone to get hurt."

The other man with the gun said, "This isn't a civil rights movement. The guy abducted your wife, possibly at gunpoint. And personally, *I* don't want to get hurt."

Uly could see heads nodding in agreement.

Bray was losing control of the situation and now stood silently. He looked beat down.

Uly said out loud to the group, "I'll go into the motorcoach and get Jo to come outside. And I'll try to talk with the man."

He stepped up the four stairs of the motorcoach. Lucas was behind him with the GoPro clipped to the bill of his trucker cap. Uly knocked on the door. No one answered. He tried the door and found it unlocked.

Jo was sitting alone at the dinette table with her face in her hands, crying. She did not look up.

"Jo?" he asked.

She didn't acknowledge him, but her sobs began to subside like she was trying to pull herself together.

"I've been helping Bray search for you. My name is Ulysses." He added, "Walker." He touched her shoulder and she flinched. "Where's the man who abducted you? Is he in the back?"

She looked up then, her face puffy and crimson. "He's dying."

"He's dying? How?"

"COVID. He's got the virus, and he can't breathe. He won't go to a hospital." The woman was not wearing a mask, and Uly touched his to make sure it covered his nose and mouth securely.

He could hear the muffled sound of a television coming from the back. "I think you need to go outside. Bray is there and you'll be safe."

Jo wiped away her tears. She was still looking at him but didn't move. She said, "What have I gotten myself into?"

"I don't know."

Uly paused, then continued, speaking louder so his voice penetrated the blue paper of his mask. "What I do know is that sometimes situations can seem like traps you can't escape. I felt trapped in college when I didn't know what I wanted to do, and I knew that what I was learning was all crap. I was trapped for a time, living in my parent's basement while my father lay dying of cancer, my life on hold. And even after he died, I felt trapped in a vision of my dying father's expectations. It was like I had to be this or that, make money, and fall into line with the other ants in the colony. I did that and then felt trapped by my business. I now think I subconsciously drove it into the ground so I could escape. And I think that maybe I sabotaged my marriage for the same reason. What I know about that trapped feeling is you think there are no alternatives, that the life you're living is like a rat's maze that you just need to navigate through. But the reality is that the world is bigger than the maze you're in."

He thought his speech was very Bronson-like, simple

reflections that revealed a sense of humanity and compassion.

Jo was still looking at him and listening. She didn't answer, but he had her attention. She then picked up a pack of cigarettes off the dinette table and reached for a lighter.

Her movements startled him. Uly's father had died from cancer-causing cigarettes—unfiltered Lucky Strikes. He said, "Those will kill you." It was an aside, a distraction, and he shouldn't have brought it up.

Jo looked at him for what seemed minutes, then calmly placed the unlit cigarette and lighter back on the table.

Now, he'd lost his train of thought, and the speech had sounded so meaningful. He took some time to regain his composure, then continued, "One of the most important things I've learned in life is . . ." he paused dramatically, "you can just leave. You can escape those cages and mazes and just walk out. And that's all you need to do right now. Just walk out."

She stood then, left the cigarettes behind, and walked past Lucas filming the scene. She stepped down and through the door.

Uly could hear clapping outside for the released abductee, a hero's welcome. It almost made him weep.

Uly walked further back into the motorcoach and stood just to the side of the bedroom door. He turned the handle and opened it slowly, half expecting a gun to go off at any moment. Nothing happened and he stepped into the doorway. The man looked at him but did not move. He lay in a queen-sized bed under a gray-blue comforter. The television was on. He wore no mask, and his breathing was labored, each breath a suck for air. Uly could see that the guy had the virus, and he stepped back from the doorway and again touched the seams of his own mask.

He spoke loudly, "You okay, mister?"

The man sat up slightly and said something Uly couldn't hear over the chatter of the television. He took one step inside. He said, "What?"

Uly saw the man's lips move to form one word. "What?"

The television was mounted on the wall just to Uly's left. He looked at it for a moment and saw a young man standing at a podium saying something that sounded like, "The leather jacket in question." Then the camera switched to an older woman in a judge's black robe, Judge Judy. Uly reached over and pressed the power button. The image and sound vanished. He said, "We know that you abducted the woman, my friend's wife, Jo."

"She . . . could . . . have left." The man could barely talk, and his eyes looked strained, like about to burst.

"Why did you do it?"

The man looked at Uly but didn't reply.

"Was it a sex thing?"

He spat out, "No."

Uly couldn't tell whether or not the man was reacting with anger or just the strain of gasping air. "Then what? Did you think you could just steal companionship like it was a Snickers bar at the checkout aisle?

The man said, "Yes."

He didn't know what to do with the unexpected answer. How do you reason with a man who thinks he can steal another human being like an inanimate object? What do you do with a complete psychopath? Uly couldn't remember any Bronson episode with that kind of bad guy. Sure, there were crazies, but they all turned out to have some inner truth that made them not so crazy. And the bad guys mostly turned out to have a soft spot somewhere. So, where was this man's soft spot?

Uly asked, "Do you love her?"

The man heard him but lay still in his bed, sluggishly moving air in and out of his lungs. He then reached over to the open nightstand drawer and lifted out a handgun. His weak and shaky arm held the gun up so it wavered in and out of his aim at Uly. "Get . . . out."

He could see the man's arm tire from holding the heavy gun until he lowered it and rested the weapon on his lap. Uly's handgun was in his pocket, and he left it there. The man tried to lift the gun again, but it barely moved.

Uly said, "I suspect the police are on their way." Just then, he heard a siren in the distance, although he was certain the police presence on Boulder Highway had nothing to do with them. The man heard it also. Uly told him, "Put the gun away so they don't panic and kill you when they see it."

It looked like the man now considered this. He lifted the handgun from his lap and swung it barrel-down toward the nightstand. But then the gun turned, now pointed at his head. The man leaned his temple against the barrel, gently like sinking into a soft pillow. He looked at Uly. The man's expression seemed totally blank, as though what he was doing was just something to be done, like brushing teeth before bed.

The sound was deafening, and Uly flinched and briefly closed his eyes, too scared to look. When his eyes finally opened, he saw the mess and damage the bullet had made. It reminded Uly of the time his wife was furious about something—he'd probably come home late for dinner, and drunk—and she took a large plate of spaghetti and threw it against the wall. The side of the bed looked messy like that.

The man, now with a partial head, lay in a pool of chunky blood.

32

A Respectable Amount of Time

Smoke from the wildfires in California drifted west and settled in the Las Vegas Valley. The monoliths of casinos that lined the strip could barely be seen, mirages of a lost city. The smoke obscured the mountains in the distance and created Instagramable sunsets of deep orange and red. To Bray, it looked as though the whole damned world was burning up.

For two days, Bray stayed in the campervan while Jo quarantined in a room at a cheap motor hotel on the highway that passed Sam's Town. She had a loss of smell, headaches, and fatigue. Her breathing was only somewhat labored. Bray cooked in the van and brought her meals and plenty of fluids. At times, *he* felt tired, and one morning, his head throbbed with a sinus headache. But he never did come down with the virus. He attributed the headache to the California smoke, which he knew would be doubly toxic for Jo. He decided to move her from the motel and drive south and east.

He wore his Chinese N95 mask that he doubled up with

a cheaper blue one. Jo lay on her separate twin bed in the back, and Bray drove with both driver and passenger windows wide open. He would need a tent to sleep outside so Jo could quarantine alone in the campervan. Bray told her he would purchase one at the nearest Walmart.

Past Henderson, he turned off the highway to take the old road crossing the Hoover Dam's spine. The first thing he saw was drought-stricken Lake Mead with a thousand-foot white bathtub ring left by the receding water. He pulled over past the dam to take photos of the dramatic ring, then the two massive deco pillars that drained water from Lake Mead, turning turbines that electrified the thousands of neon lights that adorned Las Vegas—at least until the bathtub emptied. Jo stayed in the campervan, uninterested.

Four hours later, near Phoenix, he stopped at a Walmart Superstore. Jo, double-masked and still in her ankle boot, insisted she go in on her own to purchase the tent. When Bray protested, she said, "I'd rather be the one sleeping outside. I just need to be by myself until I get over this." Bray knew she was referring to the virus but also wondered if she meant something else—they'd not yet discussed what had happened during the abduction.

He knew enough to give her time and space.

He drove north on I-17 and turned west into the Prescott National Forest. The smoke had thinned further south and east, and now he could see green hills and trees. He reached a ghost town called Cleator, where a sign just outside said you could purchase the entire town, forty acres, for one and a half million dollars. The lone business still operating was called the Cleator Bar and Yacht Club. He took a photo of the backwoods, land-locked bar surrounded by old runabouts, jets skis, a pontoon boat, and surfboards—all junk someone had hauled up there as a joke. He kept driving. One of his camping apps showed a boondocking area near another town called Crown King. Bray followed the directions ten miles up a rocky and pitted dirt road high above the town. Once there, he passed six empty camping spots until he found one that looked level and private.

Jo set up the domed tent by herself while Bray organized the campervan for what he expected to be an extended stay. He brought out her mattress and bedding, along with a battery-powered lantern and a gallon jug of water. Afterward, Jo stayed in the tent while Bray made dinner.

Two days later, dark clouds moved through the low mountains of the forest and dropped enough rain that Bray thought it safe to make a campfire. Since the day of the abduction, when he'd had trouble toting the two bundles of firewood, he'd found a used Duluth canoeing backpack the size of a large hamper he could now utilize for that purpose. He walked the road, then hiked onto a hillside. The area was covered in large pines, and he searched for dead and dried limbs that had broken off from wind gusts or the weight of snow. He liked the ones that were an inch to an inch and a half in width that he could easily break with his boot into perfect eighteen-inch lengths—thick enough so they'd burn slower than twigs and produce embers good for cooking. He foraged a stack he fit into the backpack, then moved on to another area. Within an hour, the pack was full.

Someone had built a fire ring with rocks. Bray carefully laid down pine needles, then small twigs, then larger twigs, followed by a teepee of the eighteen-inch sticks. One match, that was the goal. He struck the match against a rock and lowered it into the pine needles. They caught and flamed up, igniting the smaller twigs. He blew softly on the embers until he'd created a good fire to have a beer by and later cook a steak on. When he finally looked up from his task, he saw Jo standing and staring at him from just outside the tent.

He said, "How long have you been there?"

"Long enough to see you build that fire." Her hands were shoved into the pockets of her pants. Her graying hair hung loose and wild around her head—snarly—and Bray wondered how long it'd been since she'd showered. The motel had a shower, and it would've been a waste not to take advantage of the limitless hot water.

"Why don't you sit over here near the fire. I'll get you a beer. You'll like this one out of California called *Hopnosis*." Bray didn't wait for a response—her looking at him and being all quiet was creeping him out. He walked into the van and pulled two cans from the refrigerator. When he returned, she was sitting next to the fire and staring at the flames. She did not look up when he slid the can into the camp chair's built-in koozie.

He said, "I have a nice ribeye for dinner. I can also make fettuccine alfredo if you'd like." His alfredo was one of her favorites and made with just heavy cream, parmesan cheese, and a hint of garlic. It occurred to him then that she still might not be able to taste, but he let that thought pass.

"Okay." Jo lifted her beer and took a sip, though she said nothing more.

Bray waited a respectable amount of time before asking her a question he'd wanted to ask since that day at Sam's Town. "I'd like to know what happened. I know it might be difficult for you to discuss, but I think talking about it will help."

Again, she said, "Okay."

"Did he molest you?" He thought maybe he should have said *sexually abused*. Molested sounded so base or sick, like *child molester.*

She looked at him then. "Would it matter?"

He thought of what that answer—an answer with a question—meant or implied. Did Jo believe he'd think of her any different if that had happened—like spoiled goods? They hadn't had sex since her bout with breast cancer—there were no goods to spoil. The thought made him cringe with its callousness. He wasn't the kind of person to think, well, *that way.* Was she then maybe asking if sexual abuse would matter to *her?* Of course, it would, and she would need help. He answered, "You might want to talk to a psychologist."

Jo lifted up the can of *Hopnosis* again and looked at the label for an uncomfortably long time. She then drank the rest in gulps until the can was empty. He'd never seen her drink a beer like that, like some frat boy, and it frightened him. She said, "Hugh was a psychologist. His name was Hugh."

"I understand." The fact was, Bray didn't. He hadn't a clue what was going on in Jo's mind, what she was feeling, and now *he* was afraid to talk about it. His answer, *I understand*, in effect, ended the conversation.

———

Two days later, Bray took the Travato down to the town of Crown King to fill up his twenty-five-gallon freshwater tank and empty his tanks of gray and black water. The clerk at the general store let him use the outdoor spigot for fresh water, but the nearest dump station was all the way back toward Phoenix. He was not going to drive that far, but he also couldn't get by another day with the full tanks.

Bray was loath to pollute the environment and empty his poopy water on the side of the road, but he did find a trailhead with a pit toilet. Dumping there was strictly a no-no, but it was a lesser-of-two-evils situation. Three cars were in the parking lot, and he waited to hear if anyone was coming down the trail. When he thought the coast was clear, he stretched his extra-long, three-inch-wide hose from the tank outlet to the toilet, with the end draining down the hole. He turned on his pump and hoped no one would see him.

Just then, a Subaru Outback pulled into the parking lot on the other side of the Travato. Bray switched off the pump and then knelt down to hide. He peeked out beneath the campervan's chassis and saw two sets of hiking boots step from the vehicle. He heard the hatchback open and someone pull out equipment. They closed the car and walked toward the trail leading past the outhouse. Bray stayed as quiet as he could.

Two middle-aged women with hiking poles, sunglasses, and small backpacks passed by the van and the outhouse. They stopped and stared at the three-inch hose that stretched twenty feet from the van to the toilet. One woman removed her sunglasses and looked back at Bray kneeling on the ground. She said, "Shame on you."

And that's what he felt after the two women had left—shame.

Forty minutes later, Bray was back at the campsite, still trying to overcome the profound embarrassment. He said nothing to Jo.

———

The COVID symptoms seemed to be subsiding, and she could taste the spaghetti sauce and spiralized zucchini he cooked for dinner. It only occurred to him while they were eating that the meal of "zoodles" was the same one he and Jo had cooked the day of the abduction. Bray thought it a good omen, the two meals like bookends to a chapter in their lives best forgotten over the years to come. He kept that thought to himself.

After dinner, she started to clean. Jo hadn't been much into cleanliness in the past, which bothered Bray. In fact, he thought she was somewhat of a slob. Her cleaning started with washing dishes. The next day, while he was out on a walk, she started in on the van's cabinets, pulling drawers out and cleaning behind. She was still in the process when he returned, and he let her finish. Then she cleaned the BMW. He'd never covered it. He liked the bike's look on the back of the van and thought it was a conversation starter at campgrounds and gas stations. Normally, he cleaned it every place they camped and ran the engine to keep it in good working order, but he hadn't done either since the abduction. Jo used the outside hose and rinsed it down with their limited supply of fresh water, then detailed it with the specialty cleaners used only for that purpose.

All of which Bray thought was great, but she still hadn't washed *herself*.

That night, he started a fire again using his teepee method and just one match. He sat ten feet away from Jo on the other side of the fire, and they drank from their cans of beer. She'd still been mostly quiet, talking only in response to Bray's plans for the day or the next week. She hadn't talked about the abduction, or the man, Hugh, and Bray had waited for the right time to bring it up again. Sitting across from her, he finally asked what he'd been thinking for days. "There's something I don't understand—why didn't you just leave when you could?"

Bray let minutes go by, waiting for an answer, but she remained silent. He thought it was a simple question, possibly uncomfortable for her, but one that could have been assuaged with an easy answer like, *He threatened to hunt me down if I didn't return*. But she just sat there and stared at the fire. He felt that welling of anger that usually leaked out in some passive-aggressive manner. What's more, her dirty hair was bugging him. He said, "You should use the shower to clean yourself before dinner." He knew the tone of his voice sounded aggressive, intimating she was unclean, and he quickly backpedaled. "Afterward, I can make your favorite fettuccine alfredo again with grilled chicken thighs." The Rumaki Method, and just then, he regretted everything.

Jo stood up and limped into the campervan. Bray could hear the water running in the shower, and it ran until his precious supply of fresh water was completely depleted.

33

Not Just Another Sam

Two days after the man shot himself, Margo and Lucas drove Fabvan through the harsh wildfire smoke directly toward its source. The previous night, they'd posted the longer confrontation video on YouTube with a link from her Instagram account. Lucas had edited together the setting of Las Vegas, the group of #vanlife followers, Bray's instructions, and Uly walking into the motorcoach and confronting Jo and then the man, Hugh. Lucas was standing just outside the door to the bedroom when the gun went off. In the video, the bang was startling, like thunder. Margo knew Lucas had actually filmed the aftermath in the bedroom, but that had been edited out to avoid any real backlash—publishing a snuff film would get her censored. Overall, it was a good, dramatic story, and the ending to a longer @fabvanlife episode that had pushed their following to more than twenty-five thousand.

Lucas had done all this work and she thought it brilliant.

They didn't talk about what was next. Lucas had wanted to see his parents, then decide after that whether or not to go back on the road. Margo thought she should see her father.

Lucas drove through the thickening smoke drifting down from the fires north of LA. Margo could see the road but not much else, and it seemed they were the only ones driving west. The windows were rolled up and the air conditioner was on high, but they still breathed foul air inside the van. It wasn't until they passed Escondido that the smoke cleared.

An hour later, they were in stop-and-go traffic on Torrey Pines Road in La Jolla.

Lucas dropped himself off at his parents' home in the neighborhood of La Jolla Heights, and Margo drove home. The house she grew up in, where her father still lived, stood in a tonier neighborhood near the Pacific Ocean called La Jolla Hermosa. Margo turned up the short driveway and parked outside the garage doors too short for the eight-foot-tall campervan. The home's architecture looked modern, with boxy angles, stainless-steel railings, and bright white stucco. Her friends had called it the Ikea house, which sounded cool and modern when she was younger but now seemed ticky-tack, prefabricated like many of the other multi-million-dollar homes in La Jolla.

She did not have a key and rang the doorbell, expecting her dad to be working from home during the pandemic. No one answered. She walked around to the back patio doors and found one open. She walked in. The living room appeared the same, with lots of leather, chrome, and marble. Margo walked into the kitchen, which looked unused. No one appeared to be home or even living there.

She walked up the stairs to the second level and looked at the framed family photos along the wall. Something seemed different, and she wondered what had changed. It took her a second to realize that all the photos of her family with her mother had been taken down. Five years before, her mother had divorced her dad and taken up with another man who lived in Manhattan (Margo wasn't sure in which order). The photos had been replaced with ones of her dad and his new girlfriend, Samantha.

At the top of the stairs, she took the first right into her bedroom. It was all there as she had left it, waiting for her return—the queen-sized bed with a princess canopy of pink chiffon, her collection of stuffed animals, including a plush, actual-scale tiger, and a desk beneath a bulletin board of photos and old awards. It was the bedroom of a thirteen-year-old, and she now thought it kind of creepy.

She decided to leave all her stuff in the van and sleep out there.

She found a single-serve yogurt in the refrigerator and sat in the living room to wait. An hour later, she heard one of the three automatic garage doors lift, then lower.

The interior door from the garage opened and her father shouted, "Margo?"

"In here."

Her father, Richard, walked into the living room. "Hey, you."

As a little girl, she'd never considered her father handsome until a friend's mom commented, "Your father's so handsome," and then she realized it was true. As she grew up and her father made his millions, he seemed to become even more handsome. His head of chestnut-brown hair was still full and cut long, blue eyes like hers, and a recent brow lift Margo thought had taken off five years. Standing before her, he wore a bright cobalt-blue linen sport coat over a pressed white shirt. Even during the pandemic, when stuck mostly at home and working remotely, she'd never seen him in sweatpants.

Standing a safe COVID distance away, Margo replied, "Hey, you."

"We didn't expect you here so soon. Last we saw, you were in Las Vegas chasing down that abducted woman. Scary. We hope you're home for good."

It occurred to her that he'd said, "We." *We didn't expect you here.* What was this *we* shit?

Then, the *we* part of his life walked into the room. Margo said, "Hi, Samantha." Samantha had wanted Margo to call her Sam, but that level of familiarity still grated.

"Hi, honey." And Samantha sometimes called her honey, which smacked of parental guidance, though *Sam* was young enough to be a sister. "So how did that abduction story end up? We've been following it like a Netflix series but haven't looked online in a few days."

"The guy that abducted her shot himself. The woman is okay."

Richard said, "That's unsettling."

In a sarcastic tone, Margo said, "Ya think?" Hearing herself, she realized the response sounded more condescending than sarcastic—maybe a subconscious reaction to her bitterness over *we*. She backed off the condescension and added, "Lucas was in the guy's RV at the time."

Samantha said, "Sounds like you've been around a lot of people." She stood back behind her father, and that uncomfortable COVID question hung between them like, she guessed, leprosy or the plague. Then she remembered Lucas had been in the Thor Outlaw with the abductor and the woman. Both had the virus.

Margo said, "Yes, I guess so. I'd better get a mask."

"That's not what I meant. It's more like we haven't seen anyone in ages. I'm just starved for any social interaction. Not that your father isn't good company."

Margo thought it was more likely that Samantha was starved for any social *attention*. She reiterated, "I'll still go get a mask."

Richard said, "That would be great. I don't think we've told you—Sam is three months pregnant, and her obstetrician said that she has an increased risk of COVID-related complications."

It was the first Margo had heard—all this shit coming at her at once. She said, "Congratulations."

Samantha stood there smiling—a trophy wife (or girlfriend—she didn't see a ring) with fake tits and not a baby bump or ounce of fat showing.

A fucked-up thought just then crossed Margo's mind. *In four years, I could be a Sam—get fake tits, marry an older rich dude like Dad, and be a trophy wife.*

———

That night, she was sitting on the bed inside Fabvan and paging through the photos stored in the Dropbox account she and Lucas shared. Most were of her posing in front of some fabulous backdrop, but others didn't include her, ones she'd previously ignored. He'd gone off alone at Lake Powell and taken photos of the random people on the beach. She noticed he avoided the ones on jet skis or paddle boards but focused on those who just sat and watched. His eye caught people with something out of place or unique, like a small boy sitting in a beach chair drinking a can of soda. The kid sat like an adult— good posture, his legs crossed, the can held deftly between his middle finger and thumb—but the boy watched the action on the beach through pink swim goggles with a nose plug clamped to his nostrils. There was another photo of a woman casually standing and smoking while watching the vigilante mob pound on the reckless jet skier. Jo also found the photos he'd taken of the skateboard kid at the pool—the one who'd fallen and then trudged up to the shallow end with a pensive look on his hair-splashed face. She guessed the word she was looking for was *ironic*. There was something to these photos that went beyond the Instagram stuff they posted. She thought they were works of art.

She looked again at the ones Lucas had shot of the Mormons in their broken-down schoolie. They were beyond cool, like Diane Arbus stuff, like photos for a *Vanity Fair* piece. Then she had an idea—this *could* be a *Vanity Fair* piece.

She opened her MacBook and immediately started writing. At USC, she'd been a communication major, and though she mostly wrote posts for her Instagram page, she'd taken journalism classes. She plagiarized her share of assignments and had boyfriends to help out, but she wrote many herself and received reasonably good feedback.

The title of the article was "Hunker and Bunker." She didn't know where this would go but knew she wanted to write an article—or a blog post, or maybe a podcast—and she wanted to do it with Lucas.

Within three hours, she had a draft written, almost one thousand words, and what she read back to herself wasn't bad. There was a sense of place and otherworldliness. She thought people would want to know.

She texted Lucas, "Really miss u! Not saying LOVE, but want u around if u want to be around. Gotta get outta Jolla. You?"

Before hitting "send," she read over the text, thought about not saying, *Not saying LOVE,* and decided to leave it in.

She didn't want Lucas to get any ideas about their relationship—that's why she wrote it—but she also wanted that word out there for him to see.

Margo filled her fresh water tank from the house spigot the next morning. She stripped the campervan bed and, with her dirty clothes, started a load of laundry in the house washing machine. Afterward, Margo strapped on her tie-dyed mask and walked into the kitchen. Richard was alone and eating a late breakfast at the island counter. Margo sat down, socially distant at the nearby dining table.

It took her father only a few minutes past the pleasantries to ask what she planned to do next. Margo knew this conversation would happen, the not-so-veiled, what-are-you-going-to-do-with-your-life bullshit.

"Get back on the road, I guess."

"A guy I know runs a PR agency. With your skills in social media, I think you'd be a real asset."

"What, write posts for others? I'm doing that for myself now."

"I think that you'd find the pay generous. It would be a real career—and safe. I don't think what you're doing is safe."

All Margo heard was, "Real career." She knew her dad didn't take what she did seriously. Then it occurred to Margo that he'd already arranged this position—along with the negotiated pay—for when his daughter finally returned. She wondered who this guy was who had a job just open and waiting. She guessed Richard was a partner or investor or something. She'd known he would try to persuade her to stay in La Jolla—be a nepo baby, then a *Sam*. Again, she thought, *No fucking way.*

By noon, Lucas had texted back a simple message, "Let's go. Nothing here for me."

When she looked for Richard in the early afternoon to say goodbye, he'd gone somewhere with Samantha. Margo did not wait around for the awkward parting pleasantries.

That evening, she and Lucas were camped outside Yuma, Arizona along the Colorado River—two hundred miles away.

————

A few days later, they were in the artists' community of Marfa, Texas, taking photos of vintage RVs at a place called El Cosmico Trailer Park. The RVs were all midcentury pull-behinds painted in bright colors, some with wild drawings on their sides, and all for rent. Margo posed as a fifties pin-up girl wearing a one-piece bathing suit, neck scarf, and high heels. Lucas took the photos, but there was little exchange while they worked, and now both were just going through the motions. And frankly, Margo felt a little exposed, like they were shooting a soft-porn calendar for the gratification of some gas station grease monkey. She knew something needed to change.

The next day, after reading an Instagram post from @vanlifevagabonds, they were relieved and also excited to turn around and head back west.

34
Then Came Uly – Final Episode

Uly had quickly left Sam's Town after the messy intervention. He did not want to speak with the group of #vanlife followers who held out their cellphones like tourists to document his departure as he stepped from the motorcoach. He did not want to speak with the Las Vegas police, who would somehow try to mix him up in the death or make him feel guilty for not doing something to alter the outcome. Fuck them. He kept his head down as he walked through the group, walking straight to his Xplorer, then took off north on Boulder Highway toward City Center. At Tropicana, he turned left toward the Strip. He didn't know where he intended to go, but the Strip had always been like a tractor beam drawing him in.

The man had shot himself in the head. What did that mean? While still back in Baltimore, he had a close cousin who'd committed suicide at the age of twenty-six. She'd been clinically depressed most of her life, and she either went off her meds or they just stopped working. Her name was Faye, and she took a flying leap off the Francis Scott Key Bridge. But Uly didn't think depression was at the core of the man's motivation. He thought it had more to do with a kind of fuck-it attitude, like, *I did what I did, and I'm not going to pay the price for it—so fuck it, I'll take my own life.* Uly, in his own way, knew the impulse. It was the same impulse he had as a young man after his father died and Merl kicked him out—when he decided to go west. *Fuck it.* He knew the feeling now as an older man. Life would all come full circle, inception to dotage until he eventually metamorphosed back into a baby with some underpaid home healthcare worker wiping his ass. Time was running out, and he could either sit back and wait to get his ass wiped or—*fuck it*—get away and do something. Better to go out on a high note—not that Uly condoned abducting women. Then again, Uly had never met the man, Hugh, and had no real clue as to whatever had drifted through his obviously warped mind.

Near where Tropicana crossed I-515, just at the entrance to a Winchell's Donut House, Uly saw a kid with his thumb out. He looked clean-cut, wore a blue paper mask, and carried the kind of backpack kids used for books, not the kind a homeless person might use to tote all their earthly belongings. Uly stopped and put on his mask. He thought picking up a hitchhiker was good Bronson-like karma.

The kid pulled open the campervan door and climbed in. He said, "Thanks, mister," and set his backpack between the two seats. Up close, the kid wasn't as clean-cut as he looked on the side of the road. His brown hair hung unevenly like he'd cut it with kitchen shears. His face was boyish but slightly grimy, and Uly could see where a line of sweat had created a rivulet through accumulated dust. The kid's mask looked like he'd picked it out of the gutter, and the backpack was lumpy with possibly extra clothes and food but definitely not books. He looked older now, not a kid anymore, but maybe not an alcohol-buying adult.

Uly said, "I can take you as far as the Strip."

"Cool."

He merged back onto Tropicana. The kid made him nervous, so Uly stayed quiet.

The kid said, "You mind if I open the window? It kind of stinks in here."

It was then Uly realized that the campervan had been starting to give off a pungent odor. It smelled like rotting flesh. He didn't think it was something in the refrigerator; he didn't store much in there. Then he thought of a dying and decomposing mouse. It couldn't be one of Calypso's babies; they hadn't been weened. Then it dawned on him that Calypso must have had a mate, a mouse daddy left behind, who died amongst the pipes and wires hidden beneath the van's cabinets. Had he failed Calypso in the end? It wasn't something he wanted to think about right then. He said, "Sure, go ahead."

The kid opened the window and then looked into the back. "Cool van, mister. You, like, sleep back there and everything?"

Uly did not like being called mister, but then again, he wasn't going to introduce himself during the short ride. "Yeah, that's where I sleep and eat."

"And fuck?"

The harsh question startled Uly. "What?" He looked over at the kid, who was now smiling back.

"Fuck, isn't that what you want? Or suck? I could have taken a bus if I just needed a ride."

So, the kid was a hustler. Uly could only imagine how he got there—substance abuse, some kind of early childhood trauma, or maybe a pimp who preyed on young boys. "Sorry, I just thought you really needed a lift. I don't want sex."

"You need pills or blow. I can get just about anything." The kid's voice was crackly like he needed to drink some water.

"I don't do drugs anymore. Do you need something to drink or eat? I can help with that."

"I don't need no sustenance. What I need is some cash. Can you just spare me some cash?"

Sustenance, who says sustenance?

Uly didn't like where the conversation was going, and he didn't like that the kid was working Tropicana, turning tricks. It had to be dangerous. He'd known a few female escorts over the years, ones who hung out late at night at The Lunch Box. They'd go on "dates" with tourists and get "tips" for extra services. The girls advertised on business cards handed out by illegals on the Strip. One girl had been badly beaten up by a date before quitting for good. She later became one of his cocktail waitresses. Prostitution was a horrible, predatory business in Las Vegas. This kid was someone's son, someone's grandchild.

Uly said, "You don't have to do this. You can decide to quit, and I know there are services in town that will help."

"You'll help me, mister?"

Uly didn't know if the kid was serious or just playing him. Uly took the comment at face value. You need to trust and take a leap of faith at some point in life. Otherwise, you could shrink from humanity and become some kind of misanthrope. Bronson always had faith. "If you want, I can stop and look online. I know I've seen billboards around town, places you can call if you're homeless or a runaway, have addiction problems, or are human trafficked."

"What's human traffic?"

"Like a pimp, a person who traffics humans."

"So, you can find a place that will help me?"

"Sure, I'll pull over." Uly pulled the Xplorer into the parking lot of a Taco Bell. The sun was just dropping behind the mountains to the west, and the temperature was cooling. Uly opened his window. He slipped on the reading glasses that dangled from his neck, then stared down at his cell phone to look up resources for the kid. He asked, "How old are you anyway?"

The kid reached down and lifted the backpack onto his lap. He said, "Eighteen."

Uly put on his reading glasses and entered into the search bar, "Help For Runaway Teens." Right away, a crisis hotline came up, 1-866-AR-U-SAFE. He asked, "Do you have a phone?"

"Sure." The kid reached into his backpack. But instead of a phone, the kid pulled out a small knife. He held it deftly in his fingertips, more like how you'd hold a teaspoon to eat, rather than an instrument to stab. The handle was bright green, and Uly thought it looked like a peeling knife for potatoes and carrots.

He said, "What the fuck?"

"Listen, mister, what I need is cash. Just slowly reach into your pocket and pull out your wallet. I swear I'll stab you if you try anything."

"Hey, you don't have to do this. I was just trying to get you help. You keep going down the road you're on, you could end up in prison or worse, dead in some . . ." Uly looked up at the sign. ". . . Taco Bell dumpster. It happens to kids all the time in Vegas."

"You sound like my fucking dad. Except he'd kick my ass too. Just fucking hand over the wallet."

Uly inched closer, turned his body toward the kid, and looked at him full-on. He was pissed. "No."

"I will seriously stab you."

"Get the fuck out of my van."

The kid switched the peeling knife to his left hand and reached down with his right to pull the door's handle. The door popped open an inch. He lifted the backpack, still holding the knife toward Uly, still watching him. He said, "Last time."

The space between the point of the knife and Uly's immense belly was close to two feet. Uly looked at the kid over the readers, still perched on his nose. It seemed such a waste, this kid hitchhiking on Tropicana, turning tricks for what? Maybe fifty or a hundred bucks before the police came by and either brought him downtown or just moved him along. Then AIDs—the kid could be HIV positive for all Uly knew, and probably untreated. This kid needed help.

"Hey, let me just call the hotline . . ."

Before he could finish or touch the screen of his phone, the kid, fast as a cat, reached over and plunged the knife into Uly's gut. He just sat there and watched like it was someone else getting stabbed. The kid yanked out the knife just as quickly and was out the door, slamming it behind him and then running across the parking lot.

Blood slowly seeped from the wound and collected in the white cotton of his T-shirt. He said, "Fuck," to himself and tried to think of what to do next. He touched the blood-red spot with his fingers, and they came away wet and sticky. The spot quickly grew to the size of a softball, then seemed to slow. He climbed from the front and sat in the one bench seat of the dinette. He lifted his shirt to take a look, but the puncture wound was hidden below the arc of his belly. His cell phone was still in the front seat, and he stood up to grab it, then used the selfie function to see beneath his gut. The wound was small, the length of a fingernail, and had almost completely stopped bleeding. Uly wasn't worried—to penetrate his inches of fat and pierce an organ, the kid would've needed a bayonet.

His first aid kit was in a drawer just beneath his seat, and Uly found Neosporin and a larger adhesive pad to patch himself up. He changed into a clean T-shirt, climbed up into the front, then merged back onto Tropicana.

Something was telling him to leave Las Vegas and in a not-so-subtle way.

The day had started well enough—he'd been able to talk Jo into safely leaving the motorcoach. But it hadn't gone well with the man in the bedroom. Uly tried to think of what he could have said differently. The old the-police-are-coming routine backfired when the man shot himself. Maybe he should have dived for the gun. Maybe if he'd just listened to the man—really listened—there might have been something more meaningful Uly could have said. Then that kid. Maybe he could've offered him money to make the call for help. But the kid seemed street-hardened and had probably been through the social services safety net a few times. Uly ended up stabbed—a nice parting fuck-you from Vegas.

So far, his Bronson quest wasn't going so well. He'd need to work harder on his technique to improve his outcomes. He knew it would take time. He had time.

Uly passed the Strip without turning, then got onto I-15 going north. He thought going back east would be going back in time, and he thought of himself as a forward-thinking guy. West would put him in wildfires and smoke—California seemed to be always burning up, cracking up, or drowning. He would have gone south to Mexico if he'd spent more time paying attention in high school Spanish. So, north it was. And continuing to travel seemed like a better idea than sitting on his ass, watching TV, and waiting until he reached that latent, infantile state where he needed someone to wipe his ass. Better to go out on a high note, with purpose.

Five days later, he changed direction after reading an Instagram post from @vanlifevagavonds.

35

Josephine Takes Wing

Jo had slept poorly in the tent with upsetting, haunting dreams. Her one visceral nightmare took place in the Outlaw motorcoach. She was cooking a casserole from scratch, not one of the microwaved cans of food Hugh preferred. The oven was lit, the dial turned to three hundred and fifty degrees, and she slid in the dish minutes later. Then she lay down on the pull-out bench seat in the toy box and looked at the passing clouds through the skylight above. Then she was playing cards with Hugh, but they weren't in the motorcoach but at the tournament, and Hugh was winning. He told her, "The only luck of the game is in the cards dealt." Then she smelled something burning, and now she was back in the coach and smoke was billowing from the oven door. She turned the dial to shut off the flames, but the dial disintegrated in her hand. She saw the casserole blackening and finally bursting into flames. The fire was now on the stovetop, with flames touching the cabinets above, and she knew the whole motorcoach would burn. The flames blocked her way to the front door, so she retreated into the toy box with its drop-down rear door latched and locked. Right before waking from the nightmare, she screamed, "Hugh."

Somehow, she knew the scream was real and cut through the tent's thin walls.

There was a time when she'd dissect her dreams and explain them away by placing them in tidy categories corresponding to what was happening in her life, like fear, confidence, pleasure, anxiety, love, and longing. The process made her feel at ease and in control. Now, none of that made any sense, and that conscious examination of dreams seemed like an excuse not to change or act. It was like standing at the edge of a cliff and wanting to jump but knowing that if you *do* jump, you'll end up dead with all the repercussions for the people around you. So, you decide not to jump and instead of acting, you do nothing. Which was part of why Jo hadn't discussed with Bray what had happened in the motorcoach.

Later, around the campfire, she had an urge to touch the flames, see if the pain would undermine the shame she knew was there, that wanted to be examined.

Jo cleaned instead. She'd always hated cleaning but knew she needed it now, like a penance. She cleaned the inside of the campervan when Bray was off doing whatever Bray did. She got back underneath the beds and behind drawers where the tangle of electric wires and plastic water pipes were hidden. She found a dead mouse that had decomposed and dried up so it looked like a sci-fi zombie, a ghost mouse. She lifted it by its bony tail and tossed it into the woods. She found the *New York Times* crossword puzzle she'd been working on the day of the abduction. It was creased back and opened to the last page, the one five-letter word for weariness missing—*ennui*. She felt that sense of ennui now and knew it had been there way before

Hugh and the toybox and the tournament. She felt like the dead zombie mouse found in the confluence of wires and pipes.

She cleaned the motorcycle they'd toted around for the last year but never driven. She knew motorcycles from her past and loved the BMW. Its pre-1970s lines were sleek and elegant, almost deco. She'd learned about the women in the Berlin factory who hand-painted the trademark white pinstriping on the gas tanks and fenders, each brush stroke as different as snowflakes. The engine was simple and compact, with its two opposing cylinders sticking out horizontally, exposing cooling fins to the oncoming air. Bolted on to each side of the rear fender were Craven luggage cases with chrome strapping. Bray had a whole box of cleaners and waxes used to detail the bike for the shows they visited, and she used them all. Cleaning the bike began to feel less like penance and now more like reading a good book. She worked slowly.

When Bray told her in his special way to take a shower, Jo did as he asked without thought. Alone inside the Travato, she stripped off the clothes she'd worn since Hugh killed himself. She turned on the shower in the small wet bath and stood under the cold water until it turned scalding hot. She left the water running, scrubbed herself with soap, and washed her hair. She washed herself again, then washed a third time. She was still covered with a soapy film when the water finally ran out. She toweled off and changed into clean underwear, jeans, and a long-sleeved flannel shirt. Only later, when she passed Bray on the way to her tent, did she realize he'd be upset about the now empty fresh water tank.

She was awoken the next morning by Bray, who spoke to her through the closed tent flaps, saying he'd be gone for a few hours to run errands. She knew Bray was going back to wherever to fill up with more water. She lay in the tent as the sun rose above the surrounding hills and trees, warming the air inside. She thought about who Hugh was, and she thought about the tournament. The man had violently abducted her only to have someone to play games with. Just that idea made him monstrous but, in a way, also vulnerable. Did he act without considering the consequences, the end game? No, Hugh had thought through all of the details—he'd known how to avoid being caught, he understood how to make her believe there was no way to escape, and he'd manipulated her into feeling there existed some kind of life they could share. He knew the consequences, and death in some form was the end game. That's where they differed now. Jo had changed, and she would no longer act with that kind of premeditation, with an idea of an end game. She knew she could jump off a cliff without consequence.

And the tournament? Her thirty-thousand-dollar prize money was still waiting for her back in Las Vegas. Jo had not told Bray about the tournament; he would not have understood what it had meant. To Bray's mind, the game would have been wrapped up in the abduction and her relationship with Hugh. But the tournament was outside that. It had been exhilarating, and she did not know if she could or would feel that way again. But maybe she'd try.

Bray was back two hours later. She could hear doors opening and closing and then hear footsteps as he walked toward the tent. Through the nylon walls, he said, "Jo, I'm going to collect some firewood. There's coffee in the thermos. Feel free to make yourself some breakfast or lunch."

"Okay."

She heard him leave and knew he wouldn't return for an hour or more.

She wanted to act. On a deeper level that she was just now trying to understand, it felt as though she'd been abducted all over again. And maybe she'd been an abducted hostage her whole life. What had the small man said to her? *Act big, do something unexpected.* And what had that big man said? *You can just leave.* If she wanted to act, to leave—to jump—she'd need to move quickly.

Jo dressed, folded up her bedding, and then emptied the tent. She collapsed the tent and stuffed it into its sack. From inside the campervan, she filled two kitchen garbage bags with a few clothes and toiletries. She cast off her plastic boot and pulled on hiking boots, the one just fitting over her sprained ankle, the swelling all but gone. Her sunglasses were on the dashboard, and a Levi's jacket hung in the small closet. She put those on and then filled the Craven cases of the BMW. She tied the tent to the handlebars. She slid out the ramp for the carrier, unstrapped the motorcycle, and slowly backed it down. She opened the petcocks, releasing gas from the full tank. She put her good foot onto the kickstarter and then stamped down with all her weight.

The small engine came to life.

36

The Quest Continues

Bray came back with his full pack of sticks for the fire. He saw that the tent was gone. Jo still had a few days left in the fourteen-day quarantine period, and he thought it too soon to move back into the Travato. He called out, "Jo," but heard no response. After unpacking the firewood and neatly stacking the sticks next to the makeshift fire pit, Bray looked inside the van. Jo's walking boot lay on the floor, but she wasn't there. He stood outside and looked around. No one. Then he saw the empty carrier on the back of the Travato.

He tried to remain calm and tried to think of a reason why Jo would have taken the BMW. None came to him. He pulled out his cell phone and dialed her number. He heard the ringtone somewhere nearby and tracked the sound to the campervan. He found Jo's cell phone in the front seat. Now he was really worried.

He poured himself a cup of coffee from the thermos and tried to think. Jo had taken the BMW—why? She hadn't been herself since the abduction, and maybe she just needed to get away for a few hours and go for a ride. But then why hadn't she said something? The vintage BMW was not a toy you just took out for pleasure. They didn't even have helmets. Now he was worried for her safety.

She hadn't returned an hour later and hadn't returned by evening. It was déjà vu—Jo was missing again, though this time she hadn't been abducted. Bray figured the smart thing to do was to stay where he was and continue waiting to see if she'd return. He needed help, though, in the event she didn't. He opened his computer and found an old photo of Jo sitting on the BMW. Bray uploaded the photo to their Instagram account. He felt a surge of adrenaline and a feeling of absolute purpose as he wrote, "Jo is gone again."

Kurt Johnson
Burntside Lake, Ely, Minnesota

FIND MORE FROM AUTHOR
KURT JOHNSON

www.KurtJohnsonBooks.com

KurtJohnsonBooks.substack.com